A PROPOSAL FOR MAMA

"You look very serious, Lady Lovington. What is it that so absorbs your attention?"

"I have been busy making my plans, sir," she responded coolly. "I am about to leave the country and I wish to put my affairs in order before I leave."

"An admirable sentiment, ma'am. Are you making a very long journey?"

"It will seem so to me," she replied, smiling absently. "I am going far away to seek my fortune, sir. I think it is time that I do so."

"Would you like to see it with me, Mercy?" he asked tenderly, slipping into the chair beside her and drawing close. He took her hand and held it to his lips, watching her carefully.

"You know full well that I cannot do that, Mr. Grant," she replied, reclaiming her hand without looking into his eyes.

"We would suit, Mercy," he said, his eyes serious. "Why not go with me to Barbados?"

Her eyes flew back to his. "So you guessed where I would go?"

He grinned now, the smile lighting his eyes. "Did you think I would forget our conversation?" he asked. "I remember everything that you have said to me."

"How kind you are," she murmured, turning away from the intensity of his gaze.

He caught her arm and turned her back toward him. "It isn't kindness, Mercy. You know very well that I love you, so why n̶o̶t̶

by Mona Gedney

D1403087

BOOK YOUR PLACE ON OUR WEBSITE AND MAKE THE READING CONNECTION!

We've created a customized website just for our very special readers, where you can get the inside scoop on everything that's going on with Zebra, Pinnacle and Kensington books.

When you come online, you'll have the exciting opportunity to:

- View covers of upcoming books
- Read sample chapters
- Learn about our future publishing schedule (listed by publication month *and author*)
- Find out when your favorite authors will be visiting a city near you
- Search for and order backlist books from our online catalog
- Check out author bios and background information
- Send e-mail to your favorite authors
- Meet the Kensington staff online
- Join us in weekly chats with authors, readers and other guests
- Get writing guidelines
- AND MUCH MORE!

**Visit our website at
http://www.zebrabooks.com**

A MATCH FOR MOTHER

MONA GEDNEY

KATHRYN KIRKWOOD

REGINA SCOTT

Zebra Books
Kensington Publishing Corp.
http://www.zebrabooks.com

CONTENTS

A MATCH FOR MAMA

by
Mona Gedney

"Well, of course I think Mama should marry again!" exclaimed Reginald, striding up and down the room and rumpling his dark hair until it stood up in disordered tufts. "She's the dearest woman in the world, Bet—you know that I think that she is—but if she were married, surely she would have less time to rearrange our lives and to get herself into trouble! Perhaps we would have at least a quarter of an hour to ourselves!"

He paused a moment and stared at his sister sternly, quite as though she might be held accountable for the actions of their mother. "I don't suppose you realize that while I was out of town she repapered my bedchamber and had a talk with my housekeeper about what I should be eating—just as though I were a child instead of a man of six and twenty with his own establishment!"

"You shouldn't be surprised, Reggie," responded Elizabeth calmly. "You know how she has been fussing over you. She thinks that you've lost weight and grown a little pale. She just wanted to be certain that you're taking care of yourself—and I daresay that she repapered your room in cheerful colors—she thinks that colors have a definite influence on your mood."

Reginald nodded in disgust. "I now have a bedroom that looks like a lemon meringue—all swirls of yellow and white—but I suppose I should be grateful that she didn't do anything more outrageous than that, like coming down to Brighton with me to be certain that I ate my dinner every night."

He thought with considerable bitterness of her unexpected arrival at his snug hunting lodge just last autumn. He and three of his particular companions had just settled in for a comfortable fortnight of hunting, drinking, and masculine camaraderie when his mother had descended upon them with her excellent cook and baskets of delicacies, announcing that she was certain that they would starve if dear Reggie were left to provide for them.

She was already a favorite with the young men there, who looked upon her as a combination of mother, sister, and confessor, so they could see no difficulty with her staying with them for the entire visit, nor would they allow Reginald to say a word against her doing so. To his dismay, she had gambled with them and exchanged stories with them and ridden with them—although at least she had not taken part in the hunt herself. Their mother did not approve of blood sports.

"Come now, Reggie," she had told him. "Don't be so stuffy! Your friends are having a good time—why cannot you do so, too?" If she perceived that her stories about flirtations and love affairs somewhat inhibited his ability to have a good time, she made no mention of it. She had seemed for all the world like one of the boon companions of *his* friends. It was no less than highway robbery.

With this experience vividly in mind, he turned back to Elizabeth, and replied with emphasis, "So in response to your question, dear sister, I would again say yes! By all means, let us find Mama a husband so that she doesn't have enough time to rearrange our lives entirely or to get herself into mischief."

He ruffled his hair once more and smiled wickedly. "If there were any justice, Mama would marry someone who was forever getting himself into trouble so that *she* would be the one who had to worry and fret and expect the worst."

Elizabeth, tall and dark and slender like her brother, smiled at him grimly, thinking of their mother's brief second marriage. That husband, like her first, had been far from the type of man Reginald was describing. Sir George Lovington, a quiet and conservative country gentleman, had lived only six months after their wedding, dying, Reginald had announced to her privately, out of fear of what his beloved new wife might do next. He had succumbed to death shortly after Lady Lovington had gambled away ten thousand pounds in one night, making herself the talk of the *ton* for at least the whole of the next week. Sir George could easily pay the debt, but the notoriety had disturbed him.

"I don't believe that Mama would ever marry that type of gentleman, Reggie—or at least she has not thus far—and perhaps marriage *might* keep her that busy," Elizabeth replied doubtfully, "but I don't recall that that has been the case. Mama has far too much energy for one person."

"Don't I know it!" he agreed, ruffling his hair once more as he recalled various recent other forays his mother had made into his life, rearranging his small household staff, giving advice to his valet, inspecting whatever barque of frailty he was favoring with his attentions at the moment.

Lady Lovington appeared not to realize that there were some things that just weren't done by mothers—and the thing that perturbed him most was that he and Elizabeth—and the late Sir George—appeared to be the only ones disturbed by her peregrinations. Others were either amused by her antics or they dismissed her frequently unusual behavior as what was to be expected of a delightful eccentric.

Mercy Rochester, now the widowed Lady Lovington, was a universal favorite—sunny-tempered, kindhearted, and amusing. Only her own two children, although they loved her dearly, appeared to be troubled by her propensity to get herself into trouble.

"I think, Reggie, that her next husband had best be some-one who can have a greater influence on her actions than Sir George did," said Elizabeth, her tone even more serious than it usually was. Elizabeth had inherited little of their mother's frivolous nature and her quick humor. "I only wish that she were already married to such a man. Perhaps then we would not be at sixes and sevens at home as we are just now."

His attention arrested by her tone and her ominous remark, her brother stopped his restless pacing and stared at her, his expression suddenly fearful. He had been out of town only three weeks.

"Is there something wrong, Bet? Is that what's brought you out to see me so early this morning?" he demanded. "She hasn't gotten herself into another scrape, has she?"

There was no immediate response, and Reginald leaned toward his sister pleadingly. "Please tell me that she hasn't!"

Elizabeth, unable to give such reassurance, was silent. Her hands, daintily gloved in yellow kid, were folded in her lap, and she appeared to be studying them intently.

Able to bear it no longer, Reginald pulled her abruptly to her feet and put his hand under her chin, forcing her to look at him. "What is it, Bet? What has she done this time?"

Elizabeth shrugged. "It was another bet, Reggie—and of course everyone knows about it. She was racing Lady Vick-ery in the park and overset her curricle as she took a curve."

"Was she hurt? No," he said, answering his own question before she could reply, "you would have tracked me to the far ends of the earth if she had been injured."

"Mama wasn't hurt—but she caused a gentleman to be thrown from his own curricle and injured quite badly."

Here Reginald sank into a chair and stared at her. Their mother's antics, however wild, had never before caused any-one any serious hurt. "Was it anyone we know, Bet?"

"No—although we shall soon known him very well in-deed."

"What does that mean?" he asked apprehensively.

"Colonel Anderson is home on leave from the Peninsula and hasn't any relatives in town, so Mama had him taken to our home—along with his aide."

Seeing his astonished expression, she added defensively, "Well, she couldn't just leave him friendless, Reggie! Mama was conscience-stricken when she saw what a disaster her carelessness had caused. And she has sworn faithfully that she will never again act without thinking of the possible consequences."

Her brother snorted in disbelief.

"Well, I'm certain that you're right, Reggie," she sighed. "No doubt she will do something outrageous as soon as this is behind her—which is why we really must find her a husband who will be a settling influence."

Reginald nodded, his usually cheerful countenance creased by a worried frown. "She gets worse and worse. We're fortunate that the man wasn't killed outright. Has she thought that next time she might not be so lucky?"

"Oh, indeed she has! And you know how soft-hearted she is, Reggie. Mama would never intentionally hurt anyone. You really mustn't scold her when she is already so distressed."

He looked unconvinced, but they both knew full well that neither of them had the power to remain angry with their mother for very long.

"You haven't told me yet that this Colonel Anderson will be all right—he will, won't he, Bet?" he asked anxiously. "Mama hasn't done him any permanent damage, has she?"

"No, fortunately the surgeon assures us that he will be quite well again. And in the meantime, the poor man is besieged by attentions. If Mr. Grant, his aide, were not here to protect him from the ministrations of Mama and Aunt Lucinda, why, I'm certain—"

"Aunt Lucinda!" exclaimed Reginald, unable to let her continue. "What the devil is Aunt Lucinda doing in London?"

Elizabeth looked at him in amusement. "When she heard

that Mama had two men in the house with no proper chaperone, she closed up her home and came down to play propriety. I knew that you would be delighted to hear the news."

Reginald groaned. Aunt Lucinda, their father's sister, was a tart-tongued spinster who spoke her mind at every opportunity, and all too often he had found himself the subject of her comments. He foresaw nothing but more trouble with her presence, for she too was under Mama's spell.

Suddenly, however, his eyes brightened and he leaped from his chair to pace up and down the length of his drawing room.

"This military man that she ran down, Bet—is he truly a gentleman?" he inquired eagerly.

"He certainly appears to be so. Why do you ask?"

"And what age is he?"

"He is an older gentleman—about Mama's age, I suppose. He has a touch of gray in his hair like Sir George did, though, and Mama, of course, has none."

She looked at him suspiciously. "Why? What are you thinking of, Reggie?

He grabbed her hands and pulled her up from the sofa, swinging her round. "I am thinking, dear sister, that he may be the answer to our prayer! Who better than a military man to take a firm hand with Mama? And since he is spending time with her already, why could he not fall in love with her? Everyone else does."

Elizabeth laughed in spite of her doubts. As always, Reginald's good humor was contagious, and she found herself believing that Colonel Anderson might be the answer to their prayers—a safe haven for their irrepressible mother.

"So tell me what you know of him, Bet," he demanded a few minutes later as they bowled along the busy street toward the townhouse where Elizabeth lived with their mother.

"Well," she began slowly, "he is a well-bred man of good family."

"Good," nodded Reginald encouragingly. "That is a must, of course. We could not have Mama marry someone unsuitable. Has he ever been married?"

"Yes, but he is a widower, and he says that he has been for a good many years."

"Good—at least we know that he is not averse to marriage. Were there any children?"

"No. He has mentioned that they both regretted the fact that there were none."

"Even better," responded Reggie. "Mama does not need other children—even grown ones—to look after. Is he a kind man?" he added abruptly. "That is a necessity for Mama."

Elizabeth nodded, a smile deepening the dimples that were very like those of her mother. "He must be, Reggie. He has been at our house for some ten days with Mama ministering to him, and he has never once complained."

Reginald shuddered. "Has she been cooking for him?"

She nodded again, solemnly this time, but with a light in her eyes that denied her serious expression. "Milk toast," she said briefly, "and chamomile tea, punctuated by an occasional coddled egg and beef tea."

"Dear Lord, Bet," groaned Reginald. "My heart goes out to the poor man. Surely you've managed to sneak in other food to him or he would have wasted away by now."

"Aunt Lucinda and I—and Mr. Grant, of course—have managed well enough," she replied. "We have managed to smuggle in at least two full meals each day. However, Mama thinks that he's thriving on the diet that she has prescribed and prepared with her own hands."

"And the surgeon is right—that he is really mending?" inquired Reginald, suddenly apprehensive. "I mean, are you absolutely sure that Mama hasn't been responsible for an injury that has done him permanent damage?"

Elizabeth patted his hand reassuringly. "I admit that things looked quite wicked at first. When I got home that afternoon, Mama was wringing her hands outside the guest room and the surgeon and Mr. Grant were inside with the colonel. All Mama could tell me was that he was unconscious and bleeding and that his right leg had been bent at a very odd angle. The surgeon says that fortunately it was a clean break and Colonel Anderson will be as 'right as rain' once it has time to mend."

Reassured, Reginald heaved a sigh of relief and they turned their thoughts once more to the much more agreeable prospect of marrying their mama to her unsuspecting victim.

"Don't worry, Bet," said Reginald blithely as they pulled up in front of the house. "I promise you that if we put our minds to it, within a matter of weeks—or perhaps even days—we will have Mama safely married."

The subject of their distress had problems of her own to contend with. Lady Lovington pushed back a bright tendril that had escaped her topknot of curls and paused a moment to fan her flushed cheeks. The kitchen, situated in the basement of the townhouse, grew very warm on sunny days like this. She did not pause for self-pity, though, however little she might enjoy spending her time in such a way. She was preparing the colonel a light meal to help him regain his strength. It had seemed to her that he had a slight fever earlier that morning, even though Dr. Stout had said that he could detect none, and she had not the slightest intention of allowing their patient to suffer a relapse. She still had nightmares in which he did not recover as quickly as he appeared to be doing in real life, so she could take nothing for granted.

Settling herself on a stool safely out of the way of the bustling cook, she waited for the water to boil to fix his tea. It was there that Jack Grant found her.

"Come now, Lady Lovington," he said kindly, "you know that Colonel Anderson doesn't wish for you to be down here in the kitchen spending your time fixing things for him. He sent me down to make sure that you were doing no such thing."

"It's kind of you to come and check upon me, Mr. Grant, and kind of your colonel to send you," she replied, smiling up at him gently, "but it would be cruel to deny me this. I must feel as though I'm doing something to make amends for my carelessness."

"I've tried to get her to accept at least some of her engagements and go out instead of languishing at home in the kitchen and the sickroom, but I'm afraid, young man, that it would take an act of God to change her mind once she's decided to do something," said Lucinda Rochester, who had entered the kitchen on his heels. "That's what my brother Edward always said about Mercy, and I must say that she has proved his judgment correct again and again."

Lady Lovington laughed a little self-consciously and smoothed the skirt of her gown as she stood. "Yes, I'm afraid that I was a terrible trial to him. Edward was very sensible and patient, and so terribly logical. He always tried to anticipate what he called my 'odd fits' so that he could keep me out of trouble."

It was her sister-in-law's turn to laugh. "But I don't believe I recall a single time when he managed to do that, Mercy. You led Edward a merry chase."

"Forgive us, Mr. Grant," said Lady Lovington, glancing at him apologetically. "I'm sorry to be boring you to distraction with our memories."

"But you aren't, Lady Lovington," he replied courteously, "not at all. I'm most interested in what Miss Rochester was saying."

"A very civil young man," said Lucinda, looking at him approvingly. Then she turned back to Lady Lovington and patted her hand. "But even though you led him a merry chase, my dear, he loved every moment of it. He wouldn't have had you change a hair."

Mr. Grant smiled at them. "Then I can see that Mr. Rochester must have been a very intelligent man as well as a very lucky one," he said, bowing briefly to them before turning to leave the room.

"That young man has very pleasing manners," observed Lucinda, watching the door swing shut behind him. "He has been extraordinarily patient through all of this. Most men his age would be chafing at the bit to be free of such constraints."

Mercy nodded. "He does seem to be older than his years. Heaven knows that Reginald is not nearly so steady even though he only lacks a few years of Mr. Grant."

"Well, Reggie is a ninny, of course, but there is still time for him, Mercy," replied her sister-in-law comfortably. "He will settle down soon enough. Let him sow his wild oats and get it out of his system."

"Perhaps you're right," sighed his mother, "and heaven only knows why I would criticize anyone for a lack of steadiness. Here I am his mother and Reginald is three times as mature as I am. Why, I'm not even fit to be their mother, Lucy—I can't imagine how the two of them grew up to be such reasonable human beings with someone like me looking after them."

"That's nonsense, Mercy, and you know it," responded Lucinda crisply. "You *do* do some outrageous things, but overall you have been as loving and careful a mother as anyone could have. You know that both of your children adore you."

Lady Lovington smiled and scrubbed away a furtive tear trickling down her cheek with the back of her hand. "They are very loving, aren't they?" she agreed. "They scold me, of course, but not as much as I deserve to be."

She paused a moment, her chin cupped between her two hands as she stared at the fire. "I wish that I could do something for poor Elizabeth—"

"Why ever do you call her that, Mercy?" demanded Aunt Lucinda. "So far as I can tell, the girl has the world in her pocket. Edward left her well provided for and she is certainly handsome enough."

"Oh, she has suitors enough and she seems reasonably happy even though she won't accept any of them, Lucy, but—"

"But what?" demanded Miss Rochester.

"Well, she never looks quite . . . quite happy! I mean just think of it, Lucy. When have you seen Elizabeth look as though she were really enjoying herself?"

Lucinda looked at her blankly. "Well, I can't think of a particular time," she replied slowly, "but then she was always serious, even as a little girl."

Lady Lovington nodded in agreement. "That's very true, Lucy—and did you ever ask yourself why that was so?"

"I should imagine because she is very like her papa," responded Lucinda. "Edward never looked particularly cheerful except when he was with you."

"There now!" exclaimed Lady Lovington, clutching her sister-in-law's hand urgently. "That's precisely what I mean! Edward was happy to be with me, but Elizabeth isn't. I believe that she feels responsible for me and it makes her nervous. Reginald is happier because he doesn't feel the weight of it so much since he lives away from me. And it isn't right, Lucy—my children should not have to feel that they are responsible for my actions."

"Mercy, I don't know where you get these queer notions of yours!" exclaimed Lucinda. "I know that neither one of them has ever said such a thing to you!"

"No, of course they wouldn't," agreed Lady Lovington. "They do love me and wouldn't want to hurt my feelings— but I'm certain that they are feeling quite burdened by me. Every now and then each of them has given me a sort of little lecture on my shortcomings—very nicely, of course— but still they have pointed them out."

Both of them were distressed by the turn the conversation had taken, so it was with relief that they saw the water was boiling. Lady Lovington prepared the tray to take upstairs to the colonel, carefully placing the pot of willow bark tea beside the coddled eggs that she took from a niche in the fireplace where they had kept warm.

Reginald and Elizabeth had already arrived and been shown to the colonel's chamber. Fortunately for all concerned, Colonel Anderson was no mind reader and so he was able to greet his guests with an air of calm good sense, quite unruffled by any awareness of Reginald's plans for his future.

"I am most awfully sorry about all of this, sir," said Reginald sincerely, very favorably impressed by the man before him.

The colonel sat up in bed, half a dozen fat, lacy pillows propping him in place. Despite his broken leg and the bandage about his head, his lean, muscular form clearly indicated a man of action. As Elizabeth had said, his dark hair was touched with gray, and his alert, dark eyes assessed the young man before him without appearing to do so.

"I assure you that you should not pity me," Colonel Anderson responded, smiling. "As you can see, I am well looked after." Here he indicated the sea of pillows surrounding him.

"Then too," he continued, "Jack and I have had our leave extended so that we have extra time in London, and we are spending it in the company of three very lovely ladies. What more could we ask?"

"You're very gracious, Colonel, but I'm certain that you would prefer to spend your time in London being able to get about instead of being harnessed to a bed," replied Reginald. "Our mother should have been more careful."

"Your mother is the most charming woman I have met in many years," replied the colonel reprovingly. "And her accident could have happened to anyone. I count this mishap a most fortunate one because I have met her as a result of it."

"A very pretty speech, Colonel Anderson," said Lady Lovington approvingly, entering the room with a tray bearing the china teapot carefully covered with a quilted tea cozy to keep it hot, "but you know quite well that the accident was entirely my fault. I should never have forgiven myself if I had done you a lasting injury."

"But you did no such thing, ma'am," he reassured her firmly. "I have suffered far worse injuries than this in the field and thought little enough of them. All you have done, Lady Lovington, is to offer me the most delightful company that I have had in many years."

Reggie caught his sister's eye and winked. Things appeared to be going along famously, and he could already imagine himself taking a holiday without worrying about his mother's erratic behavior.

"And I understand that you have had some perfectly delightful meals served to you, sir!" he exclaimed merrily, his good mood overcoming his good sense. "There's nothing to equal milk toast!"

Bet frowned at him and shook her head slightly, for their mother was very proud of her ability to care for invalids, but the colonel, after a pause so slight that it was almost unnoticeable, said resolutely, "Your mother has been most kind, Mr. Rochester. She has been preparing meals for me with her own hands, which, as I have told her, is not a suitable occupation for such a lady. She should be waited upon herself, but instead, she and your good aunt have been toiling in the kitchen and bringing my food to me themselves."

Lady Lovington glanced at her graceless son, quite certain of the intent of his remark. She was a small woman, much shorter than either of her children, but her large eyes and generous mouth—and her topknot of bright, frothy curls—made her a figure that could not be lightly dismissed. At the moment, anticipating further criticism from her son, she looked a little ruffled, rather like a budgie bird when it has fluffed its feathers against the cold, becoming an indignant, downy ball.

"What Reggie means to say, Colonel Anderson," she said, her dimples deepening dangerously, "is that he believes that I must be tormenting you with my cooking. I'm afraid he has no faith in my knowledge of cookery or invalids."

"No, no, Mama," said Reginald hurriedly, anxious to keep everything going smoothly, "nothing of the sort. I am certain that you have been most attentive to the colonel's needs."

"No doubt you think that he should be eating great slabs of beef and drinking gallons of port," observed Lady Lovington a little tartly, thinking of her son's habits.

Reginald, who thought precisely that, denied it vehemently. "I am certain that you are taking very fine care of him, Mama," he replied, carefully avoiding his sister's eye.

Somewhat mollified, Lady Lovington set down her tray upon the table beside the colonel, filling a dainty china cup with steaming tea and handing it to him.

"Now, sir," she said brightly, "you must drink this immediately. It will serve to keep your fever from returning."

"What sort of witch's brew is that, Mama?" inquired her irreverent son.

"Willow bark tea," replied his fond parent shortly. "Colonel Anderson suffered from a fever after his accident, and I am determined that it shall not return."

"And she has done a splendid job of keeping it at bay," said the colonel, sipping the drink carefully and studying the faces of Reginald and Elizabeth.

"Your mother knows quite a bit about herbs," he continued, and gestured with a smile to the pillows behind him. "All of the linens have been stored with lavender leaves, which she tells me have a soothing effect upon me and take away my sleepless nights." He glanced at her fondly. "And I must say that she is quite right about that. Since the fever abated, I have slept like a babe each night."

"Indeed," remarked Reginald in astonishment, glancing at

his mother. "I had no idea, Mama, that you were so proficient in your use of herbs. You amaze me."

Before she could answer, the door opened once more and Jack Grant entered. Lady Lovington looked at him and smiled—as did everyone else in the room. Most people did smile when they saw him. His eyes were bright and his smile warm, and he had the happy gift of making each person he spoke to feel fascinating.

"Good morning again, Lady Lovington," he said, bowing to her.

Glancing toward the bed, he added, "I see that your ministering angel has returned once again, Colonel. You must count yourself a fortunate man."

"You know that I do, Jack," he responded, sipping his tea. Looking at Elizabeth and Reginald, he said, "You already know Miss Rochester, of course. Mr. Rochester, I would like for you to meet my aide, Mr. Jack Grant. Jack, this is Lady Lovington's son."

"Your servant, sir," returned the young man, bowing to Reginald. "I suppose that Colonel Anderson has been telling you how wonderfully well your mother has been caring for him."

Reginald nodded, but before Jack could say anything else, he said briskly, "It is no more than she should do, of course, since she was responsible for running him down."

There was a startled pause as the others looked at each other and Lady Lovington blinked back tears at this unexpected and sudden attack. It was not like her son to criticize her when others were present, and his words confirmed her misgivings. She was a burden to her children.

"Not at all, sir," responded Mr. Grant, his tone equally brisk. "I am afraid that you have been misinformed. Why, had I been riding at Colonel Anderson's side as I should have been, the accident wouldn't have occurred at all. I would have been in a position to see the pair of curricles coming."

He caught Reginald's eye and addressed him directly.

"Perhaps you have not heard, Mr. Rochester, that it was Lady Vickery who actually caused the accident."

Reginald and Elizabeth both stared at him, and Elizabeth said blankly, "But Mama told me that the whole matter was her fault."

"Lady Lovington has taken too much blame upon herself for all of this," he returned. "I was waiting for Colonel Anderson, and my vantage point gave me a clear view of the last part of the race and the wreck. Had Lady Vickery not pulled over and crowded your mother's curricle, almost catching its wheel, there would have been no accident at all. As it was, Lady Lovington had no choice but to move abruptly to the side as she rounded the corner. That is how she was thrown off balance and almost collided with Colonel Anderson."

"Then I beg your pardon, Mama," murmured Reginald, his cheeks flaming. "I might have known that Lady Vickery was at fault."

"That didn't seem to have occurred to you earlier," replied his mother, trying not to show how much his words had hurt her.

"Why didn't you tell me just how it happened, Mama?" demanded Elizabeth. "Reggie only knew what I told him—and that was what you told me!"

Her mother sighed and once again absently smoothed back a curl that had escaped the others. "Because it truly was my fault, Elizabeth. If I hadn't agreed to race, the accident never would have occurred. There was no point in talking about what Letty did or didn't do—it was my own thoughtlessness that brought about the colonel's wreck."

Lady Lovington smiled sadly at Mr. Grant, ignoring her two children for a moment. "Attempting to rescue me was very gallant of you, sir. Thank you."

The young man returned her smile and bowed. "It was my pleasure, ma'am. I had wondered if you would ever set the record straight yourself. I had decided that if you did not, I was going to tell the colonel the truth of the matter myself."

Colonel Anderson patted her hand comfortingly. "I repeat, Lady Lovington, that I am happier spending my time here than I would have been living at my club. I shall be sorry when I am well enough to leave you."

"Well, we certainly don't want you to think of leaving until you are quite well again, sir!" said Reginald.

As the colonel thanked him, Lady Lovington regarded her son thoughtfully, wondering just why he was so insistent that the colonel stay. She had thought that he would be quite put out over the whole matter and would wish the colonel gone as soon as possible so that there would be no more conversation about the accident. Reginald never liked notoriety, nor did he like to focus on unpleasant happenings. His behavior struck her as most curious.

"It is really quite astounding," remarked Elizabeth thoughtfully to her brother as they went downstairs to the drawing room. "In spite of his pain and inconvenience, Colonel Anderson appears to be grateful to Mama for the accident. How ever does she manage it?"

Reginald shrugged gracefully. "Why are you surprised, Bet? Isn't that the way things have always been for her? No matter what she does, no matter how outrageous it may seem to us, she still emerges as the heroine of the piece. It's Mama's gift."

"I've watched her carefully for years, Reggie, trying to determine just what she does so that I can do it, too," said Elizabeth, her shoulders drooping in discouragement, "but it never seems to serve me as it does her."

Seeing her brother's amazed expression, she added hastily, "I don't mean that I want to get into the kind of scrapes that Mama does—I just want to learn to be as charming as she is."

"Come now, Bet," replied her brother consolingly, "you don't want to have Mama's charm—you have your own particular style and charm."

"Do I?" she inquired. "I have never felt that to be so."

"You slow-top!" exclaimed Reginald. "Haven't you had offers that you have refused, and don't you have young men who wish to escort you everywhere?"

"Well, you are exaggerating a little, Reggie," she said, her practical nature reasserting itself. "I've had two offers—neither of which I would have considered for a moment—and I suspect that they were thinking more of the five thousand pounds a year that Papa settled on me than they were of me. And when those young men that you refer to come to call on me or to take me out, they invariably fall prey to Mama's charm. Then we spend half of our evening talking about her—which is scarcely what I had in mind."

Elizabeth sank down onto the sofa and smiled a little crookedly, trying her best to make light of what she had just said. "You know, Reggie, that I've always tried to have Mama's way with people—to laugh like her, to say the same kind of thing that she would say—but it has never worked for me."

"Well, of course it hasn't," said Reginald practically. "How could you expect it to, Bet? You can't be Mama—but you *can* be Elizabeth Rochester. You need to do what comes naturally to you instead of trying to borrow Mama's ways. That's like trying to wear someone else's clothes—it simply can't be done effectively. Be yourself and you will have quite enough charm."

"Do you think so, Reggie?" she asked hopefully. Having spent a lifetime in her mother's shadow, it was a little overwhelming to think of stepping out of it.

Her brother was straightening his immaculate neckcloth in the pier glass. "I know that it is so," said her brother confidently, preening a little more. "After all—look at Mama—and look at me. How could you *not* be charming?"

"You are too kind to me, Reggie," she said wryly. "And

I had no notion that you thought yourself so much like Mama. I would have been keeping a closer eye upon you."

"There you are, Bet!" he said encouragingly. "Feeling a little more the thing, aren't you? A little more ginger is what you need—that's the trick!"

He sat down beside her and slipped an arm about her shoulders, hugging her lightly. "And now," he said, "we need to plan our strategy for Mama and the colonel."

"Do you really think strategy will be necessary?" inquired Elizabeth. "It's as plain as day that Colonel Anderson is captivated by her. If Mama looked only halfway interested, he would propose to her in a moment."

"Well, then we must encourage Mama to look interested," replied Reginald confidently. "If she knows that we want her to marry him, she probably will do so. Mama has always wished us to be happy."

"Yes, I know that's so, Reggie." She paused a moment, then added thoughtfully, "Do you think she has been happy in her marriages?"

Reginald stared at her. "Of course she has. When have you ever known Mama not to be happy? And it isn't as though we're asking her to do something distasteful, Bet," he said encouragingly. "Colonel Anderson is a very attractive match for her."

"Yes, of course he is," she replied slowly. Still, she wondered if Mama really had been happy during her first two marriages. It was a thought that had occurred to her just after the accident, when she realized that her mother had been very distressed. She appeared to have come about, however. Perhaps, she thought, Mama's nature was so perennially sunny that she was untroubled even by situations that were not precisely to her taste.

Finally Elizabeth gave herself a brief shake. Of course Mama had been happy in her marriages—and she would be happy with the colonel. What they were doing was for her own well-being and their peace of mind.

* * *

The rest of the day slipped by smoothly enough, and at the end of it they left the colonel to rest as the remainder of the party retired to the dining room.

"I truly am sorry, Mama," said her penitent son in a low voice as he led her in to dinner. "You should have told me what really happened and made me mind my manners."

She shook her head firmly. "I told you, Reggie—it really was my fault. I knew that I could not control my team well enough to race Letty Vickery—but I didn't want to give way when she had challenged me."

"Mama, will you never learn that you need not accept a challenge? At any rate," he added, "Lady Vickery has always been jealous of you. You should avoid that woman like the plague."

"Reggie!" exclaimed Lady Lovington in distress. "That's no way to talk about one of my oldest friends!"

"Well, she *is* old, Mama. That's certainly true enough. But she is not so truly your friend. She has always envied you and so she tries to involve you in her harebrained schemes."

He stared down at his mother for a moment. "And just why didn't Lady Vickery explain that this whole matter was her fault?" he demanded. "Why is she allowing you to take the blame?"

"You know how Lord Vickery is," responded his mother pacifically. "He is so much older than she. If he knew that Letty had made a bet or that she had been racing, he would take away her curricle and pair—"

"Not a bad idea," commented her son dryly.

"And he would lock her in her chamber and carry the key about with him," said Lady Lovington, finishing the story.

Reginald's eyebrows shot to his hairline. "I don't believe it, Mama! Lock her in her room? No one is that old-fashioned—not even Vickery."

His mother looked at him reproachfully. "You know very

well that he would do precisely that, Reggie. So of course I had no choice but to accept the blame for everything."

He dropped a kiss on the top of her head as he held her chair for her. "You are an angel," he whispered, "and I am not worthy of tying your bootlaces, ma'am."

Kindness, he reflected, was no small part of his mother's charm. He would remember to share that with Elizabeth.

"The colonel seems a very good sort of man," he said casually, watching her expression carefully from the corner of his eye.

"Yes, yes, he is," she responded. "Very few men would have reacted to this whole beastly mess as he has. He reminds me a great deal of Sir George."

"Just so," replied her son. "I'm sure that you will be sorry to see him leave."

Lady Lovington looked up at him, a little puzzled by his remark. "Sorry to see him well again? Why would I be sorry about that?" she inquired.

"I meant that you would be sorry to lose his company, Mama," replied her duplicitous son. "I know that the house seems too quiet to you since losing Sir George."

She looked at him with raised eyebrows. She had made no such comment to either of her children. In fact, although she had made no mention of it, she had been quite relieved to be on her own again and not have to answer for her every move to someone else—no matter how beloved.

She sighed. Reggie had an agenda of his own. That much was clear to her—and she had an uneasy notion that she knew exactly what he had in mind.

And indeed, by the time the evening was over, she knew precisely what Reginald and Elizabeth wished her to do: she was to marry Colonel Anderson.

The next morning Lady Lovington leaned her forehead against the window of her chamber and watched the spring rain melt down across the splashes of color in the garden behind her house. Normally she allowed few things to distress her, her cheerful temperament minimizing problems and emphasizing the happy events that undoubtedly lay just around the corner.

Today, however, she could not manage such an attitude. Reggie and Bet were clearly united in their determination to see her married—not, she understood, simply because they wished her to be happy, although they did of course wish that, but because they found her troublesome and were hoping that the colonel would be able to hold her in check.

She sighed. Her duty was obvious. She would ease her children's minds by marrying the colonel. And, if God were good, she would not be responsible for ushering him to an early grave and once again find herself wearing widow's weeds.

Smiling into her glass, she smoothed her gown and her hair before going in to see him. Colonel Anderson had made his interest quite clear to her from the first, so she knew that securing a proposal would require no effort at all; the difficulty had been holding him at arm's length for this long. He was a good man and he was kind—but she felt quite certain that after closer acquaintance, he would not find her as completely charming as he had at first sight.

Lady Lovington was not a prophet, but she had a very fair knowledge of human nature and of her own particular weaknesses. One week after the announcement of her engagement to Colonel Anderson, she had wagered her quarter's pin money that the flirtatious Sarah Jellico would not accept the offer of Sir David Barringer. And she had won.

"But, Mercy," said the colonel, mystified, "why would you have wagered on such a matter? And why," he added, "would you have believed that she would not accept so excellent an offer?"

"Because I know Sarah," she replied simply. "She has no interest in being bored—and Sir David, no matter how excellent a man he may be, is assuredly quite boring."

"But you realize, my dear," he said, measuring his words carefully, "that betting on the matter in such a public manner is not, not—" He paused, trying to find a diplomatic way to phrase his misgivings.

"Not the ladylike thing to do?" she suggested wryly, smiling at him. "Perhaps not, but I was scarcely the only lady to lay a wager on it, sir."

"But, Mercy, I am not interested in the others—only in you, my own dear wife-to-be."

His earnest tone and expression softened her, and she bent over him and dropped a butterfly kiss on his eyebrow. "Of course you are right, my dear. I shall try to be more circumspect in my behavior."

"That's all I ask," replied the colonel, relieved. "I certainly have no wish to deprive you of your pleasures."

On her way down the stairs, she passed Jack Grant, who took one look at her face and asked abruptly, "What is wrong, Lady Lovington?"

"Nothing, Mr. Grant, nothing at all," she replied without expression. "How could there be?" She paused a moment before continuing past him, adding in a low voice, "Sarah Jellico is a most fortunate woman."

Troubled, Jack Grant watched her as she walked down the stairs and disappeared into the drawing room. Seeking out Elizabeth, who was comfortably ensconced in her own snug sitting room, he accepted her invitation and perched precariously upon a dainty chair artfully upholstered in the straw-colored silk that was all the rage among the members of the *ton.*

"Forgive me for intruding, Miss Rochester," he began, but Elizabeth interrupted him.

"You aren't intruding, Mr. Grant," she assured him

warmly. "I knew that you would come to call upon me privately at some point and I have looked forward to it."

Jack Grant looked mildly startled by her declaration, since his purpose had been to inquire about her mother. Noting immediately that it would be an error in judgment to tell her that, he decided to defer his question about Lady Lovington until later.

"You do me too much honor, ma'am," he said quite honestly. "However, I do wish to thank you again for smuggling dinner to Colonel Anderson each night. The extra food has helped him regain his strength much more quickly than he would have otherwise."

Elizabeth giggled. "Well, he could scarcely live on the bird-like diet Mama had prescribed for him. I am amazed that he keeps up the pretense even now."

"I think that the teas and broths your mother prepares have helped him immensely," Jack assured her honestly. "And her attentiveness to his comfort certainly has made all the difference in his attitude. I must admit that I am amazed by her. I didn't expect a lady of fashion to put herself out in such a manner."

"She has a guilty conscience," returned Elizabeth. "I'm sure that she feels better because she has made the effort to take care of Colonel Anderson."

"Still, most ladies would have thought it sufficient to give the orders to their servants rather than taking care of matters themselves," persisted Jack, unwilling to have Lady Lovington's kindness dismissed as a matter of salving her conscience.

"True," said Elizabeth a little reluctantly, "although Mama does like to see to things herself. Then she knows that they have been done properly."

"Another admirable characteristic," mused Mr. Grant. "She is considerably more complex than she first appears."

"So are we all," returned Elizabeth, anxious to divert the conversation from its too-familiar focus. "I daresay that both of us also possess more interesting contradictions and admirable qualities than we might first appear to have."

"I am sure that you are right, Miss Rochester," he returned amiably, bowing over her hand.

"For instance," continued Elizabeth, "I know, Mr. Grant, that you are a man with many exceptional characteristics: you are patient, for you have given no sign that this inactive life troubles you; you are discreet, for you haven't breathed a word to Mama about the extra meals that Colonel Anderson receives; you are gracious, for you make all of the inconveniences seem as though they are advantages planned especially for your benefit."

He grinned at her. "You make me sound as though I am ready for sainthood, Miss Rochester—and I assure you that you have been too kind in your estimate of my character. It's fortunate that you don't know that I am a gambler and something of a wastrel."

"Nonsense!" exclaimed Elizabeth firmly. "I'm sure that you are no such thing. You should not be ashamed of being virtuous, Mr. Grant."

He bent over her hand, glancing up at her with a bright glint in his eye as he did so. "If I were virtuous, Miss Rochester, I would not be ashamed of it. I would proclaim myself a paragon to any who would listen to me—but since I am not, I cannot falsely claim what is not my own."

Elizabeth, however, refused to discuss the possibility. "Colonel Anderson thinks you a very fine man, Mr. Grant, and that is a high enough recommendation for me."

"Now there is your paragon," returned Jack, his tone serious now. "If you would take up with a man of virtue, Colonel Malcolm Anderson has few equals."

"Tell me a little about him," said Elizabeth. "I know that he is from Scotland and that he was once married, but I really know no more than that. What happened to his wife?"

"She died in childbirth," replied Jack. "And I think it must have been the single most grievous experience in the colonel's life. He will not speak of it even today."

"How very sad," said Elizabeth slowly. "And the child? Did the child die, too?"

Jack Grant nodded, for once looking quite serious. "I don't think that he ever recovered from the loss. Your mother, I believe, will help him to live again."

"Mama?" exclaimed Elizabeth. "She will most certainly do that, whether he wills it or not. I hope that Colonel Anderson is feeling very strong, for he will need to be when he marries Mama."

Jack laughed, then added in an absentminded sort of way, "Miss Rochester, who is Sarah Jellico?"

"Sarah? Oh, you must have heard something about that scandalous bet!"

He nodded encouragingly, and she continued, "Sarah has been courted by Sir David Barringer, and a most unfortunate bet was made about whether or not she would accept his offer."

"Indeed?" inquired Jack in an absent tone, although he was listening most attentively.

"And Mama, of course, had to make her wager along with the others."

"Your mother placed a wager upon the matter?" he asked, surprised into asking more than he had intended.

Elizabeth nodded, pleased to think that he would be surprised by such a lapse in her mother's behavior. "Mama is very fond of betting, and of course she has known Sarah from the cradle."

"And how did your mother bet?" he inquired.

"She wagered that Sarah wouldn't marry him because she would be bored by Sir David." She put a hand to her mouth to smother a laugh. "Can you feature it? I wouldn't think that my mother would know what boredom is. She certainly has never been bored herself, nor allowed anyone closely connected with her to be so."

"Is that so?" he asked, remembering Lady Lovington's expression and her comment that Sarah Jellico was to be envied. "Do you think your mother has always been happy, that she has never been bored?"

Elizabeth looked at him sharply, for the questions were too much like those that she had asked herself. "Of course not!" she replied. "Even though you don't know her well, think of the times you have seen her. Has she ever appeared unhappy or bored?"

Jack stared at the toes of his boots for a moment as though studying the matter seriously. "Yes, I think that she has," he replied unexpectedly. "I think that she does not wish for anyone to suspect it, but I think that it has been so."

"Nonsense!" she exclaimed sharply. "I have known her for much, much longer than you, Mr. Grant, and I have never seen her behave in such a manner!"

"Perhaps, Miss Rochester, she wishes for you not to know it, precisely because you are so very close to her. From what I have seen, your mother appears to be a very kind woman. Why would she wish to distress you?"

Elizabeth stared at him, unwilling to accept his words as accurate. "And I suppose, sir, that you too are in love with my mother?" she inquired bitterly.

He looked at her mildly. "How could I be, ma'am?" he inquired reasonably. "She is engaged to the colonel, is she not? And are they not to be married next month?"

Elizabeth nodded miserably. "Yes, yes, of course they are to be married. Forgive me, Mr. Grant, for my shortness of temper."

"What could there be to forgive?" he asked gently. "She would not wish for you to be unhappy—nor would I."

"Truly?" she asked, blinking back tears. "Would you not wish me to be unhappy, Mr. Grant?" No one had ever expressed a particular interest in her happiness at all.

He shook his head. "I cannot think that there could be a reason for your unhappiness, ma'am," he replied. "You are lovely, you are pleasant and intelligent, you are well-situated in this world—how could you be unhappy?"

"You make a good case," she acknowledged, "but sometimes, sir, loneliness can be the root of unhappiness."

"Need you be lonely?" he asked, innocently enough.

She looked at him tenderly, her dark eyes melting as she looked deeply into his own. "Not if you are here, Jack," she replied in a low voice.

Startled, he realized too late the turn the conversation had taken. There was nothing to be done, he thought miserably. How could he tell her that he was not interested? He should have been more alert and he had not been. He thought of Elizabeth made unhappy by his indifference and of her mother's consequent unhappiness. He could not do it. Lady Lovington was unhappy enough.

Smiling gently, he looked back at Elizabeth. "I am here, Elizabeth," he assured her.

"Well, I must say that this is splendid!" exclaimed Reginald gleefully, hugging his sister. "Not only do we have Mama safely in tow with the colonel, but now you also have a very likely young man of your own!"

"Well, he isn't my own yet," demurred Elizabeth, fearful of tempting fate by being too happy. "But at least Jack has shown his interest in me."

She hugged her brother again. "Don't you think he is a marvelous man?" she exclaimed.

"Yes, of course he is everything that a young man should be," returned Reginald. He paused a moment, fearful of disturbing her happiness, but then added gently, "Tell me what you know of him, Bet. What is his history?"

Elizabeth stared at him a moment, then said slowly, "Well, I actually know little enough, I suppose. Of course we know that he is the colonel's aide, and has been for the past three years."

Reginald nodded encouragingly. "And we know that Colonel Anderson thinks very highly of him."

"Yes, we know that everyone loves Jack." Her expression darkened a moment. "Probably every young woman he sees falls in love with him."

"Now that's going it much too strong, Bet! Don't judge all young women by yourself!" He strolled to the glass and smoothed his hair carefully, admiring his reflection. "After all, there *are* other handsome, available young men. Jack Grant is not the only fish in the sea."

Elizabeth laughed in spite of herself. "Don't be absurd, Reggie. You and Jack are two completely different types."

"I know," returned her brother complacently. "And I assure you that I have my fair share of admirers, dear sister, so clearly young Mr. Grant does not overwhelm every young female who sees him."

"Very well, Reggie," she conceded, "but you must admit that he has a very pleasing presence and that everyone is inclined to like him."

Reginald nodded thoughtfully. "Yes, I will agree with that, Bet. I like him myself—or at least I like him as far as I know him."

"What else must you know about him? We know that the colonel thinks him loyal and courageous—and we have seen how well he has conducted himself here since the accident."

"Yes, he has shown himself to be well-mannered, intelligent, and agreeable. But what of his background, Bet? Before you become any more interested than you are, should we not know a little more about him? What if he turned out to be a wastrel and a scoundrel?"

His last remark was intended for a humorous effect, for he had no notion that Jack Grant was either of those things, but his sister's reaction startled him.

Elizabeth turned pale and demanded, "Tell me what you have heard about him, Reggie! What are you hiding from me?"

"Hiding from you?" he asked in astonishment. "What the devil would I be hiding from you? Do you mean to say that you think he might actually have something to hide?"

"Of course not!" Her face crumpled a little, however. "It's just that it's odd that you would use the same word—wastrel—that he used about himself. But he was only joking, I'm sure."

"Naturally," said her brother consolingly. "Did he call himself a scoundrel, too?"

"Don't be an idiot, Reggie," Elizabeth said crossly. "He did not." She thought for a moment, then added slowly, "Actually, he called himself 'a gambler and a wastrel'—but I thought that he was just embarrassed because I had been praising him."

"A gambler, eh? Well, that should be easy enough to check on."

"You're going to check on him, Reggie?" she asked, horrified. "Just as though he were a servant and you were checking his reference? How could you do such a thing?"

Reginald looked at her a little grimly. "It is quite easy, Bet. He is a guest in our mother's home, an intimate member of our little group, and an object of interest to you. I would be foolhardy not to check on him. And in the meantime, you would be wise to see what you can learn of him yourself."

If Jack Grant was a little startled by the sudden interest in his childhood and youthful adventures, he hid it well, indulging Elizabeth and her mother in several stories of riding mishaps and boyish misadventures. He was, they discovered, the youngest son of quite a large brood; his father, the younger son of an earl, had been a clergyman in Yorkshire.

"The youngest son of a younger son has limitied choices in life, I'm afraid," he said, smiling ruefully, "and so my father told me I must choose between the church and the military. I chose the military."

"But you're not in uniform," observed Elizabeth, "and the colonel calls you Mr. Grant—when he is not calling you Jack, of course."

He nodded. "I served for four years, then sold out and spent some time here in London. I had served under Colonel Anderson, and he asked me to return to his service as an aide."

To the delight of the ladies, he regaled them with a good many stories of Peninsular life, giving them intimate glances of preparations for battle as well as the day-in and day-out activities of life in a military encampment.

"But you do not choose to follow the drum any longer, Mr. Grant?" inquired Lucinda, wiping her eyes after one of his stories.

He shook his head. "No, ma'am. I discovered that I was not made for that sort of life, although I have enjoyed acting as the colonel's aide."

"But I understand that you will be leaving the colonel soon. What will you do then?" persisted Lucinda, who was not known for her reticence. For once, both Elizabeth and her mother were grateful for her forthright manner.

"That is an excellent question and I am in the process of deciding precisely that, ma'am," he returned smoothly, leaving them knowing no more than they had.

Lucinda ached to ask him just how he would earn his living once he left the colonel, but even she could not bring herself to be quite so bold.

"I would hope, Mr. Grant," said Elizabeth, "that you will make your home here in London. I would like to think that we would continue to have your company."

"You are most kind, Miss Rochester," he returned, bowing briefly. "I would very much enjoy being able to maintain our acquaintance."

"Come now, Mr. Grant," said Lady Lovington brightly. "Surely we are more than acquaintances after all that we have been through together. I hope that you will count us among your friends and not stand on ceremony with us."

His eyes grew warm as he glanced her way. "I feel very fortunate to number you among my friends, Lady Lovington. I will most certainly come to call now that I have been invited."

Elizabeth was a little annoyed by this response, for it seemed to her that he was speaking too directly to her mother; his gaze then turned to her, including her in the charmed circle, and she was consoled.

"What have you found out about Mr. Grant?" she demanded of her brother the next night when he came to dinner. "Tell me immediately, Reginald!"

Her brother turned his snuff box thoughtfully in his hands for a moment before he spoke. "There is no immediate sign of his being a gambler, Bet. I inquired at several of the clubs he would be likely to frequent and, although two of them report that he has been there, he is not a regular. In brief, Bet," he said, grinning, "as yet he has no black marks against his name—but give me time."

"Time!" she snapped indignantly. "Don't speak as though we're eager for there to be something amiss with him—we're not. I think that you have made a mountain out of a mole-hill—and I certainly hope that he never discovers that we have been checking upon him. I daresay he would hate us!"

"Not at all," protested Reginald. "He would merely think us very sensible for taking such precautions."

"Pshaw!" exclaimed Elizabeth inelegantly. "He would be indignant, just as I am on his behalf."

"By the way, dear sister, where is your prize pigeon? I haven't seen him yet this afternoon."

"Nor have I," she said restlessly, "even though he always joins us for dinner. I hope that he hasn't found out what you're doing. He could be avoiding us because the investigation annoys him."

"I doubt that," said Reggie. "Whatever he may be, wastrel or not, he has courage and good manners, so he will be here—even if he only comes to call us to order for investigating him."

Somewhat comforted, she joined her mother for a game of cards to help to pass the time until his arrival.

"You seem quite taken with Mr. Grant," said Lady Lovington to Elizabeth, after some fifteen minutes of play.

"He is a very pleasant man, Mama. You must admit that," replied Elizabeth, unwilling to commit herself.

Her mother nodded. "Even Lucy acknowledges that he has very pretty manners," said Lady Lovington lightly. "In fact, I haven't ever seen her quite so taken by a young man. Mr. Grant had better watch his step."

Elizabeth's eyes flew to her mother's face, startled by her comment. Seeing her mother's quizzical expression, she relaxed. "Oh, you're only funning, Mama. I should have known, of course. Aunt Lucinda has been a spinster for sixty years, so I daresay that she won't change her ways."

"You can't be too certain of that, my girl," announced her aunt from the doorway. "I might just decide to take a young husband to show all of you just how it's done."

Reggie laughed. "I don't know who's worse, Aunt Lucy—you or Bet. Bet can never see a joke and you never stop making them. I would think that by now, Bet, you would know that Aunt Lucy and Mama are always funning."

Before Elizabeth could reply, her aunt returned quickly, "And just how do you know that I'm not serious, young man? For all you know, I might have every intention of sweeping Mr. Grant off his feet and carrying him away to Gretna Green."

"And I would be ready at a moment's notice, dear lady," said Jack Grant, his green eyes merry. Being a member of the household, he had come in without announcement and slipped behind Lucinda, who was now somewhat pink-cheeked. "I had no idea that you were interested, or I would have been more attentive, ma'am."

He took her hand and bowed low. "Just when does the carriage leave for the border, Miss Rochester?" he inquired.

Lucinda snapped him on the shoulder with the fan she always carried, a holdover from her younger, more flirtatious days. "And where would you be, sir, if I were to say that it leaves at ten o'clock tonight?" she retorted. "You would look no-how if you didn't come and left me waiting by myself."

Mr. Grant pursed his lips and regarded her intently. "So it is at ten o'clock we meet, Miss Lucinda?" he asked, his tone passionate. "I may call you Lucinda, may I not, since we shall soon be bound together in marriage? Shall we meet at the foot of the stairs here in the house so that I may escort you to the carriage or would it be more romantic to meet secretly at the carriage?"

"You rascal!" exclaimed Lucinda, laughing. "I believe that I just may accept you, sir!"

"I really think that this is quite tasteless," said Elizabeth stiffly. She was always uncomfortable when her mother and her aunt began to joke. She could never quite perceive where the joke lay, and she was always fearful that she was somehow being laughed at herself.

"Oh, come now, Bet! Enjoy yourself a little!" exclaimed her brother. "You needn't take a pet just because Aunt Lucinda has finally decided to marry!"

Seeing that he had joined forces with the others, Elizabeth rose and removed herself from the drawing room, ignoring the invitations to remain and enjoy herself.

"I believe that I should check upon Colonel Anderson," she said. "We have quite forgotten him in the merriment, and I'm sure he wonders what all of the noise is about."

Excusing herself, she left the others to laugh and lay careful plans for the elopement and wedding of Jack and Lucinda. She sat with the colonel through dinner, having her own brought up on a tray, and read to him from *Julius Caesar,* his favorite work by Shakespeare.

"You look very despondent, Miss Rochester," he said gently, removing the book from her hand after the death of Cassius, "and I don't believe it is entirely because of the play. May I ask what is troubling you?"

He looked so concerned that her heart was warmed. It was a rare thing when she felt that someone was truly interested in what she had to say.

"Do you think, Colonel, that it is a great handicap for a young girl if she is not a jokester?" she asked shyly.

"I shouldn't think it a handicap at all," he responded promptly. "In fact, I should say it is quite the opposite. If a young girl *were* a jokester, I should imagine that would be a handicap indeed."

"Really?" she asked, her eyes brightening. Then she remembered. "But, as you know, Colonel, it is no handicap for my mother."

"Your mother?" he asked, startled. "I should not say that your mother is a jokester, my dear."

"Well, perhaps not just as you are thinking of it, sir—but she does have a sense of humor and she does laugh a great deal. She and Aunt Lucinda have always been great ones for laughing—and Reggie is not much better. I am the one who is the slow-top. I can't quite seem to do it properly, even when I try."

The colonel was still looking at her, his expression shocked. "I have never seen your mother in such a sportive mood as you describe, Elizabeth. Are you quite certain that you are not ascribing some of Reginald's humor to her?"

Elizabeth shook her head emphatically. "Mama is the heart of it all," she said firmly. Then, realizing how shocked he appeared, she thought about the matter for a minute or two.

"Do you know, Colonel Anderson, I don't believe that I have seen Mama merry when she is here in the sickroom with you. Possibly because of the accident, she is always serious when she is with you."

"Is that so?" he said thoughtfully. "Yes, I can see where

that might be possible—but she seems so natural when she is with me. She doesn't appear to be in the dismals—just quiet and rather reserved. Even though she seldom smiles, her expression is always pleasant."

Elizabeth shook her head. "Mama is usually smiling. I expect that she has just been worried on your behalf."

There was a brief silence, then Colonel Anderson nodded. "Perhaps so, my dear. At any rate," he added more briskly, "I would not worry about trying to change yourself to suit others. You are a lovely young woman, very quiet and peaceful and pleasant. You should not alter a thing about yourself."

"Really?" asked Elizabeth, her eyes wide. Never had anyone indicated to her that she was quite perfect as she was. Always she had felt that there was something wanting about her, something that she should be trying to improve. When she went downstairs to join the others, she walked with a lighter, more confident step. The colonel really was most kind.

Thinking of her conversation with the colonel, Elizabeth made her way to her mother's chamber that evening before retiring to bed. Lady Lovington was surprised but touched by her daughter's visit. Elizabeth was not inclined to seek her mother out for private conversation.

"Is there something wrong, Elizabeth?" she asked, her eyes wide with concern. Elizabeth stood silently for a few moments, apparently unable to articulate her thoughts.

"Not wrong precisely, Mama," she began, "but—not exactly right, either. May I ask you something quite personal?"

"Why, yes, of course, my dear. What is it that you would like to ask?"

"Tonight when you and Reggie and Aunt Lucinda were laughing about Aunt Lucinda eloping with Mr. Grant—"

"Oh, I am sorry that we upset you, my dear. We didn't intend to do so. We were just teasing."

Elizabeth waved her hand impatiently. "Yes, I know that you were. That isn't what I meant to talk about." She paused a moment and glanced around, as though looking for inspiration.

"What I mean to say," she continued, "is that I always think of you being cheerful, like you were today. But then I wonder—" Here she broke off and stared down at her hands.

"You wonder what?" asked her mother curiously.

"I wonder if you were really happy in your marriages to Papa and Sir George. It didn't seem to me that you laughed as much when Sir George was present—and when I thought about that, I remembered that you were not always the same when Papa was present. It's just that he was gone so frequently that I forgot the differences in your behavior—until I saw you with Sir George."

"And whatever is making you think of this now, Elizabeth?" inquired her mother carefully. "Is it just because of our playing this afternoon?"

Elizabeth shook her head. "No. Actually, in part it's because of Jack Grant. He said that you are unhappy but that you don't wish for us to know it." She looked at her mother sharply. "Is that true, Mama?"

Lady Lovington shrugged lightly. "Perhaps there is some truth in what Mr. Grant says," she conceded.

Elizabeth stared at her a moment. "But how would Jack have known it when Reggie and I didn't?" she asked blankly. "He hasn't known you for much more than a fortnight."

Her mother shrugged again. How indeed, she thought. "He appears to be a very perceptive young man," she replied.

"Once he said that," Elizabeth said slowly, "I started thinking about your engagement to Colonel Anderson. He is a great deal in manner like Papa and Sir George, isn't he?"

Lady Lovington nodded, a slight smile curving her lips. "Yes, my dear. It seems that I am drawn to—and draw—the same kind of men again and again."

"But, Mama, are they men that make you happy?" she demanded. "And if they don't, why do you keep seeking them out?"

From the mouths of babes, thought Lady Lovington. Aloud, she simply said, "Colonel Anderson is a very good and honorable man. He will make a good home for us."

"Yes, I know, Mama—but do you love him? Does he make you happy?"

In the brief silence that ensued, she hurried on. "Colonel Anderson seemed quite surprised when I told him that you liked to joke, Mama. Then I remembered that you always are so quiet and serious when you are with him—and I told him that perhaps that was because of the accident."

"And did you tell him that I am different with other people?" asked her mother, and Elizabeth nodded silently.

"Yes, I suppose I am," said Lady Lovington, staring into the glass as she brushed her hair.

"Is it because of the accident that you are quieter with him?" persisted Elizabeth.

After a brief pause, her mother sighed. "I suppose it is because of that, Elizabeth—at least in part. But that certainly isn't all of the reason. I think that I try to behave differently with the colonel—just as I did with your father and Sir George."

"But why would you try to behave differently, Mama, when they have fallen in love with you for who you are?" she asked, more puzzled still.

"Yes, they do fall in love with me, my dear—but then, once we are married, the things that they thought charming about me are not necessarily so charming any longer—and so they try to change me."

"Change you?" said Elizabeth blankly. "Why would anyone wish to change you?" Then, remembering their plan to marry her safely to someone who *would* perhaps not change her but at least limit her, Elizabeth flushed brightly and buried her face in her arms.

"That's horrible!" she exclaimed vehemently. "Too awful to think that once you were married, someone would want to try to remake you!"

Lady Lovington patted her daughter's dark head. "You needn't be concerned for me, Elizabeth—nor for yourself."

Elizabeth raised her tear-stained face from a damp sleeve. "Of course I would have to be concerned for myself, Mama. Good Lord! If someone would wish to change you, they would wish to remake me entirely! I would not have a prayer of being accepted!"

"Of course you would!" exclaimed her mother, pulling her close. "We are very different people, Elizabeth—and I know that you sometimes compare yourself to me and think that you are lacking, but it isn't true. You have qualities that every gentleman must admire—you are well-bred and quiet and you think before you speak."

"I sound deadly dull," returned Elizabeth wearily.

"Nonsense!" said Lady Lovington. "Those are qualities that endure and make everyday life pleasant and livable."

"But, Mama, you are lively and amusing and you like to laugh. Aren't those qualities that make life 'pleasant and livable'?"

"Not always, my dear—not for everyone. But you won't have to worry about it, Elizabeth, because you are sensible. When the time comes for you to marry, you will choose a man who appreciates you."

She hugged her daughter again, then pointed her toward the door. "And now, my dear, it is time for both of us to get some rest. I will see you tomorrow."

Before Elizabeth closed the door behind her, she turned back to Lady Lovington once more. "Colonel Anderson told me that I didn't need to alter my behavior at all," she said shyly. "That was very kind of him, was it not?"

"He was being truthful, Elizabeth. It is just as I told you— gentlemen do admire the qualities that you possess."

After the door clicked shut behind her daughter, Lady Lovington sat and brushed her hair until it shone like a new guinea. Finally, she laid down the brush and stared at herself in the glass. Once again she had chosen a path for her future.

She thought about Elizabeth's questions. Why had she chosen to marry the colonel? Because of her children, of course. Would he make her happy? Not particularly. Would she please him? Only for a little while.

For a moment she thought about Jack Grant. What on earth had made the young man so aware of her unhappiness? She had thought that she had concealed it well, and, judging by her family, she had succeeded. But she had not fooled him. Very curious, that.

The candles burned low and flickered out as she sat and stared at her reflection. When darkness surrounded her, she finally moved slowly to her bed, opening the curtains around the bed and the drapes at the window so that she could lie and look up at the stars. That at least gave her lasting pleasure.

What would it be like, she wondered, to marry a man that she loved, one that she could enjoy? For a moment she allowed her mind to wander, and she pictured a laughing-eyed, dark-haired young man.

Impossible! she thought to herself. And she turned her back, even on the stars.

Lady Lovington sat back in her carriage, closing her eyes and breathing deeply as they rolled quietly into the greenness of the park. The soft freshness of spring filled her sore heart and for a moment she forgot her unhappiness.

"Foolish woman!" she thought to herself sharply. "Foolish, ungrateful woman!" For what had she to be unhappy about? She was well, her children were happy, she was about to be married to an excellent man. In short, she had no reason to repine.

She thought again of Sarah Jellico—bright, happy Sarah, who had refused Sir David and just yesterday happily married the young man who had won her heart—a man not so successful nor so handsome as Sir David, but a man who made her happy. She had attended the wedding and wished her friend well—and had come home to complain of a headache and go to bed early—something quite unheard of for her.

She opened her eyes just in time to see a pair of lovers disappearing down a garden path together. "Fool!" she muttered to herself. "How could you be such a fool, Mercy Rochester?" she asked herself sharply.

She wanted no part of the painful misery associated with love. Her first two marriages had been loveless on her part, although in both cases she had grown very fond of the men. Still, there had been none of the sharp pain associated with love—no eager waiting for his eye to catch hers, no warm glow when his hand touched hers, no loss of breath when he pressed close to her.

She shuddered. How could she be thinking such things just days before her third wedding? And how could she be feeling such things for a man that she was not to marry? Colonel Anderson was a good man and a kind one. She would have a good marriage. How could she be so ungrateful as to be thinking the thoughts that were presently haunting her?

The driver stopped at her favorite walk, and Lady Lovington allowed the footman to help her down. Perhaps a brisk stroll in the fresh air would free her of the hobgoblins that were troubling her. Smiling at the footman, she signaled her wish to take her stroll unaccompanied, as she often did. Her carriage and her servants would wait patiently until she emerged again from her stroll in the green glades.

She had scarcely begun her walk when someone else fell in beside her, measuring his pace to hers.

"Good day, Lady Lovington," he said, a smile deep within his bright eyes. "I hope that you are doing well."

"Very well, Mr. Grant," she returned coolly, glancing at him instead of looking at him directly. "What brings you here at this time of day?"

"The hope that I might see you, ma'am," he said quietly.

Her heart began to beat too quickly and she suddenly found it difficult to breathe. Nonetheless, her reply was crisp. "Well, and you have seen me now, have you not, sir?"

"You know that's not what I meant, Lady Lovington," he said gently, a smile curving the corners of his lips. "Are you playing with me, ma'am?"

She carefully avoided looking directly at him, and was profoundly grateful that she had told the footman that she would not need him for the walk. She could tell from the warmth of her cheeks that she was flushed, and it annoyed her a little that he should have her at such a disadvantage. Surely her *tendre* for him was more than obvious.

They walked on in silence for a minute or two until he caught her hand and they came to a stop.

"Are you indeed playing with me, ma'am?" he asked, looking deeply into her eyes before she could look away and feign a lack of interest.

She shook her head. "Why did you wish to see me, Mr. Grant?" she inquired simply.

"Because I wished to," he replied.

"What sort of answer is that?" she demanded, annoyed by what she considered to be his cavalier attitude.

"An honest one, Lady Lovington," he said. "I wish above all things to spend more time with you—and I wish to see you happy."

"And do those two things go together in your mind, sir?"

He nodded. "Perhaps not in yours—but in mine they certainly do. I believe that we could be happy together."

She stopped and faced him squarely. "You know perfectly well that such a thing is impossible, sir. My daughter is in love with you and I am engaged. It appears to me that there are obstacles."

"I will acknowledge that, ma'am, but I see no insurmountable ones."

"Then we differ greatly," she said shortly, turning her steps toward her carriage. "I would say, sir, that we have seen about enough of each other today. I trust that by the time we meet again you will have had time enough to rethink this matter and behave in a more sensible way."

Lady Lovington calmly put the matter behind her, spending her energy on preparing for her wedding, which was to occur in a few days. It was, after all, up to her to be the rational one. Jack Grant was too young to realize the impossibility of what he was suggesting. She talked cheerfully with him—although his responses were brief—and with her son and daughter, both of whom were very pleased with her since she was doing just what they wished her to do. If Elizabeth wondered from time to time about her mother's real feelings, she made no further attempt to discover what they were. The colonel, of course, was also pleased, and if he had any misgivings, he hid them manfully. In short, everything appeared to be going well.

It was just two days before the wedding that the storm broke. It was suddenly brought to Lady Lovington's attention that her beloved son had been spending an unusual amount of time in various gaming hells, and she had grown uneasy. Since he had not taken her into his confidence about his background check on Mr. Grant, the obvious conclusion for her to draw was that her son had developed a gambling problem.

She decided to investigate the matter further, and took herself to Reginald's home. He was out—naturally enough, she thought—probably recuperating at his club after a late night of gambling. Unfortunately for both of them, Jarvis, his valet, was at home.

Having called in the wary valet, who could not ignore her summons but knew full well that his master would be livid,

Lady Lovington proceeded to question him as though he were a soldier caught behind enemy lines.

"Has Mr. Rochester been out every night this week?" she asked sharply.

The valet did not move nor speak for a moment, but catching her eye, he nodded—one quick, careful nod.

"And was he gambling every night?" she demanded.

"How am I to know, Lady Lovington?" he said pitifully. "I don't mean to be rude, ma'am, but Mr. Rochester don't confide in me. He could have been doing anything these nights."

"I should like for you to make it your business, Jarvis," she announced.

"Do you mean to spy on him?" he gasped, horrified. "Why, he'd let me go without a character if I did such a thing."

"I don't mean actually to spy on him, of course, but you could encourage him not to smoke and to stay away from those hells—couldn't you?"

Thus appealed to, Jarvis acknowledged that he could do that much—but he pleaded with her not to tell the master that they had talked because his master would be beside himself.

His mother was only too aware that this statement would be no more than a mild description of his state when he discovered that she had made another invasion into his private domain. Reginald considered himself an independent young fellow, quite a man about town, and his mother was interfering with the image he had of himself. When he found that his mother had again been guilty of taking his home by storm, he paid an unwonted midday visit to her to express his displeasure.

"Well, damn it all, Mama, why have you been at it again?"

"Been at what, Reginald?" she asked blandly. "Are you asking why I had a chat with Jarvis?"

"A chat?" he snorted. "More like the bloody Inquisition

from what he says about it! What on earth did you hope to achieve by doing this, Mama?"

"I hoped to keep you from gambling, Reggie," she replied.

He stared at her. "Gambling?" he asked blankly. "What makes you think I've taken up a life of gambling?"

"My sources tell me that you've been seen in some of the lowest dives in London, Reggie, drinking Blue Ruin and betting on the ponies. What was I to think?"

"You were to think, ma'am, that I am a grown man and am capable of making my own decisions. As it happens, I have *not* been gambling, although I cannot see that it is any of your business if I have."

Before she could say anything, he snapped, "And I do want to say, Mama, that I do not expect you ever to interfere with another servant of mine. Your interrogation of Jarvis was a shameful thing—both for him and for me! Mama, I'm afraid that I must forbid you to come to my home unless I have expressly invited you. Do I make myself clear?"

His mother looked at him for a moment, then nodded her head slowly. "Very clear, Reginald." She watched him stalk from the room, the very picture of affronted dignity.

It was there that Jack Grant found her an hour later. When he glanced into the drawing room and saw her there, he started not to enter the room at all. Unable to stay away from her, he had "accidentally" bumped into her during her daily walks in the park, and he knew that he was distressing her by the attention. Giving her privacy now in her own home seemed the kindest thing to do—until he realized that she was crying.

He shut the door quietly behind him and hurried to her side.

"What has happened, Mercy?" he asked gently, offering her his fresh handkerchief.

She took it gratefully, but the tears continued to stream down her cheeks.

"Tell me what's wrong. Is someone ill? Has there been another accident?"

Lady Lovington shook her head.

"I'll ring for tea. Perhaps that will help."

She shook her head violently, so he returned to the sofa and seated himself beside her.

"It's Reggie," she finally managed to say, her voice broken, "but it isn't just Reggie—it's everything! I have made such a mess of everyone's life!"

"That's not true, Mercy," he said, putting his arms firmly around her and stroking her back comfortingly. "No matter what has just happened, you certainly have not harmed anyone."

"How I wish that were true," she murmured, burying her face in his waistcoat, "but just look at us now! We shouldn't even be talking to each other!"

"Not talk to each other?" he asked in surprise. "Why shouldn't we at least be able to talk?"

"You know very well why we shouldn't, Jack Grant!" she exclaimed impatiently. "We don't even remember that Elizabeth and Malcolm exist when we talk. We concentrate only on each other!"

Jack caught her closer and put his hand under her chin so that she was forced to face him. "That's just it, isn't it, Mercy?" he asked, his voice low. "We do concentrate only on each other. And how will that be after you are married? And what if I were to marry Elizabeth? Do you not see a problem coming?"

Lady Lovington shook her head vehemently. "There is no problem, Jack, unless we allow there to be one! We will go quietly about our respective lives and make them successful. It won't matter to us that there ever was a time when we thought only of each other."

"Do you really believe that, Mercy?" he demanded, trying to force her to look into his eyes again.

"You know that I do!" she said sharply, avoiding his gaze.

"There is nothing for me with you and there is nothing for you with me. I am marrying Malcolm."

Once again he turned her chin firmly toward him so that she was forced to look into his eyes. "Do you love me, Mercy?" he asked. "You need only tell me yes or no."

There was a long pause, but finally, in a small, quiet voice, she said, "Yes—yes, of course I do."

"Then marry me, Mercy—marry me!"

Crushing her to his chest, he kissed her eyelids and the corners of her lips and the wide expanse of tender skin above the ruched bosom of her lilac gown.

Before he could say anything else, Mercy suddenly broke free of his embrace and ran from the drawing room to the stairway. As he sat there, he could hear her footsteps growing fainter. If there was an easy solution to their problem, one that would hurt no one, he could not see it.

Dinner was a quiet affair that evening. Lady Lovington stayed upstairs with a headache, Reginald did not join them, and Mr. Grant dined at his club. Lucinda and Elizabeth, left to their own thoughts, ate in virtual silence, each of them keenly aware of the tension in the house.

When she came down to breakfast the next morning, Elizabeth was dismayed to discover that her mother had left the house with her maid, leaving behind a note for her daughter and one for the colonel. In them she announced that she was not feeling herself and that she needed to be alone for a while. If the colonel still wished to marry her when she returned, they could have the wedding then. She did not tell them where she had gone.

A footman sent hastily round to Reginald brought him there in short order.

"Whatever did you say to Mama that would have made her run away like this?" demanded Elizabeth. "And don't tell me that you aren't responsible, Reggie! I know very well that Mama talked to Jarvis yesterday and I am sure that you were as mad as fire!"

"Well, of course I was, Bet!" he responded, burying his face in his hands as he tried to think. "But I was entitled to be angry—and I didn't think that she would do such a rattlebrained thing as running away."

"I think that you might ask yourself just what she is running away from, Reggie. You still haven't told me what you said to her."

He sat quietly for a moment, and finally said in a low voice, "I forbade her to come to my house unless I had invited her."

Elizabeth stared at him. "How devastatingly rude, Reggie! How could you say such a thing to her?"

"She made me lose my temper, Bet! You know that she can do it!"

They sat for a moment in silence, but then he said, "There must be more to it than this, Bet! Mama has more ginger than to give way before something addlepated that I say to her. What do you suppose she's up to?"

The butler appeared in the doorway, bearing a salver with a folded note upon it.

"This just came round by a messenger, miss," he said, offering it to Elizabeth. "It's addressed to Lady Lovington, but I thought that in the circumstances—"

"Yes, thank you, Roberts," she replied, taking it and staring at it for a moment before opening it.

Reginald watched her while she read through its brief contents. "Well?" he demanded impatiently. "What does it say?"

"You may be right, Reggie," she said. "Maybe Mama is in another scrape."

"Why? For heaven's sake, Bet, tell me what's going on!"

"This is from the owner of a jewelry store on Oxford Street. He writes to Mama that he would like to buy the rest of the set that the diamond necklace belongs to. It is, he writes, a particularly fine piece."

She stared at her brother. "She has been selling her jewelry? Why would she do such a thing?"

Reginald looked no happier than his sister. "Why would you ask such a reasonable question, Bet?" he responded. "Remember that we're talking about Mama. Why would she run away? There is absolutely no telling why she has done it!"

"She ran away because she's unhappy," she said flatly. "I knew it because Jack told me, and Mama as much as admitted it when I asked her."

"Unhappy?" her brother said blankly. "Mama? And why would Jack Grant have known anything about her unhappiness? Why didn't I know?"

"You are always too wrapped up in yourself to notice anyone else, Reggie," returned Elizabeth. "But I suppose that I'm no better. I knew and I still did nothing about it."

"I don't think that I'm following this properly," said Reginald. "Just what could you have done about Mama's unhappiness?"

"Kept her from marrying Colonel Anderson," she returned briefly. "But of course that's what we wanted her to do, so I wasn't going to go against that."

Reginald's expression indicated that he was having some difficulty following all of this, but he pushed back his chair and stood up, saying in a decisive voice, "We have to find her, Bet. She must be using the money from that diamond necklace for some sort of scrape. Heaven only knows what it is, but we've got to find her and help her."

They agreed that he would begin the search and Elizabeth would remain at home, hoping that they would receive a message. Elizabeth went upstairs to waken Lucinda and tell her about it and to see how Colonel Anderson was faring, and she passed Jack Grant on the way down.

"Mama's gone, Jack, and I am just on my way to check on the colonel."

"Gone?" he said, stopping abruptly. "Gone where?"

"That's just it," she explained. "She didn't tell us, so we really have no idea at all. She could be anywhere. And we know that she needed money for something."

"How do you know that?" he asked curiously.

Elizabeth explained about the necklace, and Jack began to look grim. He went back up to his bedchamber for a moment and emerged carrying a satchel.

"Are you leaving, Jack?" she asked. "Do you have an idea where she may be?"

He nodded. "There's one place I can think of. If she's there, I'll have her back in the blink of an eye."

And so the two men set out on their separate journeys, each of them looking for Mercy Rochester. The first stage of Reginald's journey took him to the jeweler on Oxford Street, the first stage of Jack's took him to Liverpool.

The little jeweler nodded when Reginald came in. "Your mother is a lovely lady," he said. "You were certainly fortunate to be born to such a woman, for her loveliness goes beyond her beauty."

Eager to hurry him a little and uncover some more helpful information, Reginald nodded. "It does indeed," he agreed. "Did she, by any chance, give you an indication of what she was planning to use the money from the necklace for?"

The jeweler shook his head. "I have no idea," he responded. "All that she ever said was that all of her money shouldn't be tied up in stocks and jewelry. She wanted some of it free so that she could spend it."

Reginald stared at the jeweler. No doubt his mother had another wager. What on earth had she found to bet on now? Hopefully it was nothing dangerous—and he would find her before any more harm could befall them. Unable to think of any other tactic, he began a round of the clubs, inspecting all of the betting books and trying to imagine which wagers would hold the greatest appeal for his mother. Inquiries among his friends and acquaintances yielded no news of his mother, however, and the end of that day found him back at her home, hoping against hope that she might have returned or at least sent a message.

To his sorrow, though, there had been no news. Depressed, he sank down beside Elizabeth, who had sent one of the footmen to make discreet inquiries of all of their mother's friends. Again, however, the search had yielded no results.

"Very well, Elizabeth, there is no need to say it, I will say it for you. 'Reggie, you are an insensitive brute. If you had behaved in a more gentlemanly fashion, she would still be here.' "

Elizabeth, busy with her own thoughts, did not respond at first. Only after her brother's repeated efforts was she able to listen to and understand what he was saying.

"Of course you shouldn't have treated Mama as you did," she agreed at last, "but that isn't what made her decide to leave, Reggie. I've already told you that she was unhappy. That's why she is gone."

He nodded. "Surely she knows that she wouldn't have to marry the colonel if she really doesn't wish to do so," he said reluctantly.

"How would she know that? You two have certainly made it clear to Mercy that you want her to do just that," observed Lucinda, who was standing in the entrance to the drawing room. "Naturally, she would try to please you, simply because she feels guilty."

"Guilty?" Both of them stared at Lucinda. "Guilty of what?"

"Of being a burden to you," responded Lucinda.

"That's ridiculous!" exclaimed Reginald. "Mama could never be a burden!"

"I don't believe that's the same tune you were singing yesterday," his aunt responded dryly. "I don't think I've ever seen your mother suffering from the megrims until yesterday. I've never seen her so low."

"You don't think she would do anything desperate, do you?" asked Elizabeth, turning to Lucinda fearfully.

To their dismay, their aunt did not have an immediate rejoinder, and when she did speak, she offered little encouragement. "Until yesterday," she said slowly, "I would have said absolutely not—that Mercy would never dream of taking her own life—but now I am not so certain. Elizabeth is quite right—Mercy is unhappy and she has been for a very long time."

She sat and studied their faces for a moment. "You know, there is a certain irony here. She has been worried about you, Elizabeth, because she knows you are unhappy. It has taken the two of you a very long time to notice that about your mother."

"I didn't realize that Mama is so observant," replied Elizabeth slowly, "or that she paid that much attention to me."

"She apparently is more observant than either of you two," returned Lucinda crisply.

"You're right," Elizabeth said glumly. "After all, it was Jack who noticed her unhappiness, not us. We were too absorbed in ourselves to spare any attention for her."

"Well, I hope that Jack has some notion of how to find her," said Lucinda. "The rest of us don't seem to have listened to her closely enough to know what she might do."

As a matter of fact, Jack Grant had a much better idea of where to look for her. As he rode toward Liverpool, he recalled a conversation he had had with Lady Lovington when he and the colonel had first arrived. Her genuine concern for the colonel's well-being had caught him off guard and he had found himself talking much more freely than he normally did. He could remember the conversation clearly.

"So, Mr. Grant, if you wanted to get away from your present life and you could have a wish granted that would take you anywhere in the world, where would that place be?"

She had asked him that one evening when the two of them were on the terrace after dinner. She had been staring up at a tiny chip of golden moon and he had thought then that she was the loveliest woman he had ever seen.

"Well, I'm not certain, Lady Lovington, but I think that I might go back to Barbados."

"To Barbados!" she exclaimed. "You have been there?"

He nodded. "Once when I was a boy, and again last year."

"Is it very beautiful there?" she asked, her eyes bright with interest.

"Yes—beaches of white sand and bright blue waves lapping in across them. It is wonderful."

She had continued to stare dreamily at the moon. "It sounds delightful. Perhaps someday I'll go to such a place."

If she were thinking of breaking her engagement to the colonel, she might well have decided that she would adventure to such a place. Possibly she had sold her necklace to buy her passage for the journey so that no one would be able to trace her immediately. At least, he thought, it was the only idea he had.

When he arrived in Liverpool, the docks were alive with activity and the harbormaster's office was crowded with businessmen, so he stopped at a nearby tavern frequented by sailors to see if any of them knew of a ship about to sail for Barbados. To his delight, he discovered that the *Sally T* would weigh anchor the very next day for that destination and that her captain was in the tavern. His description of Lady Lovington brought a smile of recognition to the captain's lips.

"Ah, yes!" he exclaimed. "Mrs. Sterling will be sailing with us. She booked her passage just yesterday."

"Do you happen to know where she is staying?" asked Jack eagerly.

The captain jerked his thumb in an easterly direction. "She

is putting up at the Pig and Whistle. It's not the best place for a lady, but it will serve for a day or two."

Jack found her there, seated in a corner of the busy taproom, writing letters to be delivered to her children and the colonel. He stood unobserved for a moment, noting sadly that there was no note for him. Apparently she was imparting her plans only to her nearest and dearest—and he was not among them.

Ignoring his own unhappiness, he stepped closer and greeted her cheerfully. "You look very serious, Lady Lovington. What is it that so absorbs your attention?"

"I have been busy making my plans, sir," she responded coolly. "I am about to leave the country and I wish to put my affairs in order before I leave."

"An admirable sentiment, ma'am. Are you making a very long journey?"

"It will seem so to me," she replied, smiling absently. "I am going far away to seek my fortune, sir. I think that it is time that I do so."

"Would you like to seek it with me, Mercy?" he asked tenderly, slipping into the chair beside her and drawing close. He took her hand and held it to his lips, watching her carefully.

"You know full well that I cannot do that, Mr. Grant," she replied, reclaiming her hand without looking into his eyes.

"Why is that? Are you not breaking your engagement with Colonel Anderson?" he asked, indicating the letter in front of her.

"Yes, I am, but I am not doing so because I am running away with you, sir. I am doing it because I know that marrying him would be the wrong thing to do. We would both be unhappy."

"I think you are very wise," said Jack slowly. "I don't think that the two of you would suit—any more than you and Edward or you and Sir George were suited to each other."

She looked up at him then and smiled. "You're right, of

course, Jack," she replied, falling easily back into the habit of calling him by his Christian name. "And it is so comfortable that you know that."

"We would suit, Mercy," he said, his eyes serious. "Why not go with me to Barbados?"

Her eyes flew back to his. "So you guessed where I would go?"

He grinned now, the smile lighting his eyes. "Did you think that I would forget our conversation?" he asked. "I remember everything that you have said to me."

"How kind you are," she murmured, turning away from the intensity of his gaze.

He caught her arm and turned her back toward him. "It isn't kindness, Mercy. You know very well that I love you, so why not run away with me?"

She smiled at him, and for a moment he thought that he had convinced her. Then the smile faded, and her gaze dropped to the letters in front of her.

"Elizabeth loves you, Jack. How could I possibly marry you and make her unhappy?"

"You would prefer that you and I be unhappy, Mercy?" he demanded. "Is that the price of Elizabeth's happiness?"

"Not your happiness, Jack," she said in a low voice. "You could be happy with Elizabeth."

He snorted. "Not when I am in love with you, ma'am. I can assure you that I will not be marrying Elizabeth, even if you run away to Barbados. So why should you throw our happiness away?"

"I can't do it, Jack," she replied, turning away from him. "Don't press me to do so."

"Very well," he said, becoming somewhat exasperated with his beloved. "Will you at least come back to London with me? You can tell the colonel face-to-face that you are breaking off your engagement. That would be the courageous way to do it, instead of sending him a letter."

Stung by his criticism, Lady Lovington rose to her full

height and looked down at him, still seated on the chair beside him.

"Very well, Jack. I know that you're correct about facing the colonel. I was taking the coward's way because I was afraid that I wouldn't have enough strength to do so if he and my children argued with me about it."

"Do you think that you have the courage now?" he asked gently. "I will come with you, if you like, and then escort you back here to put you on the next ship for Barbados."

She nodded. "Thank you, Jack. And I will do precisely that. I will not give way on this matter."

"And I will not ask you to," he replied.

Elizabeth sat beside the colonel's bed as he ate his dinner, once again reading to him to try to raise his spirits. The past three days had taken their toll on him, and she had made it her business to look after him.

Finally, noting that his expression had not lifted even though she was reading a most amusing part of *A Midsummer Night's Dream,* she sighed and laid down the book.

"I am certain, Colonel Anderson, that Mr. Grant will find Mama and bring her back."

"I'm afraid, Elizabeth, that that is the problem. He *will* find her and bring her back. The question is—why is she so unhappy that she ran away to begin with? Is it that she doesn't wish to marry again?"

"It isn't because of you, Colonel Anderson," Elizabeth assured him warmly. "Why, marrying you would be a wonderful thing. Any woman would be pleased to become your wife."

He smiled at her. "I'm afraid that you are overstating the case, my dear, but it's very kind of you to try to spare my feelings."

"I'm not!" she replied indignantly. "You should think better of yourself, Colonel, than to consider for a moment that she might be leaving because of you. The problem is not with you—it's with Reggie and me."

He looked at her in astonishment. "What could be the problem there?" he asked. "I had the impression that she adored you and that the feeling was mutual."

"It is," she sighed. "Well, it almost is," she added reluctantly. "Mama thinks that she is a burden to us because she has a slight tendency to—to get herself into difficult situations."

"Like the race," he observed.

"Like the race," she agreed. "And I'm afraid that, since neither Reggie nor I has the same happy temperament as Mama, that we have criticized her more harshly than we should have."

"And she ran away because of that?" he demanded. "Because you said something critical of her? Are you certain of that, Elizabeth? It seems very weak-minded. I had thought your mother a stronger woman than that."

Dismayed by his reaction, Elizabeth hastened to try to undo the damage without mentioning that they were afraid that they had forced her into the engagement.

"Oh, Mama is far from weak-minded, Colonel. It's just that Reggie and I are very important to her, and I think she takes our comments too much to heart."

"That still seems a little—well, I hate to say it of your mother, but it seems a little flighty. I had not thought her so easily swayed. One should be in charge of one's children, not vice versa—and it is the child who runs away from home, not the mother. Why, you are much more sensible than your own mother, Elizabeth."

Even though she was distressed by his reaction, Elizabeth could not help flushing with pleasure at his compliment.

"You are too hard on her, sir," she assured him. "When she comes home again, everything will be as it should be."

The colonel moved restlessly, causing the pillows behind him to slip out of their proper places. "I don't think that we can go back to the way things were, Elizabeth. Your mother should have come to me for help if she was distressed. When I am her husband, I would expect her to do just that—and I don't believe now that she would."

"Oh, she would, Colonel, she would," Elizabeth reassured him, anxious to undo the damage she had done. She leaned close to him to rearrange the pillows in a more comfortable arrangement.

"Thank you, my dear," he murmured. "You are very kind to an old man."

"Oh, I don't consider you old!" she exclaimed indignantly. "Just look at yourself, Colonel. How could anyone think of you as old?"

With a satisfied smile, the colonel sank back into his pillows. Bending close to him once more, she tucked the covers around him. As she did so, her hair brushed softly across his cheek and, almost involuntarily, he leaned forward and kissed her—a kiss that she warmly returned.

"I can see that it is just as well that Mercy delayed the wedding, Colonel," said Lucinda dryly.

Scarlet-faced, the two jerked apart. "It is not what you think, ma'am," said Colonel Anderson. "Elizabeth was just straightening the bedcovers for me."

"That isn't what we called it," returned Lucinda, "but then I am rather old-fashioned in my ways."

"And I in mine, ma'am," replied the colonel stiffly. "I am accustomed to having people accept my word."

"And I am quite accustomed to accepting the truth of what I see," said Lucinda, her tone grim. "I think that Mercy was very wise in waiting to marry."

"Why was Mama wise in waiting to marry?" demanded Reginald, who had entered the chamber just in time to hear the last part of Lucinda's comment.

"I believe that Colonel Anderson is having second thoughts about the wisdom of his choice of a bride," replied Lucinda.

"It isn't that," began the colonel, and Elizabeth burst into tears.

Reginald stared at his sister and then at the colonel and his aunt. "What is taking place here?" he asked. "I have spent every hour combing London for any sign of Mama, and I come home to find the colonel reconsidering his marriage and my sister in tears. Could someone please tell me what is happening?"

"Don't listen to Aunt Lucinda!" exclaimed Elizabeth tearfully. "I wasn't trying to take the colonel's love away from Mama!"

It was at this inauspicious moment that Jack led Lady Lovington into the colonel's chamber.

"Are we intruding?" he asked coolly, glancing at Mercy to see if she was bearing up under the weight of Elizabeth's exclamation. To his delight, he could see that a little of her natural color was returning. She had been far too pale on the journey back from Liverpool.

"Mama!" exclaimed Reginald, turning to embrace her fiercely. "Where the devil have you been? I've had the most frightful time trying to find you, knowing that it was my fault that you ran away."

"Of course it was not your fault, Reggie. Don't be a goose," replied Lady Lovington, hugging him back and then patting his cheek maternally. "It was quite my own decision, and I apologize to you for frightening you."

She looked at Colonel Anderson, her gaze direct. "And I apologize to you, sir, for letting you know my plans only through a note. I handled everything very thoughtlessly."

Before he could respond, Lucinda said, "Your handsome colonel has something to tell you, Mercy. I believe there has been another change in your wedding plans—but perhaps you'll be able to keep him in the family."

Colonel Anderson again turned a fiery red, as did Elizabeth. The others stared at them, open-mouthed.

"Miss Rochester takes too much upon herself," said Colonel Anderson stiffly. "She misinterpreted something that she saw—"

"He was kissing her," explained Lucinda briefly to Mercy. "I saw it with my own eyes. And she was returning the kiss."

"Oh, Mama!" exclaimed Elizabeth, horrified by the betrayal of which she had been guilty. She rushed to Lady Lovington and buried her face in her shoulder. "I am so very sorry! I did not intend to fall in love with the colonel!"

"In love!" exclaimed the object of her affections, looking at her warmly. "Do you mean that, my dear?"

Elizabeth raised a tear-stained face from her mother's shoulders. "Yes—I mean, no—no, of course not! You and my mother are being married! I would do nothing to interfere with your happiness."

"I should say, dear heart, that our marriage doesn't sound destined for happiness if you and the colonel are in love," replied Lady Lovington, smiling at her.

"Are you, sir?" demanded Reginald, outraged by the lack of decorum. "Are you in love with my sister?"

Colonel Anderson nodded, smiling at Elizabeth and holding out his arms to her.

Elizabeth looked at her mother questioningly and Lady Lovington gave her a little push toward the colonel. She hurried around and sat lightly on the edge of his bed, her head on his shoulder.

"And you assuredly plan to marry Elizabeth after this outrageous behavior," said Reginald stiffly.

"Of course I will marry her—if she will have me," replied Colonel Anderson.

"If you're certain, Mama, that I'm not breaking your heart—" she began, looking across the room at Lady Lovington, who shook her head.

"Not at all," she replied. "The colonel would be an excellent choice for you, my dear."

"Then, yes," sighed Elizabeth, happy at last. "Yes, of course I will marry you, Malcolm."

"And now," snapped Lucinda, her bright eyes darting to Lady Lovington and Mr. Grant, "they're not the only ones in the room smelling of April and May. Go ahead, Mercy. I've never known you to be afraid of telling the truth—once you know it—even if it brought the walls tumbling down on you."

"Well, Elizabeth dear, since you are happy—and since you have no wish to marry Jack—"

"Then I can ask you properly, ma'am," interrupted Mr. Grant, sinking down upon one knee. "Will you do me the honor of becoming my wife?"

"Becoming your wife?" repeated Reginald in astonishment. "Have you all lost your minds?"

He turned to his mother. "We don't know everything we need to know about this man before you marry him, Mama! Why, he has admitted himself that he is a gambler and a wastrel."

"Even so," said Lady Lovington, smiling at Jack Grant, "I am going to marry him."

"If it is any comfort to you," said Jack to Reginald, "I said that I am a gambler because I invested my small savings in the cargo of a ship sailing to the Orient, and the colonel and my friends informed me that I was wasting the ready with both hands."

"And were you?" asked Reginald.

Jack shook his head. "Although I am no nabob, I can keep my wife in comfort—if she doesn't mind the idea of having a husband in trade."

Mercy turned to him and walked into his open arms, smiling. "A husband who is in trade and who lives in the Barbados," she said, and kissed him tenderly.

Outside, a small chip of golden moon shone gently over the scene, and she was sure that she could hear the distant lapping of bright waves on white, sandy shores.

LADY RADCLIFFE'S RUSE

by

Kathryn Kirkwood

For Bob Menadier—thanks for the breeches!

ONE

"I beg your pardon, my dear."

"Think nothing of it, Lord Pomroy." Lady Claire Radcliffe drew back as far as the figures of the country dance would allow in an attempt to achieve a safe distance between Lord Pomroy's feet and her new dancing slippers. Through quick footwork and lucky chance, she had managed to narrowly avoid his missteps thus far, but the dance had not yet ended. Lord Pomroy was by far the clumsiest dancer she had ever had the dubious pleasure of partnering and she had spent the past several minutes avoiding the stomping of his wayward heels.

There were several more apologies from Lord Pomroy before the music concluded and Claire sighed with relief as she glanced down at her feet. The integrity of her slippers had been preserved. For an elderly widower, Lord Pomroy was amazingly vigorous, stamping through the dance with no regard for its figures or its rhythms.

"I do believe the waltz is next." Lord Pomroy took her arm in a proprietary fashion and smiled down at her. "I have always been partial to the waltz. May I have the pleasure, Lady Radcliffe?"

Claire kept the polite smile on her face as she shook her head. The waltz would force her into even closer proximity to the very feet that had threatened her new slippers in the first place. "I fear it would be most unwise, Lord Pomroy.

Two successive dances with the same partner should surely cause speculation as to my propriety."

"Yes, yes. I quite forgot." Lord Pomroy nodded quickly. "Not used to these silly rules, you see. Been in the country too long, I dare say. But you must guard your reputation, of course. Perhaps later in the evening?"

Claire merely smiled again, avoiding a direct answer, and as they began to make their way round the edge of the floor, she gazed with longing at the chair she had vacated to dance with him. It seemed dreadfully far away, and the crush of guests in the ballroom did much to impede their forward progress. Perhaps, if the music began again before she reached the sanctuary of her chair, she would be spared the necessity of further dancing—at least for the duration of the waltz.

It was exactly as Claire wished, for she did not reach her chair until the lilting strains of music had commenced. She sank down gratefully, thanking Lord Pomroy quite nicely for his attentions, and sent him on his way.

"Your daughter looks lovely tonight." The elderly matron in the next chair, a cousin of their hostess, leaned close for a private word. "Such a dear girl. You must be very proud. And she seems intent on assuring a steady stream of partners for you."

"Yes, Lady Jenkins. She does." Claire smiled, but she felt more like frowning. Her daughter, Willow, a vision of loveliness in a shade of golden silk that rivaled the beauty of the sun itself, was in the process of engaging yet another older and eligible gentleman in animated converse.

"It is most generous of her. Most newly engaged young misses would not give a thought to their mothers' happiness. It is clear that your dear Willow wishes for you to share in her good fortune."

Claire nodded, not trusting herself to speak. If Willow did not cease and desist in her infernal matchmaking, she should ring a peal over her head the instant they gained the privacy of their rented town house.

As she watched Willow smile and chat politely, Claire's pride in her daughter's accomplishments replaced her momentary fit of pique. Willow had been judged an Incomparable the instant they had set foot in London. With her laughing brown eyes, shining tresses just a shade darker than auburn, pleasing features, and perfect figure, she had enjoyed a popularity that the other young hopefuls had only dreamed of achieving. Rather than turning her head, this immense popularity had spurred Willow to befriend several other young misses who had not been so fortunate, bringing them into her circle of admirers and assuring them the favorable notice that they might not have otherwise achieved.

To Claire's immense relief, Willow had wasted no time on the pinks of the *ton*. These dandies with their foppish mannerisms and their modish clothing had held no allure for her. Instead, she had sought the company of more thoughtful and earnest young gentlemen, and Claire was the first to admit that her daughter had made a superb match. Just last week, Willow had accepted a declaration from the Marquis of Northrop's eldest son, Lord Ralston. At twenty-one years of age, Philip had assumed his maternal grandfather's title of viscount. Educated at Eton and then at Oxford, Lord Ralston had effected many improvements on his estate. Claire had been most gratified to hear her high-spirited and vivacious daughter discussing the further changes that they should make together. Willow had even gone so far as to enter Lackington's Bookstore in Finsbury Square to request several volumes on the new agricultural methods, and she had approached Claire to ask her advice in setting up a school for the children of their tenants.

One had only to gaze at the proud sparkle in Claire's green eyes to be certain that she regarded her daughter with fondness. Indeed, Claire thought Willow to be perfection itself, if not for one small fault. Somehow, Willow had latched onto the notion that Claire must remarry; she had spared no effort in arranging a suitable parade of suitors for her mother.

A weary sigh escaped Claire's lips as Willow's companion turned and she recognized his features. He was Lord Dankworth, a dour widower in his fifties who had recently re-entered the Marriage Mart. Lord Dankworth was rumored to possess a poor sense of humor and a shocking lack of conversation, and Claire had no doubt that his wife had been driven to her grave by sheer boredom. Lord Dankworth did own a fine estate to the north and several of the older widows had set their caps for him, but if Willow had any notion that her mother should find such a gentleman in the least bit attractive, she was sadly mistaken!

Both Willow and Lord Dankworth glanced over at Claire. He raised his quizzing glass to inspect her features more closely, and his thin lips curved upward in a slight smile. Claire immediately averted her eyes and did her utmost to pretend that she had not noticed the gentleman's interest.

Under the spell of Lord Dankworth's scrutiny, Claire felt the heat rise to her face. Perhaps it was her new gown that had caused Lord Dankworth to smile. She had foolishly allowed her daughter to choose it, since it was to be worn tonight, at Willow's engagement ball. Rather than the gray or lavender hue that Claire had deemed appropriate for her age and status, Willow had insisted that the gown be fashioned of emerald green silk, a shade that exactly matched the color of Claire's eyes and set off her blond hair to perfection. Willow had even gone so far as to hide Claire's lace fichu, guessing quite accurately that Claire should try to tuck it in the stylishly low *décolleté*.

Claire sighed deeply, wondering what new arguments she could devise to convince Willow that she had no intention of marrying again. The truth of the matter was that Claire fully enjoyed her unencumbered status. Once Willow had married, she intended to travel and pursue her interest in unusual artifacts, but this excuse should carry no weight with her daughter. Willow was firmly convinced that a lady could not possibly be content unless she were wed.

Over the past several weeks, Claire had done her utmost to convince Willow to cease her matchmaking efforts. Their last discussion of the matter had taken place only this evening, while they had awaited Lord Ralston's arrival. Claire and Willow had been sitting on chairs in the Drawing Room of their rented town house in Half Moon Street, taking care not to wrinkle their skirts.

Their converse had begun innocently enough, when Willow had complimented her mother's appearance. But then she had announced that she had found a likely match for her dear Mama, a wealthy widower whose appearance was not unattractive and who should be certain to provide Claire with a most generous allowance.

"I have no desire to seek a wealthy husband, Willow." Claire had sighed deeply. Though they had gone over this ground several times in the past, it bore repeating. "The widow's portion your dear father left for me is more than adequate for my needs."

Willow had rolled her eyes to the ceiling. "That is nonsense, Mama. I have no doubt that dear Papa did the best that he could, but only yesterday I observed you gazing with longing at a lovely pearl bandeau in Newman's. I know that you desired to purchase it. Do not deny this, dear Mama. But you did not do so."

"The price was far too dear, Willow, and I did not need the bandeau. You must realize that there is a great difference between desire and need."

"That is precisely my point!" Willow had given a triumphant smile. "If you were to marry this particular gentleman, you should not have to consider the difference. You could have a dozen pearl bandeaus, for he should be happy to buy them for you."

Claire had sighed once again. Willow was well aware of the limitations of her purse. Instead of continuing on this

course, Claire had attempted another. "I have been a widow
for twelve long years, and I have become accustomed to making my own decisions. Most gentlemen should not desire
such an independent wife."

"That thought is hopelessly Gothic, dear Mama." Willow
had waved this argument aside. "The times have changed
and gentlemen now desire more independence in a wife. She
is no longer his chattel, existing for the sole purpose of bearing his heirs and keeping his home in order. A modern husband respects his wife's opinion and relies upon her
intelligence to assist him in running his estates."

Realizing that she had lost ground, Claire had taken another approach. She had asserted that it should be unfair to
the current group of debutantes if she actively sought another
husband. These young misses had not yet experienced the
joys of love and marriage while Claire had already enjoyed
five years of wedded bliss with Willow's dear father.

"Ridiculous." Willow had pronounced, dismissing this argument as well. "I would not expect you to desire a union
with a young gentleman who has but recently reached his
majority. We must concentrate our efforts on the group of
older and well-established widowers who find themselves
desirous of taking a second wife."

Switching directions once again, Claire had presented
what she had assumed was the perfect argument. "But it is
quite impossible for me to marry again, my darling. My heart
is still fully engaged by the fond memories I shall always
hold for your dear father."

"Yes. I am certain that is quite true." Willow had remained
silent for several moments, and Claire had begun to hope
that she had finally put a stop to her daughter's matchmaking
attempts. But once again Willow had effectively parried the
thrust of her mother's objection. "Perhaps you doubt that an
equally worthy gentleman exists. From what you have told
me of my father, I admit that locating such a paragon shall
be most difficult, but it cannot be impossible. You must take

heart, dear Mama. I am determined to find your perfect match."

"But I do not wish for you to find him!" Claire had winced, knowing that she had only caused her daughter to become more resolute. "And even if you do, you cannot be certain that he will desire to marry me. You must remember that I am well past the first bloom of youth. Most gentleman, older or no, should prefer to choose a younger and more attractive bride."

Willow had stared at her mother in shock and then she had burst into peals of laughter. "You are completely in error, dear Mama. You forget that you are a lovely young widow, not an old relict. All you need do is gaze into the glass and you shall see that you have lost none of your beauty. Why, when Philip first set eyes on you, he assumed you to be my sister!"

Claire had found herself unable to dispute this point. Several younger gentlemen had actively sought her favor, laboring under the same misconception, for it was most unusual for a lady of Claire's years to have a grown daughter. She had married Baron Radcliffe, a contemporary of her father's, at an age when most girls were still in the schoolroom. He had come to offer for her shortly after her parents had perished in a carriage accident, and Claire had accepted him most gratefully. In the five years that they had spent as husband and wife, Claire had not regretted her hasty decision for a single instant. She had loved her older husband with all her heart and mourned him still.

"I do not intend to remarry, darling." Claire had stated that fact most resolutely. "I am certain that your actions have been solely prompted by your desire to see me happily settled, but I shall be most displeased if you continue in your efforts on my behalf."

Willow had just opened her mouth, no doubt to make a further objection, when they had heard the sounds of Philip's arrival. Claire had silently given thanks for this timely intervention and turned to her daughter with a smile. "We shall not speak of this further, Willow. My decision is firm. And now let us go to greet your dear fiancé and depart for Lady Bollinger's mansion at once. The hour grows late and I am certain that you wish to arrive promptly at your engagement ball."

Assuming that the subject had been settled to her satisfaction, Claire had set off with her daughter and Lord Ralston. But now, barely an hour into the festivities that Philip's aunt had so kindly arranged, Willow was once again indulging in her matchmaking.

Reaching up to pat an errant blond curl into place, Claire glanced around the beautifully decorated ballroom. Lady Bollinger had spared no expense in preparing for this affair. Lengthy garlands of flowers in riotous bloom had been cleverly attached to the chandeliers and they draped across the ceiling to provide a colorful bower under which to dance. The heady perfume of the flowers intermingled, giving the air a most delightful scent, and the French doors that overlooked the gardens had been opened to the warm night breezes. Hundreds of candles, glittering brightly, provided a lovely illumination, and an excellent orchestra had been hired for their pleasure.

Glancing in her daughter's direction once again, Claire gave a sigh of pure exasperation. Lord Dankworth had just taken leave of Willow and he was making his way toward her chair. Claire was not aware that she had sighed so audibly until Lady Jenkins, who was seated in the next chair, responded.

"Is something wrong, my dear?" Lady Jenkins raised her brows inquiringly.

"No, indeed." Claire quickly assumed a pleasant expression. "For one brief moment, I thought that I had misplaced my reticule, but it is here beneath my chair, exactly where I placed it."

Lady Jenkins laughed, her sharp eyes returning to survey

the dance floor once again. "Just wait until you reach my age, Lady Radcliffe, and you will consider yourself fortunate if the only item you misplace is your reticule. Now do put on your best smile, dear, for I believe Lord Dankworth is headed in our direction. Could it be that he is coming to claim you for this dance?"

"I do hope that he is not." Claire rose from her chair with one quick motion. "I have just remembered a matter of some importance that I must discuss with Lady Bollinger. Perhaps you will be so kind as to accommodate him, Lady Jenkins?"

Lady Jenkins nodded quickly, all smiles. "Of course, my dear. Such a handsome gentleman, and so well situated. I shall be delighted, to be sure."

Claire's eyes scanned the ballroom anxiously and she noted that Lord Dankworth's forward progress had been halted by an acquaintance. She quickly headed off in the opposite direction, breathing a sigh of immense relief as the distance between them widened.

Escape foremost in her mind, Claire spotted their hostess taking her leave from a group at the far end of the ballroom. Her position could not have suited Claire's purpose better, for once she had reached Lady Bollinger's side, she should be separated from Lord Dankworth by the entire length of the dance floor.

Claire quickly traversed the distance and had just requested a word with their hostess, when there was a stir at the doorway to the ballroom. Though the orchestra was still playing and the dance floor was crowded with couples, all conversation ceased as the assemblage caught sight of the handsome gentleman who stood there surveying the crowd.

Despite her best efforts not to stare, Claire's eyes were drawn to the stranger, who was dressed quite properly in formal attire. He appeared to be approximately her age and he carried himself with an air of authority. His hair was dark, a midnight black, and it was worn a bit longer than was fashionable. His skin was tanned darkly by what Claire surmised was a tropical sun, and his eyes gleamed like sapphires as they roamed over the crowd. His expression was aloof, almost arrogant, Claire thought, his pose studiously casual.

Conversation began to flow once again, but Claire noticed that more than a few couples had left off dancing and taken up positions that afforded them a better view of the doorway. Though she knew full well that it was impolite of her to stare, Claire found that she could not tear her gaze from the handsome stranger who appeared to be regarding them all with a critical gaze.

His chin was firm, his nose was perfectly shaped, and his dark brows swept upward at the outer corners, giving him a sardonic look. His broad shoulders and slim waist were encased in a coat that fit him to perfection; he appeared both capable and powerful. A thin white scar, extending from the upper edge of his left brow to a point midway down his cheek, gave him a roguish appearance. Visions of pirates and an adventuresome life on the high seas flashed through Claire's mind. This handsome newcomer was either the quintessential hero or the fundamental scoundrel. Claire could not decide which category suited him better. It did not matter, for he intrigued her completely and she found herself clutching her hands tightly together as he strode into the room and made his way round the crowded dance floor.

"Oh, dear!" Lady Bollinger, the daughter of a duke on her father's side and an undisputed leader of the *ton,* began to ply her fan most anxiously. "I assure you, Lady Radcliffe, that I did not invite him. I did not even know that he had returned to our shores."

"Him? Who?" Claire was aware that her grammar was imperfect, but this was no time to quibble about semantics.

"The new Earl of Sommerset. He is my late husband's nephew. Perhaps you have heard him referred to as El Diablo?"

Claire shook her head, but her eyes widened, recognizing

the Spanish word for devil. "He is a Spaniard, Lady Bollinger?"

"He is English, though Spain was his mother's country. She came here to marry my late husband's brother and died giving birth to his heir. He called her *condesa,* but their titles are different from ours, you know. She was the last of her line and when she died, her family's wealth passed to her son."

Claire nodded, intrigued. "Did you ever have occasion to meet her, Lady Bollinger?"

"Only once. She possessed a dark beauty that captivated all who set eyes on her. I found her to be most charming, though her command of our language was slight. The earl assumed the part of her translator and we enjoyed a delightful afternoon in their company."

"The earl spoke her language?"

"Yes, indeed." Lady Bollinger smiled. "He was a most remarkable gentleman and I was inordinately fond of him. He traveled most extensively and possessed the ability to speak in several tongues quite fluently."

Claire smiled as she pictured the beautiful Spanish lady and her noble English husband. The *condesa* must have loved him dearly to leave her home and live with him in a land where she did not even speak the language. It was a most romantical story until one considered the poor little baby who had never even known his mother.

"He was such a sweet little babe," Lady Bollinger continued, as if she had read Claire's thoughts. "I remember feeling quite sorry that he was to be raised by servants and such, as his father was so often away."

"The earl did not see fit to remarry to provide a mother for his son?"

"No." Lady Bollinger sighed. "My late husband raised the issue once, but the earl dismissed it out of hand. He became quite agitated, claiming that his son was receiving excellent care and asking us not to concern ourselves further. Naturally, we did not broach the subject again."

"Naturally."

Lady Bollinger leaned close and lowered her voice. "It was quite apparent to me that the earl was suffering from a broken heart. He had truly loved his *condesa,* you see, and he could not bring himself to take another wife."

"But what of his son? Was he not lonely?" Claire also lowered her voice.

"I do not believe so. He had a delightful governess and the earl saw to it that the children of the estate were made welcome as his friends. When he grew older, he enjoyed a fine education and then he went on to travel with the earl. During those years, they spent almost every moment together, dividing their time between their holdings here and in Spain. It was only when the earl grew ill that he ceased his travels and repaired to his favorite English estate. He died there at Michaelmas, after a long and debilitating illness, and I assume that is why my nephew has returned."

Claire could not help but be curious. "The new earl was in Spain, Lady Bollinger?"

"Yes. He sailed there shortly before the conclusion of the past Season. No doubt he has returned to collect his father's inheritance and assume the duties of his new title."

"I see." Claire nodded.

"I must admit that I have always regarded him fondly." Lady Bollinger gave a small smile. "He is a most charming rogue. But you must warn your sweet daughter to have a caution in his presence, for I fear he is not a gentleman."

Claire's mouth opened and then quickly closed again. She did not quite dare to ask Lady Bollinger in precisely which way the new Earl of Sommerset was not a gentleman.

Lady Bollinger leaned close once again. "I fear my dear nephew is not to be trusted in the company of young ladies. Indeed, a dreadful scandal hangs above his head like an evil cloud."

Claire glanced at the earl again. Though she knew she was indulging in absurdity, she half expected to see a dark haze hovering round his shoulders. "Is this scandal the reason that some call him EL Diablo?"

"Yes." Lady Bollinger nodded. "Now that he is earl, none will dare to call him El Diablo to his face, but I am certain he shall still be the subject of more than a few whispered *on dits*. A scandal of that magnitude shall not easily be forgotten."

Claire began to frown. "Please enlighten me, Lady Bollinger. What did the new earl do to cause such a scandal?"

"You must be told, I suppose." Lady Bollinger sighed deeply. "If I do not tell you, another of my guests shall be quick to do so and I would rather you learn the truth of the matter from me. I do hope that it will not cause you to change your opinion of our family."

"I assure you that it will not." Claire smiled kindly at Lady Bollinger. "It should be most unusual not to have at least one bounder in a family so large as yours."

Lady Bollinger appeared much reassured by this comment and she returned Claire's smile gratefully. "My husband's brother took a turn for the worse last year and he sent for his son to attend him. He urged my nephew to take part in the Season, to find a suitable young lady to marry, and to remain in England to manage his estates. But while my dear nephew was here in London, he compromised two young debutantes."

Claire's eyes widened and she bit back a most inappropriate giggle. "Two? At the same time?"

"Yes. Both were discovered in his town house, hidden in his bedchamber. And though he was not in residence at the time, both young ladies produced notes from him, inviting them there at that precise hour for an assignation."

Claire lifted her brows, curious as to why the new earl had gone to the trouble of arranging two assignations that he had not planned to attend. "Tell me, Lady Bollinger, was your nephew considered a desirable catch?"

"Yes, indeed." Lady Bollinger nodded quickly. "His inheritance from his mother was immense and it came to him when he reached his majority. As if that were not enough, he was also the sole heir to his father's title and fortune."

Claire permitted a flicker of a smile to cross her face. Lady Bollinger's answer had borne out her suspicions. "I do believe I can surmise the rest, Lady Bollinger. The mothers discovered the notes that the young ladies had left behind and rushed off to his town house to discover their daughters there?"

"That is precisely correct! How did you know, Lady Radcliffe? Have you heard this distressing tale before?"

"No, I have not." Claire smiled as she shook her head. "But I should not put it past an anxious mama to use every means, fair and foul, to assist her daughter in making such a desirable match."

"Oh, surely not, Lady Radcliffe! Why, I am acquainted with one of the mothers and she should never stoop so low as that."

"Not even for the opportunity to welcome the earl's heir into the family? A gentleman who already possessed vast holdings and who should soon be richer than Golden Ball?"

"Lady Radcliffe!" Lady Bollinger looked askance. "I regard myself as an excellent judge of character and I am certain that this particular lady should never give way to such trickery, not even to save her husband's estate."

"Such an alliance should have been welcome then?"

"Why, yes. It should have been *most* welcome in this instance." Lady Bollinger assumed a thoughtful expression. "Dear Lady Radcliffe, I dislike to view things with a suspicious eye, but now that I think on it, the parents of the other young lady were also in dire financial straits. You do not suppose that . . ."

Lady Bollinger stopped speaking as her nephew approached and she quickly assumed her most welcoming smile. "How good to see you, nephew. Had I known that you had arrived in Town, I should have hastened to send you an invitation. You are always most welcome."

"Thank you, Aunt Marcella." The gentleman Claire had come to regard as El Diablo bowed quite formally. Then he noticed Claire's curious glance and he favored her with a smile. "I do not believe I have had the pleasure."

Lady Bollinger wore a look of some concern as she turned to Claire. "Lady Radcliffe, may I present my nephew, the Earl of Sommerset?"

"I am delighted to meet you, Lady Radcliffe." The earl gave her a devilish grin. "It is most kind of my aunt to introduce me to the loveliest lady at the ball. Your husband is the most fortunate of men."

Claire smiled back, despite herself. Though she was certain he was merely being polite, his comment was most delightful. "I am pleased to make your acquaintance, sir, and I am certain that my late husband would have been gratified to hear your compliment."

"Late husband?" The earl's roguish smile was quickly replaced by a compassionate expression. "My condolences, Lady Radcliffe. No doubt it is difficult to be widowed at such a young age."

"It was indeed, and though it was twelve long years ago, I miss him still. I am most fortunate that he left me with the comfort of a lovely daughter. Her name is Willow and she has recently become engaged to your cousin, Philip."

"I had heard that Philip was engaged." The earl's smile reappeared and he turned to survey the ballroom. "Your daughter is the charming young miss in the golden dress who is preparing to waltz with him?"

Claire glanced around to see Willow and Philip taking the floor and she nodded quickly. "Yes, that is Willow."

"Will you join me in this waltz, Lady Radcliffe?" He raised his brows inquiringly. "When it is concluded, I should be grateful if you would introduce me to your daughter. I am most eager to meet my cousin's fiancée."

Lady Bollinger, who had been scanning the room most anxiously, turned back to address them. "I fear Lady Radcliffe is not free, nephew, as I see Lord Dankworth approaching. Did you not promise him this waltz, Lady Radcliffe?"

Claire glanced up and saw that Lord Dankworth was striding purposefully in her direction, a most determined expression on his face. Claire had no doubt that Lady Bollinger had gestured for him to rescue her from the clutches of El Diablo, but Claire was not certain that she wished to be saved. Her dear husband had uttered an old maxim in similar situations: *From the frying pan into the fire.*

"Lady Radcliffe?"

The earl smiled as he extended his arm. He was waiting for her answer and Claire came to a hasty decision. If Lord Dankworth was the frying pan, she should much prefer the fire. With great dispatch, she placed her gloved hand on his arm and smiled up at him sweetly. "By all means, sir. I am not yet engaged for this waltz and I should be most delighted to dance it with you."

TWO

Claire gave a small chuckle of amusement as the Earl of Sommerset escorted her to the dance floor. Lord Dankworth had appeared quite dismayed to see her on the earl's arm and though Claire did not like to be uncharitable, she could not help but rejoice that she had escaped the dour widower's attentions.

"You obviously find my company a source of amusement, Lady Radcliffe." The earl began to grin. "How refreshing that is! Most ladies of your caliber should be mortified to be seen with me."

"I am not like most ladies." Claire smiled as they assumed the correct pose and the earl swept her across the floor. He was a skilled partner and she soon found that she was enjoying their dance most thoroughly.

"Perhaps you are more charitable than most, but I should not like to take unfair advantage of your good nature." The earl's eyes darkened perceptibly. "I know that you are a relative newcomer to the London scene. Is it possible that no one has seen fit to warn you about me?"

"I have been warned, sir, and I have dismissed it out of hand. I shall dance with whomever I please."

"You have courage!" The earl's smile returned. "Still, you should give a care for your reputation, Lady Radcliffe. If I were a true gentleman and if I were not enjoying our waltz so completely, I should promptly escort you to your daughter in an attempt to still the tongues that are certain to wag when you are observed in my company."

Claire giggled. "I fear it's far too late for that, sir, as the tongues are already wagging. If you doubt my word, you have merely to observe your cousin's mother, Lady Northrup."

"Amelia Northrup has always been a peahen." The earl laughed. "My father was used to say that she had bewitched poor, stammering Gerald with her charms and revealed herself to be a vain and silly chit only after they had spoken their vows. Still, it is the best he could have done, I imagine, as poor Gerald is missing a few cards in his deck. It never ceases to amaze me that Philip has turned out as well as he has."

Claire stared at Lord Sommerset in shock and then she gave a delighted laugh. He had put into voice her own thoughts when she had first met the Marquis and Marchioness of Northrup. Searching for some polite comment to make, Claire settled on the earl's last statement. At least he appeared to approve of Willow's fiancé. "You are acquainted with Lord Ralston then?"

"I am. His land adjoins one of my country estates and he has had the good manners to greet me pleasantly when our paths have crossed. Perhaps he is one of the few who do not believe that I have disgraced myself beyond redemption."

Claire nodded. "You refer to the two young ladies who were discovered in your town house last Season?"

"You know then?" The earl's eyes widened as she nodded. "And still you agreed to partner me? You are indeed an amazing woman, Lady Radcliffe!"

"Not so amazing as all that. Any fool could surmise that those silly young misses and their grasping mamas were attempting to manipulate you into an alliance."

"You are not only beautiful, you also have good sense." The earl threw back his head and laughed. "Are you endeavoring to save my reputation, Lady Radcliffe?"

"Of course not. I have no standing with the *ton* and such an effort on my part would yield little or no result."

"Then why did you agree to join me in this waltz?"

Claire hesitated to tell him, but she knew she must be truthful. "I must admit that I am using you, Lord Sommerset."

"Using me?" His brows shot up in surprise. "For what reason?"

Claire was about to answer when the orchestra played the final bar. Her waltz with the earl had concluded, but she could not leave him without explaining. "I did not care to dance with Lord Dankworth. You saved me from that duty, and I thank you most gratefully."

The earl began to frown. "You jeopardized your reputation by dancing with an assumed rake rather than join Lord Dankworth in the waltz?"

"Yes, indeed. And I shall be delighted to do it again, if the occasion arises. You are an excellent partner, sir, and I enjoyed myself thoroughly."

"As did I, my dear lady." The earl dipped his head in a bow. "I shall not, however, embarrass you further by asking you to introduce me to your daughter. Instead, I believe I shall join one of the tables that Aunt Marcella has set up for a hand or two of whist."

The earl led Claire to the group surrounding her daughter and thanked her most politely for the dance. After she had given the proper response, he turned on his heel and left the ballroom, looking neither to the left nor the right as he strode out the door.

"I must have a word with you, Mama!" Willow came immediately to Claire's side and drew her quickly away to a secluded alcove. "Whatever were you thinking? We saw you dancing with . . . with . . ."

"The Earl of Sommerset?" Claire supplied the name that her daughter appeared so reluctant to utter.

"Yes! I did not know that he would be in attendance, or

I should certainly have warned you. He was the cause of a dreadful scandal last Season!"

Claire smiled sweetly at her daughter. There were times when Willow's sense of propriety interfered with her good sense. "I know, dear. Lady Bollinger told me all about it."

"Then why on earth did you consent to dance with him?"

There was a disapproving frown on her daughter's lovely face and Claire had the irrepressible urge to laugh. "Because, my darling, I did not care to dance with Lord Dankworth for fear I should die of boredom. And El Diablo is a simply marvelous dancer!"

As the minutes ticked by, Claire found herself watching the door to the ballroom, hopeful that the earl should return to claim her in another dance. She had performed her duty on the dance floor with Lord Dankworth and she had found him to be every bit as tedious as she had imagined. She had also taken a turn round the floor with Lord Chatsworth, another older gentleman whom Willow had sent her way. Lord Chatsworth was a bachelor and after a few moments in his company, Claire had discovered the reason for his unmarried state. Though Lord Chatsworth had a pleasing appearance, his brainbox was filled with nothing but straw. While some unfortunate gentlemen of diminished capacity were charming in their own way, Lord Chatsworth was simply a dullard with nothing but his title to recommend him.

At the end of the second hour, Claire came to the unhappy conclusion that the earl had taken his leave. Rather than stay and endure Willow's further matchmaking attempts, Claire retrieved her shawl. She was about to plead the headache and depart when she saw the object of her fascination standing at the open doorway of the ballroom.

Without realizing that she had done so, Claire's eyes began to sparkle and a smile turned up the corners of her lips. The most interesting gentleman she had met this entire Season was back!

Filled with a desire to speak with him again, Claire attempted to meet his eyes. But before he could glance in her direction, a lovely young lady hastily crossed the floor to claim his attention. She was Willow's friend, Miss Dorinda Fellows, a true beauty and a flirt of the first water.

Claire watched as Miss Fellows placed her gloved hand on the earl's arm and smiled up at him charmingly. Even Willow, who had been raised to be charitable, had confessed only last evening that she feared dear Dorinda's morals did not bear close scrutiny. Claire had been shocked at this criticism as Miss Fellows was Willow's bosom bow, but her daughter had admitted that though they were still friends, she could not approve of Dorinda's latest plans. It seemed that Lord Fellows had lost heavily at the gaming tables and now faced utter ruin. If his daughter failed to bring a wealthy gentleman up to scratch by the conclusion of the Season, he should lose the family estate. Dorinda's response to this distressing situation had been to declare to Willow that she would stop at nothing to make a match that would save her father from financial embarrassment.

Claire sighed as she watched Miss Fellows converse with the earl. Dorinda plied her fan and posed quite charmingly, even going so far as to drop her handkerchief so that the earl should have to retrieve it. Her flirtation was obvious to all who observed her and Claire could not help but wonder whether the earl had heard of her desperate need to find a wealthy husband. It seemed unlikely, for Willow had been taught not to carry tales and she had mentioned that Dorinda had confided in none other.

Just as Claire was debating whether or not she should intervene, the earl took his leave from Miss Fellows. He bowed, smiled politely, and removed himself to join the group surrounding his aunt, Lady Bollinger. Claire breathed a deep sigh of relief as Dorinda crossed the floor to Willow's side.

She appeared quite overset and Claire had no doubt that Miss Fellows was piqued at her failure to claim the earl in a dance.

Lady Jenkins gave an amused laugh and leaned close to Claire. "Did you see *that*, Lady Radcliffe?"

"See what, Lady Jenkins?" Claire's expression was perfectly composed, though she was certain she knew what had prompted the lady's interest.

"Miss Fellows and the Earl of Sommerset. She was flirting quite shamelessly with him. It appeared that the gel was angling for a dance, but the earl wisely refused to take her bait. Perhaps he is not the rapscallion we have been led to believe?"

"Perhaps not." Claire smiled politely. "I had occasion to waltz with the earl, and I found his behavior most proper."

"You do not say! It is always possible he has reformed, of course, in the aftermath of his father's death."

Claire merely nodded. She did not wish to be drawn into taradiddle with Lady Jenkins, who was reputed as the source of more than a few *on dits*. But before she could think of a suitable reply to make to discourage any further converse about the matter, Willow gestured to her from across the room. "Will you excuse me, Lady Jenkins? My daughter is signaling for me to join her."

"Of course. Run along, dear. And when you return, you must tell me all about your dance with the earl."

Claire felt a palpable surge of relief as she took leave of Lady Jenkins. She vowed that she would not return to this particular chair, now that she was warned of Lady Jenkins's desire to quiz her about the Earl of Sommerset. Claire arrived at Willow's side in short order and turned to her daughter with a smile. "You wished to speak to me, dear?"

"Yes, Mama." Willow appeared anxious as she drew her mother away from the group. When they were well removed from curious ears, she reached out to take her mother's arm. "I need your advice, Mama, on a matter of the greatest importance."

Claire nodded quickly. "Of course. What is it, dear?"

"I have just spoken with Dorinda and I fear that she may be up to some trickery."

"And this trickery concerns the Earl of Sommerset?"

"Why, yes!" Willow's eyes widened in surprise. "How did you know, Mama?"

"I observed Miss Fellows plying her wiles on the earl. She appeared quite overset when he did not respond as she wished."

"That is it, exactly." Willow assumed a frown. "Dorinda has set her cap for the earl and I know that she will use any means possible to gain her objective. I fear what she may do, Mama. Dorinda is desperate enough to cause a terrible scandal."

"I daresay you are right, dear. Perhaps I should keep a sharp eye on Miss Fellows."

"Would you, Mama?" Willow appeared much relieved when Claire nodded. "She is my friend and I should not like to see her reputation compromised."

Claire smiled at her daughter. It was to her Willow's credit that she was more concerned about her Dorinda's reputation than she was about the possibility that her engagement party could be the scene of a scandal.

"There is one other thing, Mama." Willow looked anxious again. "Lord Dankworth complained that you did not appear to welcome his company. I told him that he was mistaken, of course, but I think it wise if you seek him out to assure him that you value his attentions."

"But I do *not* value his attentions. Lord Dankworth is a stuffy old bore."

"Mama!" A startled expression crossed Willow's lovely face. "I have it on the best authority that Lord Dankworth is a prize catch. Why, there are a half-dozen ladies here this evening who have set their caps for him!"

"Then I shall let one of them have him."

"But Mama . . ."

"I do not wish to marry, Willow." Claire interrupted what was certain to be an objection from her daughter. "We discussed the matter earlier this evening. Have you forgotten?"

"No, but Philip and I have reached the conclusion that you have not as yet met your perfect match. I would not be so bold as to choose for you, Mama. You know I would not! We are simply endeavoring to present suitable gentlemen to you, that is all. I really do have your best interests at heart, Mama. Surely you cannot doubt that!"

"I do not doubt it, dear." Claire gave a resigned sigh. It would not be so simple as she had thought to convince Willow to cease her matchmaking efforts. "We shall discuss this again, when we are in private. In the meantime, dear, please do not send any more gentlemen my way. I cannot succeed in my observation of Miss Fellows if I am distracted."

Willow nodded quickly. "Of course, Mama. I did not think of that. I promise that I will not . . ."

Claire turned to her daughter in alarm as Willow abruptly stopped speaking. "What is it, Willow?"

"Dorinda was standing by the French doors to the garden, but now she is gone."

"Then I shall go after her straightaway." Claire gave her daughter a reassuring smile. "No doubt she is simply taking the air on the veranda."

"Shall I ask Philip to accompany you?" Willow looked a bit anxious.

"No, dear. I am quite capable of crossing the floor under my own steam. You must go and enjoy your evening. It is a party for you, after all."

"Thank you, Mama."

Claire smiled as she watched her daughter walk away. At least she would be safe from further matchmaking efforts on this night. But Willow had been correct in her observation. Miss Fellows was indeed absent from the ballroom. Thankful that a widow of her standing could come and go as she pleased without the necessity of a chaperone, Claire made her way to the French doors and stepped out onto the wide veranda that overlooked Lady Bollinger's pleasure gardens.

Miss Fellows was nowhere in sight on the veranda. Claire did not think she would be so bold as to enter the gardens alone, but she stood at the rail and scrutinized the vista that was spread out below her, watching for any sign of movement on the garden paths.

As she watched, a slight breeze caressed her heated cheeks and Claire sighed with pleasure at escaping the overheated and crowded ballroom. It was a romantical evening with the stars glittering brightly overhead and the perfumed scent of night-blooming flowers wafting gently up from the foliage below. She stood lost in thought for a moment, leaning against the rail and surveying the gardens with unseeing eyes. But then her senses sharpened as she heard loose stones crunch on the path that led to the fountain. Someone was in the gardens below, enjoying this lovely evening.

Claire frowned slightly as she caught sight of a gentleman alone. Did he choose to be so, or had he failed to convince the lady of his choice to accompany him?

Flambeaux shed light on the path at intervals and Claire waited for the gentleman to enter the nearest circle of illumination. She gave a gasp of surprise and shock as she recognized the features of the Earl of Sommerset. How odd to discover him all alone in Lady Bollinger's gardens!

No sooner had the earl gone round the bend in the path than Claire heard the sound of pursuing footsteps. These were lighter and much softer than the earl's had been, and Claire surmised that they belonged to a lady. As the female figure passed by the very same torch, Claire gave another gasp of shock. It was Dorinda Fellows and she was clearly pursuing the earl.

There was nothing for it but to follow them. A scandal would result if the earl and Miss Fellows were observed together in the darkness. Thankfully, Claire was a suitable chaperone and her presence should provide the appearance of respectability. But what if the earl did not wish to be rescued from Miss Fellows's attentions and had arranged for their assignation in the garden?

Claire squared her shoulders and walked resolutely down the steps, heading toward the path that the earl and Miss Fellows had taken. She would be very quiet so as not to make her presence known to them. If she discovered that she was in error and that their rendezvous had been previously arranged, she would simply retrace her steps.

Rounding a bend, Claire stopped in mid-step as she heard an unusual noise. It sounded like fabric tearing, and she parted the thick leaves of a flowering tree to discover the source of the noise. What she saw made her press her hand tightly to her lips to stifle a shocked cry. Miss Fellows was standing at the edge of Lady Bollinger's garden pond, deliberately ripping the bodice of her lovely ball gown!

A disapproving frown crossed Claire's face as she realized the ramifications of Miss Fellows's act. No doubt the silly chit was intending to blame the Earl of Sommerset for her own devious action!

Claire felt her anger rise at this outrage. The earl had already been accused of two scandals during the past Season. Another such incident, during this current Season, should certainly dash any good will he might have left among the members of the *ton*. If he did not marry Miss Fellows straightaway, the earl should be cut by the gentry and nobility alike and his reputation would be irrevocably ruined.

Before Claire could step forward to confront Miss Fellows, footsteps sounded on the path. The earl came into view and his eyes widened as he caught sight of Miss Fellows's dishabille.

"My dear Miss Fellows! Are you hurt?" The earl rushed forward with a frown on his face. "Tell me the name of the gentleman who treated you so shabbily and I shall demand satisfaction in your name."

Miss Fellows smiled quite calmly, an act so incongruous

in light of her disarray that Claire could not help but gasp. And then she began to shriek. "How dare you take such liberties with me! Unhand me, sirrah!"

As Claire watched, Miss Fellows whirled on her heel to return to the ballroom, no doubt intending to claim that she had been accosted by the earl. But before she could gain more than a step, Claire moved forward to stop her.

"Lady Radcliffe! You must save me!" Miss Fellows managed to sound quite desperate as she threw herself into Claire's arms. "He . . . he tore my gown and attempted to ravish me! Now I am compromised and I shall be ruined unless he agrees to marry me!"

Claire knew that she must act quickly to defuse this unfortunate situation. The earl looked quite ready to explode at this unfair charge and Claire gave him a warning glance. "But the earl cannot marry you, my dear Miss Fellows, as he is already engaged to me."

"You . . . you are engaged to *her?*" Miss Fellows turned to the earl, her eyes wide with shock. "But . . . I did not know!"

The earl glanced at Claire and his lips twitched with amusement. "That is most understandable, Miss Fellows. I also find it difficult to believe."

"It *was* quite sudden and most unexpected, but I have no doubt that we shall soon become accustomed to our happy decision." Claire gave the earl what she hoped was a convincing smile. "Do not be concerned, my dearest. Poor Miss Fellows is quite understandably overset and I am certain that when she returns to her senses, she will thank you kindly for saving her from tumbling into Lady Bollinger's pond."

Miss Fellows pulled back to frown at Claire. "But I did not fall!"

"Yes, Miss Fellows, you did." Claire removed her shawl and draped it around Miss Fellows's shoulders, tying it firmly in place to cover her torn gown. "I was standing here the entire time, you see, and I observed you catch your lovely gown on that branch beside the pool. When you attempted to free yourself, you came dangerously close to a most unpleasant dunking. You owe my dear fiancé your thanks for rescuing you most handily."

Miss Fellows hesitated for a moment, staring into Claire's determined eyes. Then she nodded quickly and turned to the earl. "It all happened so quickly that I was confused. Please accept my apology, Lord Sommerset."

"Of course." The earl nodded gravely, but his eyes were twinkling as he glanced at Claire once again. "You will see to the repair of Miss Fellows's lovely gown, my . . . my dear?"

Claire dipped her head in assent as she turned to Miss Fellows. "I have no doubt that one of Lady Bollinger's maids shall be able to mend your gown, my dear. And you shall wear my shawl for the remainder of the evening so that none shall know of this unfortunate incident."

"Thank you, Lady Radcliffe. You . . . you and the earl are truly engaged?" Miss Fellows looked as if she could not believe this turn of events.

"Yes indeed, Miss Fellows." Claire smiled brightly at the thoroughly flustered girl. "It happened only this evening, you see, and we have not yet seen fit to make our announcement. We did not think it kind to draw attention to ourselves at my daughter's engagement ball. We prefer to keep it a secret for some time longer, perhaps until after dear Willow and Philip are wed. I do hope that you will not give us away?"

"N . . . no. I shall not." Miss Fellows shook her head.

"Allow me to assist you, Miss Fellows." There was a hard gleam in the earl's eye as he grasped the girl's arm. "We shall go round by the side entrance. From there it is only a few steps to the ladies withdrawing room."

Their return to the mansion was accomplished in silence and the hall was deserted when they made their entrance.

The earl took his leave of them at the bottom of the staircase and Claire and Miss Fellows managed to traverse the distance to the ladies' withdrawing room without being observed. Once Claire had summoned one of Lady Bollinger's maids to see to the mending of Miss Fellows's gown, she left the girl in her capable hands and exited the chamber with a grateful sigh. She was about to make her way back to the ballroom when the earl stepped out from a nearby alcove and took her by the arm.

"La, sir!" Claire gave a shaky laugh. "You startled me!"

"Then we are even, for you startled me in the garden. Come with me, madame. We have much to discuss."

Claire was silent as the earl led her to a small sitting room. He poured her a glass of sherry without bothering to ask whether or not she wanted it, handed it to her with no preamble, and gestured toward a settee. Rather than object to his obvious conclusion that she could do with a taste of spirits, Claire took the seat he indicated and found herself sipping the sherry gratefully.

"You claimed to be my fiancée." The earl took a seat on a neighboring chair and swirled the brandy that he had poured for himself. A ghost of a smile crossed his handsome face and he regarded her with amusement. "Whatever possessed you to come up with *that,* Lady Radcliffe?"

Claire shrugged, taking another fortifying sip of her sherry. "It was obvious that Miss Fellows thought to trap you into marriage and I did not wish to see you so ill used. I also wished to avoid such a scandal at my daughter's engagement ball."

"And you thought that if you claimed to be my fiancée, I could plead a previous commitment?"

"Precisely." Claire nodded. The sherry she had consumed had created a warm glow throughout her body and she found that she was much more relaxed than she had anticipated. "I saw Miss Fellows follow you into the garden, you see, and my daughter had previously informed me of her desperate need for a husband."

"So you thought to save me from her clutches, Lady Radcliffe?"

"Indeed." Claire nodded again. "It does sound ridiculous when you state it in that manner, but I did not wish to see you forced into marriage."

"And you gave no thought to your own reputation?"

Claire watched his brows rise with the question and she was puzzled. "Of course not. It was not my reputation at stake, sir. It was yours."

"I beg to differ, Lady Radcliffe." The earl took a healthy sip of his brandy. "Your reputation shall surely suffer when it becomes known that you are engaged to a known rake."

"But it will *not* become known. Miss Fellows has promised not to divulge it."

The earl chuckled ruefully. "I fear you are wrong, Lady Radcliffe. As we sit here quietly conversing, the news of our engagement is sweeping through the ballroom."

"But how can that be? Miss Fellows has given her word not to betray us."

"You are truly an innocent!" The earl threw back his head and laughed heartily. "Miss Fellows may not intend to betray us, but mark my words, she will let it slip. She will trust one friend with the news, swearing her to silence. And that one friend will tell another. This is the manner in which *on dits* begin, Lady Radcliffe. Our engagement is simply too juicy a tidbit to stay secret for long."

Claire's cheeks flushed with embarrassment. He was right, of course. "What would you wish me to do, Lord Sommerset?"

"Do? Why, nothing, my dear." The earl began to grin. "We must keep up our pretense for the remainder of the Season and then you shall cry off."

Claire opened her mouth to object, but she quickly closed

it again. If she admitted that she was not engaged to the earl, he should be fair game for Miss Fellows's scheme.

"I assume this is acceptable to you, Lady Radcliffe. Unless, of course, you are in the market for a new husband and our counterfeit engagement will stand in your way?"

"Oh, no!" Claire shook her head quickly. "I am most definitely not in the market for a husband!"

The earl raised one eyebrow. "Are you certain, Lady Radcliffe? I assumed that to be the reason your daughter was sending a stream of eligible gentlemen your way."

"That is *her* reason, but I have no intention of marrying again and I have told her so countless times. Unfortunately, Willow will simply not cease in her matchmaking schemes."

"She shall be required to cease now." The earl chuckled. "She cannot attempt to make a match for a mother who is already engaged."

Claire began to see the humor of their situation and she laughed with delight. "You are quite right, Lord Sommerset. If we do not admit that we are *not* engaged, Willow shall be foiled. But what of you, sir? Will our counterfeit engagement disturb your plans?"

"Quite the opposite, dear lady." The earl shook his head most emphatically. "It shall be of great benefit to me as it will serve to keep the conniving mamas and their eager daughters at bay. You see, Lady Radcliffe, I share your sentiments regarding marriage."

"Then you do not intend to marry, either?" Claire was a bit surprised.

"Not at this time, no." The earl stood up and crossed to her, extending his arm to draw her to her feet. "I find that I am delighted to have declared for you, Lady Radcliffe."

Claire smiled up at him. "And I am delighted that you have done so, Lord Sommerset."

"John." The earl corrected her. "If we are engaged, you must call me John."

Claire's smile grew wider, thankful that her impulsive action should prove to be of benefit to them both. "Yes, John. And you must call me Claire."

"Claire." The earl smiled back. Then he slipped both his arms around her and gathered her close to him. "I believe it is customary for a gentleman to kiss his intended bride?"

"Yes, indeed." Claire obediently raised her face, anticipating a chaste kiss upon her cheek. But instead of touching her cheek lightly with his lips, the earl cupped her chin quite firmly in his hand and placed a kiss upon her lips.

His kiss was initially polite, a mere brush of his lips against hers. But then it deepened and Claire drew her breath in sharply. Despite her intentions, she began to respond to the sweet pressure of his mouth against hers. Kissing her dear husband had been most pleasant; Claire had enjoyed it thoroughly. But the Earl of Sommerset's kiss was so passionate, it took her very breath away.

Was she becoming unhinged by the events of this startling evening? Claire gave a swift, fleeting thought to her own sanity, but she found it impossible to concentrate when the earl's warm lips demanded her full attention. A soft moan escaped her throat and then she was returning his kiss with a passion she had not known she possessed.

Their kiss seemed to last forever, the melting of two souls in a fierce, searing heat. Their bodies cleaved together, his hard and strong, hers soft and womanly, until Claire no longer had any sense of where she ended and where he began. When he released her at last, Claire discovered that she was quite breathless and she clung to him, her senses reeling. He also appeared shaken, and they stared at each other in amazement.

After a moment of silent bemusement, the earl released his hold on her and took her arm quite properly. "I do believe that our counterfeit engagement should prove to be quite interesting, dear Claire."

His voice shook slightly and Claire discovered that she

could not find hers at all. She merely nodded, a telling blush settling on her cheeks.

"Shall we return to the ballroom to accept our congratulations?"

Claire nodded again and found just enough of her voice to say, "Yes indeed, dear John."

THREE

"Is it true, sir?"

"Indeed it is, Hartley." John Pierpont, the Earl of Somerset, grinned as he nodded to his loyal retainer. Hartley had served his father before him; that gave him a certain license to ask questions that would be considered impertinent if they had come from another member of the staff. It seemed that word of his impromptu engagement on the previous evening had reached his valet's ears. This did not surprise John in the slightest as Hartley had a sister in his Aunt Marcella's employ.

"I do not believe that I have made the lady's acquaintance." Hartley's statement was properly formal.

"That is not surprising, for neither had I, until last night." John's grin grew wider at his valet's shocked expression. "Please ring for my coffee, Hartley. I intend to pay a morning call on my fiancée and I shall leave it to you to see that I am properly dressed."

As Hartley hurried to the clothes press, John belted his dressing gown and strode to the small study that adjoined his bedchamber. A cheery fire had been laid in the grate and he took a seat in his favorite chair. His pot of strong coffee arrived almost instantly, proof that Hartley had alerted the kitchen before he had climbed the stairs to his master's chambers. John poured out a cup of the bracing brew that he had learned to enjoy in his mother's country, and sipped it gratefully as he stared thoughtfully out the window that over-looked the quiet residential street.

The kiss he had shared with Lady Radcliffe had been an amazing surprise. He had intended to merely brush her lips with his, but the feel of her smooth, heated skin on his hands and the sweet manner in which she assented to his demand had unleashed a powerful force within him. He had kept a mistress in Spain and had thought to do the same in London, when he found a suitable woman who captured his fancy. Lord knew that he was no stranger to passion, but Lady Radcliffe's response to his kiss had taken him completely unawares. Claire Radcliffe had a wealth of hidden depths and he only wished that he might plumb them. But though he was well-known as a rake, this was not a true assessment of his character. His reputation had been created by the tales of others, not made up of whole cloth. If the truth were known, John Pierpont was a gentleman and he could no more take unfair advantage of the delightful situation in which he found himself than he could teach the fish to sing or the birds to breathe water. Though Lady Radcliffe was the most infinitely desirable woman of his acquaintance and she had come quite willingly into his embrace, he could not allow himself to fully enjoy her charms. He must remain strong and not attempt to coerce this delightful and impulsive lady into an action that she should later come to regret. She had trusted him to observe the proprieties and he must be worthy of her trust.

Though John did not regret for an instant the events that had occurred on the previous evening, he now found himself at a loss. He had never entered into an engagement before and he had not the slightest notion of how to proceed. He suspected that he should be required to gift Lady Radcliffe with a piece of jewelry to commemorate the event. At least that aspect of their betrothal should not present a problem as he had a cask of gems in his safe from which to choose.

Thinking to accomplish this task immediately, John retrieved the cask and set it on the piecrust table by his chair. As he lifted the lid, a brilliant array of jewels met his eyes. There were diamonds and rubies, sapphires and emeralds, pearls and finely worked pieces of gold and silver. He picked up a magnificent emerald ring, thinking that it should compliment her sparkling eyes quite nicely, but he feared it was not appropriate. Emeralds of this size and quality were far too dear for an engagement present.

John dumped the contents of the cask quite unceremoniously on the tabletop. He considered each piece for a moment and then he replaced them all in the cask. These jewels had belonged to his father's family and it was clear that the Pierponts had been fond of displaying their wealth. He must give Lady Radcliffe something much more subtle, a gift that would please the gossips, but not be a source of embarrassment to her.

The moment John thought of it, he returned to the safe to retrieve a cask that had belonged to his mother. The *condesa* had amassed an extensive collection of Spanish doubloons. One particularly exquisite coin had been fashioned into a pendant that hung from a lovely gold chain. This would be a perfect engagement gift for Lady Radcliffe as she had mentioned that she was fond of unusual artifacts from foreign shores.

John located the pendant and replaced the casks, locking the safe securely. Though he was not well enough acquainted with Lady Radcliffe to be certain, he suspected that she should be delighted with his thoughtful gift. Of course it would be hers to keep, even after they had ended their engagement. It was little enough payment for the peace of mind he should enjoy when he was viewed as ineligible for the remainder of the Season.

His coffee forgotten, John dropped the pendant into the pocket of his dressing gown and returned to his bedchamber. There he found Hartley engaged in the task of laying out his clothing. It was apparent that his valet had not expected to see him reappear so quickly for he gave an audible gasp.

"I see that my clothing is assembled." John smiled at his valet. It was no wonder that Hartley was astonished for it was John's habit to linger upwards of an hour over his morning coffee. "I find that I am most eager to dress and be on my way to meet with my fiancée."

"Yes indeed, sir."

It did not take Hartley long to recover; his expression was carefully impassive as he went about the business of helping his master dress. John had no doubt that his whole household should soon hear that Lady Radcliffe had already effected a change in the earl's habits, and he felt a bit guilty for misleading his loyal valet. Unfortunately, this could not be helped. The members of his staff would be quizzed by the servants of other households, and John knew that he must play the part of a gentleman in love to successfully continue the deception he had agreed to perpetuate with Lady Radcliffe.

When all was accomplished but the tying of his neckcloth, Hartley turned to his master. "I shall tie the Mathematical if you have no objections, sir."

"Is it appropriate?" John frowned slightly. Since he had never had occasion to pay a morning call on a lady who was believed to be his fiancée, he would have to rely on Hartley's judgment regarding matters of dress.

"It is not only appropriate, it is *de rigueur.* I have no doubt that any other gentlemen who arrive shall sport the Mathematical."

"Then tie something else, Hartley. I should like to stand out from all the rest. And be quick about it. I must be her first caller and I should not care to be late."

Hartley looked as if he wished to say something, but was not quite certain he should voice his comment. The inner struggle was quite evident on his face and John gestured impatiently for him to speak. "You obviously have something on your mind. Out with it, Hartley!"

"You will not be late, sir. Morning calls are not made in the morning. It is customary for them to take place in the early afternoon."

"The devil you say!" John frowned at this absurdity. "If morning calls are not made in the morning, why are they called morning calls?"

A smile threatened to turn up the corners of Hartley's mouth and his eyes twinkled in amusement. "I am sure I do not know, sir. It is the simply way things are done in Town. Perhaps it is because morning does not begin for the members of the *ton* until the sun has been up for hours. Let us not forget that they often retire in the wee hours of the morning and they seldom break their fasts before eleven."

John glanced at the clock atop his mantelpiece and frowned as he saw that it was only five minutes past nine. "Thank you, Hartley. You have kept me from making a complete cake of myself and I am grateful to you. You must not hesitate to tell me if I am about to do something inappropriate."

"Yes, sir." Hartley nodded quickly.

"What time do you think I should depart, Hartley?"

Hartley considered it for a moment and then answered, "I am certain that if you order your curricle brought round at eleven, you shall be the lady's first caller."

"I shall indulge in breakfast then." John began to smile. "I had thought I should be required to forgo it, but you have convinced me that I have ample time."

As John made his way down the stairs to the breakfast room, he felt strangely impatient. Though he was anticipating his breakfast with a great deal of pleasure, it would be another two hours before he should set eyes on Lady Radcliffe. He was eager to see his fiancée again so that they could plan the particulars of their most unusual and thoroughly enjoyable engagement.

* * *

"Be reasonable, Mother. You simply cannot marry him!"

"You are wrong, darling. I can and I will." Claire helped herself to one of Cook's excellent blackberry tarts and sighed deeply. When she had left her bedchamber this morning, Willow had been waiting for her in the breakfast room. Their discussion had begun immediately and it had lasted until Claire had finished her cup of morning chocolate. Reinforcements had arrived in the form of Willow's fiancé and Philip had added his arguments to Willow's. Now they were seated in the Drawing Room, awaiting their first callers, and the topic of conversation was still Claire's unexpected betrothal on the previous evening.

The earl had been entirely correct when he had predicted that all would hear about their engagement. When Claire and John had re-entered the ballroom, all conversation had ceased for one breathless moment and then an excited murmur had filled the large room. It had been quite evident that news of Claire's engagement to the Earl of Sommerset had swept through the crowd with the speed of lightning. Dear Lady Bollinger, always the consummate hostess, had rushed forward to lead the other members of the *ton* in offering congratulations. She had appeared most perplexed at this unexpected turn of events, and had invited Claire to pay a late call this very afternoon, no doubt to garner the details of Claire's whirlwind courtship with her nephew.

During the frantic moments that had ensued, Claire had glanced at Willow and found a most unattractive frown upon her daughter's face. They had departed shortly thereafter, and the short carriage ride from Lady Bollinger's mansion to their town house had been filled with tension. It had been quite obvious that Willow had been waiting until they were alone to quiz Claire about the startling news. Claire had avoided that confrontation quite neatly by pleading the headache and taking refuge in her quarters, after promising to discuss all with Willow this morning.

"Mother?"

"Yes, dear." Claire nodded, fortifying herself with a sip of tea. Willow was wearing a new morning frock made of printed muslin patterned with a design of red cherries with green stems and leaves, and she would have looked quite fetching but for the frown upon her face.

Philip cleared his throat. "Neither Willow nor I were aware that you had met the Earl of Sommerset before last evening's ball. And we had no suspicion that you had entered into an . . . an understanding with him."

Rather than address Philip's unspoken query, Claire nodded again. She did not wish to tell a falsehood unless she was forced to do so.

"Mother?" Willow leaned forward, putting herself directly into Claire's line of vision. "How *did* you meet the earl?"

Claire sighed and decided to be truthful, rather than be caught out in telling a bouncer. "I met the Earl of Sommerset last evening, at the ball. Lady Bollinger introduced us. I am certain that you observed me partnering him in the waltz."

"And that was when he declared for you?" Philip's brows shot up disapprovingly.

"Yes, indeed. And I accepted him."

"After only one waltz?" Willow blinked, doing her utmost to maintain her dignity.

"Yes, dear." Claire smiled sweetly. "After only one waltz."

"Mother! How could you?"

Willow's mouth dropped open and Claire stifled a giggle. She had the urge to tell her daughter to close it before the flies flew in, just as she had when Willow had been a child.

"Lady Radcliffe," Philip said and drew a deep breath, "I must confess that I find my cousin a pleasant enough fellow, but as I am soon to become your daughter's husband, I feel it is my duty to inform you of a distressing fact. I fear that the Earl of Sommerset is not the gentleman that he appears to be."

Claire shrugged. "I know all about the earl's reputation, Philip, and it does not concern me in the slightest."

"But Mother! The Earl of Sommerset is a known rake!" Willow blinked several times and Claire hoped that she would not turn into a watering pot. Though some young ladies appeared quite beautiful when they cried, Willow was not among them.

"I have heard the gossip, Willow." Claire felt the heat rise to her cheeks as she remembered the earl's kiss. Perhaps experience in matters of love was to be desired in a suitor. But Willow was watching her with eyes that were slowly filling with tears, and Claire felt compelled to set her fears to rest. "The Earl of Sommerset was falsely accused, dear, and I intend to set those rumors to rest. He is a kind and personable gentleman and I desire that both you and Philip treat him with the respect he so justly deserves!"

"Bravo, madame!"

Claire turned toward the door and her face drained of color as she met the amused gaze of their first morning caller. It was the Earl of Sommerset, himself!

"Perhaps I should have waited to be announced, but your butler became quite witless when I stated that I was your fiancé." The earl grinned at Claire and crossed the room to take a seat at her side. "The poor man rushed off in a taking and left me to find my way here unassisted."

Claire felt a smile spread over her face as the earl took her hand. She was glad that he had come and she should not have to face the children alone. "Jennings has not been informed of our engagement. I should have thought to tell him, but our decision to marry was so . . . so sudden."

"After one waltz." Willow frowned at the earl in clear disapproval. "Mother has told us that you declared yourself only last evening."

The earl smiled. "It would have been difficult to do so earlier, as I had not met your dear mother before."

"Now see here, Sommerset." Philip faced the earl squarely. "I am certain that you can understand why my fiancée and I do not approve of this match. It is simply not done, you know. What kind of a gentleman declares for a lady upon their first meeting?"

"A gentleman who is firmly smitten." The earl gave Claire's hand a comforting squeeze and turned to face Philip. "I should say that you describe a gentleman who is so completely in the grips of an overwhelming love that he cannot imagine life without his intended bride."

"But why did you not come to us before you declared for my mother?" Willow's voice was shaking with anger.

"Because there was no need to seek your approval. Dear Claire has informed me that you are soon to marry and that you and Ralston have encouraged her to do the same. Do you deny that you have been presenting gentlemen to your mother for that exact purpose?"

"No." Willow's voice was tentative as she shook her head. "It is true that we have encouraged Mother to find a match."

"Ah. Am I to assume that you do not approve of me as a prospective husband for your mother?"

Willow had the grace to blush as she nodded. "Yes, that is it exactly. We know nothing about you, sir. And . . . and I do not wish to see my dear mama hurt."

"I should never hurt your mother. You need have no worry on that score." The earl's voice was gentle as he answered her.

"Perhaps, but we do not know you well enough to judge that fact." Philip re-entered the conversation. "Though you are my cousin and I have made your acquaintance before, it was only in passing. I must admit, however, that I found you most personable."

"Thank you." The earl nodded gravely.

"But that was before we heard the rumors," Willow spoke

up. "Mother has told us that they are not to be believed, but it is exactly as Philip has stated. We do not know you well enough to be assured that you are truly an honorable man."

"Then I shall provide you with the opportunity to become better acquainted with me. I have secured a box for the opera this evening and I should like both of you to accompany us."

Willow exchanged a glance with Philip and then she nodded. "We shall be delighted, Lord Sommerset."

"John," the earl corrected. "Since I shall soon be your mother's husband, there is no cause to be so formal."

"J . . . John." After another glance at Philip, Willow repeated his name with some reluctance.

"Until this evening, then. I shall collect you in my carriage." The earl rose from his seat and extended his hand to Claire. "You will see me to the door, my darling?"

Claire was smiling as she rose to accompany him. The earl had handled the situation with Willow and Philip most admirably and she was eager to tell him so.

As they walked across the floor and into the hallway, Claire found herself blushing like a schoolgirl. If the earl lingered a bit before he took his leave, perhaps he would even see fit to kiss her again. They were engaged, after all, and couples who were engaged were allowed to take leave of each other with a fond kiss.

FOUR

John glanced at Jennings, who was stationed at the door, holding his gloves and hat at the ready. He was eager to present the doubloon to Claire, but not in the presence of her butler. Before he could ask Claire if it would be proper to enjoy a moment in private with her, she walked up to Jennings and relieved him of the gloves and hat.

"That will be all, Jennings. I wish a moment in private with my fiancé."

"Are you certain, my lady?" The butler's haughty demeanor held more than a hint of disapproval.

"Yes. You may leave us now, Jennings."

Claire's tone brooked no nonsense, but the butler cast an icy glance at John before he turned and disappeared down the long hallway. It was clear that Jennings did not approve of the earl as a suitable companion for his mistress.

John chuckled as he turned to Claire. "I would venture to say that your butler does not like me."

"It should be most unusual if he did." Claire looked most apologetic. "Jennings has decided that his sole mission in life is to protect our reputations. It was a full sennight after Willow's engagement before he would consent to admit Philip without the formality of first presenting his card. The worst of it is, Jennings tends to hover about most persistently when his presence is least wanted."

John nodded. "I see that. I do believe he is peeping out of that half-closed door even now."

"He is?" Claire whirled to gaze in the direction of the door that John had indicated and they both observed it slide shut, closed by an unseen hand. "Perhaps we should retire to a place where Jennings cannot observe us. You wished for a private moment with me, did you not?"

John nodded, a teasing glint in his eye. "I did. And you, Lady Radcliffe, have managed to read my thoughts accurately. Have I entered into an engagement with a witch?"

"No, indeed. I simply knew that I wished to be alone with you and I hoped that you shared my sentiments. If you will join me in my sitting room, we shall close the door."

John raised his brows in an attempt to appear scandalized, but he knew the amused twinkle in his eyes threatened to give him away. "For shame, Lady Radcliffe! Have you no care for your reputation?"

"None." Claire laughed. "As you so aptly stated last evening, my good standing with the *ton* has already been destroyed by affiancing myself to a known rake."

John grinned as he took her arm. "And you are enjoying it immensely, are you not?"

"I am." Claire nodded. "I find it gives me a marvelous sense of freedom to flaunt society's silly conventions. Come with me, sir, and we shall see what further damage I can do."

As she directed him down the hallway, John could not help but smile. Claire possessed the charm and spontaneity one might find in a willful child. He wondered whether she had always been this way, or whether he had caused this aspect of her personality to surface. He must make an effort to learn more about this delightful lady who had agreed to act as his fiancée for the remainder of the Season.

Claire opened the door to her sitting room and John's eyes widened. It was decorated with a treasure trove of interesting artifacts from faraway places. The carpet was exquisite, a

woven tapestry from India bordered with a design of ele-
phants that were both artistic and humorous. It was most
unusual and unlike any that he had ever seen. A pedestal
table placed in front of a window held a lovely blue glass
bowl; John surmised it was from Venice as that city was
known for its colored glass. A shining silver goblet of a Rus-
sian design sat on a corner of the small secretariat, and both
a Tomahawk from the Colonies and an Egyptian scarab were
displayed in glass-topped cases. Two ceramic creatures sat
high on the mantelpiece and John walked over to examine
them. Their features resembled both dog and dragon and he
was intrigued.

"They are temple pieces—I have placed them here to protect the house." Claire smiled at his interest. "I am told that
it is the custom in the Orient."

John nodded, returning her smile. Claire was indeed fortunate to have rented this particular town house. The owner
had excellent, as well as charmingly eclectic, taste.

"You must see the piece that pleases me most." Claire led
him to a teakwood cabinet against the fall wall. "It is a clock-
work toy from France."

John smiled as he gazed at the lovely figurine of a mini-
ature lady seated at a tiny spinet. Claire pressed a small lever
that activated a concealed music box and the figurine began
to move. The lady's hands swept over the keys in perfect
time with the music. Her head bobbed as if she were counting
the measures of the tune that she was playing, and after an
interval, one small arm raised to turn a page on the music
rack.

"It is delightful." John smiled as the music came to a conclusion and the figure was motionless once more. "This
whole chamber is delightful. I am surprised that the owner
of this house did not pack her treasures away."

Claire laughed. "She did. These are my treasures, given
to me by my husband's younger brother. Before he assumed

my husband's title, he traveled the globe. He was aware of my interest in artifacts and he brought me these gifts."

"It is a charming collection, but you have nothing from Spain." John began to grin as he drew the small box containing the pendant from his pocket. "I should like to rectify that oversight."

Claire's hand shook as she accepted the box and opened it. Her eyes widened as she drew out the pendant and examined it, and then she turned to him with an anxious expression. "This is one of the very first Spanish doubloons and, as such, it must be at least two hundred years old! I cannot accept such an expensive gift."

"Nonsense." John took the pendant and quickly fastened it around her neck before she could protest further. It nestled against the soft, sweet hollow of her throat and he found that his hand trembled slightly as he drew it back. "It belonged to my mother. She was fond of collecting Spanish doubloons and her possessions came to me when she died. I thought that it should make a perfect engagement gift to you."

Claire reached up to touch the lovely pendant and then she sighed. "It *is* a perfect engagement gift and I should be delighted to accept it if we were truly engaged. But we are not."

"Only you and I are aware of that fact." John searched his mind for a way to make her accept his gift. For some unknown reason, he found that it was most important to him to see his mother's pendant against her lovely neck. "I should like you to have it, Claire. The members of the *ton* know that I am wealthy. If I do not present you with an engagement gift, some may speculate that our engagement is less than sincere. Surely you can see that you must accept some token from me."

Claire nodded. "Yes. What you say makes perfect sense. But this lovely pendant is more than a token. It is so personal and you have admitted that it is a family heirloom. Can you not find something more ordinary?"

"I could give you the family emeralds, but I thought this pendant to be more to your taste. If you would prefer the emeralds, I can certainly . . ."

"Oh, no!" Claire interrupted him quickly. "This pendant is . . . well . . . it is simply perfection! You are entirely right, John. I should adore to wear it. And you may be sure that I shall return it to you the moment that our ruse is concluded."

John shook his head. "You must keep it as a gift from me. It is such a small thing and I owe you a debt much greater than its worth. Why, only this morning my butler told me that not one single young lady attempted to gain my attentions by claiming that her carriage had broken down at my door."

"Good gracious!" Claire stared at him in shock. "Does this sort of thing occur often?"

"More often than I would wish. I am considered a prime catch, my dear, and on one particular afternoon during the past Season, no fewer than five carriages, all carrying attractive and eligible young ladies, had mishaps on my street."

"And I have saved you from all that?" Claire's eyes began to sparkle.

"You have. Please keep the pendant, Claire. It is yours with my gratitude. I shall be most overset with you if you attempt to return it."

"I shall keep it, then!" Claire gave a delighted laugh. "It is truly the most exquisite gift that I have ever received. Thank you, John. You are the kindest and most thoughtful of gentlemen!"

As John grinned, feeling proud that he had chosen the perfect gift to delight her, she rushed to throw her arms around him. Before John could consider the rashness of his action, or renew the vow he had taken not to kiss her again, he pulled her even closer and turned so that his lips met hers.

The feel of her delightfully curved body against his and the willingness of her lips as they eagerly parted, drove John's cautions to the wind. She was even more passionate than she had been the previous evening and John groaned as he was swept away on a tide of blazing need. He had not enjoyed a woman's intimate charms since he had left Spain and he was hard pressed to contain his lust. Without conscious thought, his fingers sought the rounded curve of her bodice and he groaned deep in his throat as she welcomed his every advance.

John felt her body tremble under his caress and the soft moans that escaped from her throat served to fuel his ardor. She pressed herself against him in wild abandon and his fingers shook as he began to unfasten the bodice of her gown. It was more than even the most perfect gentleman could bear, and John was not a perfect gentleman. He picked her up in his arms and carried her to the settee, intent on ravishing her most thoroughly.

It was at this point, as she lay trembling so willingly beneath him, that John heard an impatient knock on the door. A deep voice intruded from the hallway and he recognized Jennings's disapproving voice.

"Lady Radcliffe? I have brought the tea tray."

"Damme!" John's voice was a whisper, but his anger was as apparent as if he'd shouted the word. "It's your butler, protecting your virtue."

"And just in the knick of time." Claire sat up, giggling like a schoolgirl, her gown in complete disarray.

"What shall we do?" John smiled as he caught the humor of the situation. "If we allow him to enter, what little reputation you have left will be compromised."

Claire sighed, blushing prettily. "Compromised? What a lovely word, and so well chosen! I do not suppose you could simply open the door a crack and tell him that we are otherwise engaged?"

"I do not think that would suffice. Have you any other suggestions?"

"Yes." Claire nodded quickly. "I shall take care of the

problem. Follow me, sir, and help me lift the lids on those trunks under windows."

John raised his brows, but he followed Claire to the large trunks that sat under the windows and helped her lift the lids. Inside were books, hundreds of them, packed carefully and neatly in stacks.

"Please remove several large volumes and bring them to me." Claire took up a position by the empty bookcases that lined the far wall and accepted the armload of books that he carried to her. She glanced down at her gown, signed deeply, and shook her head. "I believe another four volumes should suffice. "Please bring them to me and then remove another stack of volumes for yourself. And then, if you will but climb the ladder and shelve one or two of those books, we shall be ready for Jennings."

They had just assumed their respective positions when Jennings knocked upon the door once again. Claire favored John with a conspiratorial smile and then she called out in a loud voice. "Come in, Jennings. We are unable to reach the door."

The door opened with great dispatch and John watched with no little amusement as Claire balanced her stack of books against a shelf. She swiveled her head in Jennings's direction and gave him a guileless smile. "Place the tray on the table, Jennings, and then you may leave us. I shall pour when we have finished with the placement of these books."

"Yes, my lady." Jennings nodded and placed the tray on the table. "Have you need of my assistance?"

"No, Jennings. We have the situation well in hand. But do close the door as you leave. These volumes are dusty and the hall was cleaned only this morning. I should not like to be the cause of more work for the staff."

"Very good, my lady." The butler's disgruntled expression thawed considerably at this thoughtful comment from his mistress. "Do not hesitate to ring if you have further need of me."

"Thank you, Jennings."

John barely managed to maintain his composure as Jennings took his leave, sliding the door tightly closed behind him. Then, shaking with suppressed laughter, he turned to Claire. "You are brilliant, Lady Radcliffe."

"Thank you, sir." Claire grinned at him impishly, struggling to maintain her balance under her heavy load. "And now that you have concluded your congratulations, would you please come down off that ladder and relieve me of these massive tomes?"

John laughed and hopped down from the ladder, taking her stack of volumes. He glanced down at one title and raised his brows. *"The Care and Perpetuation of Prime Cattle?"*

"My husband's books." Claire shrugged. "I had thought to give them to Philip to augment the library at his country estate, but now I am not so certain I should like to part with them."

"You have recently developed an interest in animal husbandry?"

"Yes, indeed." Claire favored him with another impish smile. "I have found these volumes to be of great value."

A smile twitched up the corners of John's lips as he regarded this delightful minx. "How so, Lady Radcliffe?"

"They are the perfect size to hide a lady's dishabille when she is nearly compromised in her sitting room. If this should reoccur, I should not like to be caught without them."

John threw back his head and laughed. And then he sobered quickly as he realized precisely what she had said. "Do you wish it to reoccur, my dear?"

"No gentleman should ask that question of a lady." Claire dropped her eyes to the carpet and a heated blush rose to stain her cheeks.

"You forget that I am not a gentleman. We must be honest with each other if our ruse is to succeed. Please tell me, Claire. I wish to know your answer."

John waited as she considered the question. His heart was

pounding rapidly and his ardor rose, even though he tried his utmost to control it. After long moments of perfect silence, she finally raised her trusting eyes to his.

"Yes, John. I know it is most improper, but I should most definitely wish it to occur again."

The morning callers had come and gone and the favorite subject had been Claire's engagement. Willow and Philip had handled all of the queries with polite and appropriate responses, agreeing that Claire's engagement was most unexpected, but not divulging any further information. When the last caller had departed, Willow excused the servants, informed Jennings that they should not be accepting any further guests, and gave a deep sigh of relief as she sank down upon the cushions of the sofa.

"You must be exhausted, my dear." Philip poured a celebratory glass of sherry for Willow and a snifter of brandy for himself.

"I am, but I am also delighted." Willow accepted the glass and sipped gratefully. "Is it not delicious that they have so easily fallen into our scheme?"

Philip nodded and raised his glass to Willow's in a salute. "I am as delighted as you are, my darling. And I must say that you expressed just the right amount of restraint regarding your mother's match, without expressing your open disapproval."

"It was most difficult, dear Philip. I was required to pretend that I objected to the match without actually stating it to our guests. If I had done that, I should have been accused of disloyalty."

"Just so." Philip nodded. "I found it much easier to deal with your mother in private when we could openly voice our discontent."

"You are quite right, Philip. It was much easier, and I am

almost certain Mama believes that we do not approve of Lord Sommerset."

Philip laughed. "I wager to say she will never suspect that we arranged it all in the first place."

"I pray she will not!" An anxious expression crossed Willow's face. "If Mama learns that we deliberately chose Lord Sommerset to be her husband, and that we had a hand in the events that took place in the garden last evening, she will cry off before she tumbles into love with him."

"You must not concern yourself, for that will not happen. I paid careful attention to your mother's demeanor when Sommerset arrived, and I would bet a monkey that her heart is already engaged."

"Do you truly think so?" Willow looked hopeful.

"I do. There was a light in her eyes that I had not seen there before and she blushed quite charmingly when he took her hand. And I also believe that he harbors a similar affection for her. He could not tear his eyes from her face, even when we were addressing him."

Willow clapped her hands in excitement. "It shall be the match of the Season! If not for us, Lord Sommerset and Mama should never have exchanged more than a few polite words."

"Yes, indeed. Miss Fellows must have played her part to perfection. I had not thought the engagement should take place so rapidly as it did."

Willow laughed as she nodded. "I had the opportunity to exchange a quick word with Dorinda, and she said that Mama tumbled into her trap without the slightest hesitation. I truly believe that dear Dorinda could have made her fortune on the boards."

"I imagine that Winslow might have something to say about that." Philip chuckled at the thought.

"Do not say that, Philip!" Willow glanced around for fear that the servants might hear his comment, but none of the staff was about. "You must take care not to mention Dorinda and Winslow in the same breath. We are the only ones who know that they are secretly engaged."

Philip smiled and pulled his fiancée into his arms. "You are right, my dear, and I shall take care not to give their secret away. But I had thought that Winslow might have some objection to Miss Fellows's part in our scheme. How did you come to secure his approval?"

"It was child's play." Willow looked inordinately pleased with herself. "I simply persuaded the dear man that any suspicion of an alliance between Dorinda and himself should be thoroughly quashed by rumors that she must marry a wealthy nobleman."

Philip gave a chuckle of amusement. "You have a devious bent, my love. Winslow will not receive his inheritance until the beginning of the *next* Season. And if one believes the gossip that abounds about Miss Fellows, she must make her match immediately to cover her father's gambling losses."

"That part is true, Philip. Lord Fellows has signed markers in every gambling hell in London, and he will lose his estate if they are not redeemed by the conclusion of the Season. Dorinda told me that, herself. She should have been forced to marry a gentleman with enough money to save father, if not for our intervention."

"Our intervention?" Philip raised his brows.

"Yes. Dorinda has promised me that she shall personally redeem father's markers and see to it that he does not gamble again."

"But Miss Fellows has no means to redeem her father's markers." Philip began to frown slightly. "It is only through her grandmother's charity that she is able to take part in the Season. Has this same grandmother agreed to cover Lord Fellows's losses?"

"No, indeed. Her purse is not that large. But Dorinda shall come into quite a tidy sum at the conclusion of the Season and she will use every penny to pay her father's debts."

Philip stared long and hard at his fiancée, a suspicious

glint in his eye. "Tell me the truth, my love. What, precisely, did you promise Miss Fellows for her part in our scheme?"

"Why . . . nothing of significance, surely!" A telling blush rose to stain Willow's cheeks. "I . . . I merely offered her the use of my bridal inheritance."

"Your bridal inheritance?"

"Yes." Willow nodded quickly. "My father set aside a sum for me to inherit on my wedding day. He believed that a wife should not be completely reliant upon her husband's charity and should possess some money of *her* own. I agreed to make Dorinda a loan of this sum, and Winslow has promised to repay it promptly when he comes into his own inheritance next Season."

Philip's lips twitched and he struggled to maintain a stern expression. "I have no doubt that Winslow shall repay you. He is an honorable gentleman. But have you considered the full results of your rash action, my dear?"

"N-no, not precisely."

"If you have no coin, you shall be unable to order a new gown or spend a single coin at the bazaar. You shall not have the means to give vails to our friends' servants, and you shall be unable to purchase the books that you desire to read. Your purse shall be quite empty until Winslow is able to repay you. And that shall be a full twelve months from now."

Willow thought about it for a long moment and then she shrugged prettily. "It does not signify, Philip. I have enough new gowns to last me for the next several years and I shall not require any trinkets from the bazaar. If I cannot pay vails, I shall not make country visits and I shall be quite content to reread the books I already possess."

"Are you certain, Willow?"

"Yes, Philip. I pledged my inheritance for a worthy purpose. I am quite convinced of that. I should pledge my life itself if it should insure my mother's future happiness."

"And so should I." Philip smiled and gathered her tightly into his arms. "You must not be concerned about your expenses, Willow. I shall be glad to settle a generous sum on you, to do with as you wish. And I shall be happy to assume any expenses that you might incur."

"That is exceedingly kind of you, Philip." Willow's voice quavered slightly and she gazed up at the gentleman she loved with a hopeful expression on her face. "Then you do not think that I was wrong to make a loan of my inheritance to Dorinda?"

"No, my darling. In this particular case, you were entirely correct. And I should have done it, if you had not. I should desire, however, that you first discuss with me any financial arrangements that you are tempted to make in future."

"Oh, I shall! I should have asked you before I agreed to give Dorinda my bridal inheritance. Are you dreadfully disappointed in me, Philip?"

"Not in the slightest." Philip bent over to place a chaste kiss on her cheek. Then he glanced round the room and began to smile. "Do you expect the servants to refresh the tea tray at this late hour?"

"I should not think so, Philip. The time is long past for social calls."

Philip rose to his feet and walked to the door to close it. Then he smiled and gestured to Willow to join him on the most comfortable sofa in the drawing room. "Come and kiss me, my darling, and we shall truly celebrate your dear mother's engagement."

FIVE

The sun was hovering low on the horizon as Claire presented her card to Lady Bollinger's footman. She was not anticipating this audience with pleasure, but one did not send excuses when one was invited to take tea with a lady of Lady Bollinger's standing.

"How lovely you look, my dear Lady Radcliffe." Lady Bollinger rose to greet her as Claire was ushered into a charming salon done in shades of deep green and silver. "They say that a lady is even more beautiful when her heart is engaged and this is certainly borne out in your case. I do not believe that I have ever seen you appear so radiant."

"Thank you, Lady Bollinger." Claire felt the heat rise to her cheeks, certain that her hostess was merely being kind. She had tarried so long with John in her sitting room that her toilette had been made in great haste. Claire had barely had time to change her gown and give a quick pat to her curls. Perhaps Lady Bollinger had mistaken the high color of her complexion for radiance, rather than the result of her frantic rush to arrive on time.

Once Claire was seated in the chair that her hostess indicated, a footman dressed in splendid livery arrived with champagne. He filled their glasses and then Lady Bollinger gestured for the room to be cleared. Once they were completely alone, she lifted her glass and turned to Claire with a smile. "To you, my dear Lady Radcliffe. And to your most surprising engagement. I take great pleasure in welcoming you into our family."

"Thank you, Lady Bollinger." Claire took a small sip of her champagne and waited for the inevitable questions that should be asked of her.

"As we soon shall be related by marriage, you must call me Marcella. And I shall call you Claire. It that acceptable to you?"

"Most acceptable." Claire nodded quickly. "I am aware that my engagement to your nephew is sudden, Lady Bollinger, and no doubt you have . . ."

"Marcella," Lady Bollinger interrupted to correct her.

"Marcella." Claire repeated the name obediently. "No doubt you have questions and I shall do my best to answer them."

Lady Bollinger laughed and leaned a bit closer. "I must admit that I did have questions when I asked you to call. I had thought to quiz you precisely about your engagement to my nephew. But now that I have seen you, I have no further need to know the particulars."

"Why is that, Lady Bollinger?"

"Marcella."

"Why is that, Marcella?" Claire repeated her query with a smile.

"It is apparent to me that you love my nephew, and that is all that matters. Perhaps he was a bit of a rogue and a scoundrel in the past, but I have never been able to stop off liking him. And your love for him, dear Claire, will surely suffice to make him a better man."

"Thank you, Marcella." Claire winced inwardly as a wave of guilt washed over her. She was not certain how Lady Bollinger had reached the conclusion that she loved John, but she could not deny it without giving up their ruse.

"I should like to host an engagement ball for the two of you." Lady Bollinger's eyes began to sparkle. "I shall invite all the luminaries and I believe it should go far to reclaim

John's standing with the *ton*. Will you indulge me in this effort, Claire?"

Claire nodded quickly. An engagement ball, given by Lady Bollinger, would serve to throw a cloak of legitimacy over their ruse. "Of course I shall. It is most generous of you to offer, Marcella."

"Nonsense! You are doing me a kindness as I simply adore large parties! And your engagement to my nephew is the perfect opportunity to present a truly spectacular event. Shall we set the date in three weeks time?"

Claire nodded quickly. "That is most acceptable, as it shall give me ample time to secure a new gown for the occasion."

"Would you prefer it to be a traditional affair?" Lady Bollinger favored Claire with a conspiratorial smile. "Or would you indulge me even further by consenting to something a bit more unconventional?"

"Unconventional, most definitely." Claire smiled, thoroughly charmed by Lady Bollinger's candor. "After all, there is nothing in the least bit conventional about our engagement."

Lady Bollinger laughed appreciatively. "Splendid! What would you think of a costume ball?"

"It should be delightful, Marcella, so long as John does dress as a rogue or a scoundrel."

"Well said!" Lady Bollinger laughed so heartily, she was forced to avail herself of a napkin with which to wipe her eyes. When she had composed herself enough to speak again, she turned to Claire with a question. "Are there any guests, in particular, that you would have me invite?"

Claire was about to shake her head and leave the arrangements in Lady Bollinger's capable hands, when a radical thought popped into mind. "Yes, Marcella. I should like you to include the two young ladies who made accusations against John."

"My dear Claire! Why would you wish to issue invitations to the very young ladies who . . ." Lady Bollinger stopped speaking in mid-sentence and stared at Claire with an expression of dawning appreciation. "You have a reason for your request, do you not?"

"I do. If you issue the invitations, will they accept?"

"Most assuredly, my dear. It should be very bad *ton* to decline. And once arrived, they shall be on their very best behavior since all who know them will be in attendance. Do you have a plan to expose their trickery?"

"No, indeed." Claire shook her head. "It shall suffice if they are observed dancing with John."

Lady Bollinger began to laugh as she caught Claire's meaning. "Of course it shall! You are most astute for having thought of it, dear Claire. All who see them will assume that they have apologized for their escapade and John has been kind enough to forgive them."

"That is precisely correct." Claire nodded. "There is only one flaw in my plan and I must ask your assistance to overcome it."

"You have it, of course. What would you have me do, Claire?"

"I cannot ask John to dance with every young lady at the ball to be certain that he has partnered them. Is there a way that you could discover which particular costumes they will wear?"

"Of course." Lady Bollinger nodded quickly. "You must leave that to me. I assure you that I shall possess a full description long before the date we have set. And I must say that your plan is both simple and brilliant. Indeed, it cannot fail."

Claire sighed and rose to her feet. "I hope that you are right, Marcella. I should like to see John's good standing restored. Though he claims that it means nothing to him, I am certain that it does. And now I must take my leave. John is escorting us to the opera this evening and I must look my best."

"Yes, indeed. All eyes will be upon you." Lady Bollinger

also rose to her feet. She pressed Claire's hand in farewell and regarded her with a smile. "We are friends, then?"

"We are most certainly, Marcella." Claire returned her smile.

Once Claire had been ushered from Lady Bollinger's mansion and had gained the privacy of her carriage, her smile was replaced by a frown. She did not like to deceive Lady Bollinger for she had found she liked her immensely. Still puzzling over why Marcella had believed her to be in love with her nephew, Claire ordered her coachman to spring the horses and leaned back against the squabs to consider with care each nuance of the conversation that they had enjoyed.

When Claire arrived at her rented town house, she was no closer to an answer than when she had left Marcella's side. She hurried to her chamber, rang for her dresser, and sank down, exhausted, on the edge of her bed. Though she attempted to turn her thoughts in another direction, the question still plagued her. Why had Marcella believed her to be in love with John?

The next hour was a whirlwind of frantic activity. A hip bath was ordered, Claire chose the gown that she wished to wear, and her dresser rushed to gather her accessories. Once Claire had availed herself of the scented water, she sat down at her dressing table so that her hair could be properly arranged. When this task was accomplished, she was assisted into her gown, and the exquisite pendant that John had given her that very afternoon was clasped round her neck. Within the space of an hour, Claire was descending the staircase armed with her favorite pair of gloves, the ivory fan that her brother-in-law had brought to her from Asia, and the lovely cashmere shawl that had belonged to her mother.

Since Willow was not yet dressed, Claire seated herself in the drawing room to await John's arrival. As she sat quietly, perched on the edge of a chair so that she should not wrinkle the skirts of her blue satin gown, she realized that her heart was beating much more rapidly than was normal. The very thought of seeing John again filled her with a most delightful anticipation.

With no intention of doing so, Claire's thoughts turned to the kiss that they had shared in her sitting room. She could not help but remember the strength of his arms as he had held her, and she shivered slightly as she recalled how his heated lips had etched a blazing trail down the softness of her neck. She sighed in longing as she remembered the touch of his fingers upon her skin and how he had loosened the fasteners of her bodice to touch her smooth, feminine flesh. She had thought that simple passion had caused her knees to go weak and all thoughts to flee from her mind, but now she was not so certain. Could Marcella be right? Was she truly in love with John?

John frowned as his carriage rounded the corner of Half Moon Street. He should arrive at Claire's town house in very short order, and he found that he was eager to see her again. The kiss they had shared in her sitting room had left him shaken, and as he had dressed for their evening together, he had cautioned himself most severely. He must not kiss her again. He could not even go so far as to raise her lovely hand to his lips. His feelings for Claire had grown so volatile, he could not trust himself to behave in a manner that befitted a gentleman.

What was it about Claire that so intrigued him? John considered what little he knew of her. She was both gracious and charming, that was quite evident, and her generosity was unequaled in the character of any other lady that he had previously met. She had saved him from scandal without a thought for herself. And even if she had taken the time to assess the consequences of her rash action, John was certain that she should still have come to his aid.

He could find no fault with her humor. Indeed, it was delightful. Claire knew how to laugh without the slightest embarrassment, and she seemed not to care a button if her eyes streamed with mirth or her peals were heard across the room. Unlike most ladies, she did not take offense if the joke was aimed at her. Claire's marvelous spontaneity and fine sense of the absurd perfectly matched his.

Added to the mix was the fact that Claire was lovely. She was not a classic beauty in any sense of the word. Her mouth was slightly too generous to be perfect and her figure was a shade too thin. But her nose was straight and perfectly formed and her ears resembled nothing so much as the delicate pink shells that could be gathered on the beaches of his mother's homeland. Her chin was small and firm, with just a hint of stubbornness, and her movements were graceful and agile. Her green eyes were so luminous he could lose himself in their depths, and her hair was a shining curtain of spun gold.

John pictured her golden tresses spread out on his pillow and he groaned softly, deep in his throat. He knew that he could seduce her if he wished. She had confessed as much this very afternoon when she had fallen captive to his ardor. If any other lady had declared herself so boldly, John should have suspected her character. But he had no doubt that Claire was virtuous and he was certain that she should allow this pleasure to no other gentleman.

Was it possible that this pattern card of his perfect match had somehow come to love him? John was not certain, but the very thought caused his hands to shake. She was all that he could have wished for in a wife, and more.

John began to smile as he remembered the near disaster in her sitting room and how she had cleverly covered her dishabille with the tall stack of books. He had not dared to gaze at her for fear he would chortle with laughter. Claire was quick-minded and resourceful, another aspect of her character that he found most pleasing. Was there anything about her that did not please him?

The carriage stopped and John drew back the curtain to

see that they had arrived at Claire's town house. Though it
was a charming little place, quite adequate for a widow and
her grown daughter, he wondered if Claire ever had cause
to long for a larger and grander home. He should like to
show her Sommerset Park. He was certain that she would
delight in the fine Tudor architecture that made up the west
wing, and glory in the soaring cathedral ceilings of the grand
hall. The ancient ruins to the east would please her immensely, and he chuckled as he imagined her armed with a
shovel, digging up the earth for the treasures that some believed were buried beneath the crumbling stones.

Claire would also be partial to the castle, though it was
drafty and ancient. It had a sense of history that more than
compensated for its lack of modern convenience. Perhaps
they could spend the summers there, and winter at one of
the more commodious of his estates. If Claire so desired,
they could even reopen Sommerset House, his father's town
mansion. It should have to be thoroughly renovated and decorated, but Claire might welcome the opportunity to exhibit
her exquisite taste.

Where would Claire choose to live? John considered the
question for a moment, but he could not be certain which of
his estates should please her the most. Once they were married, he would take her on a tour of all his properties and
leave the choice to her.

Instructing his coachman to wait, John jumped smartly
from his carriage and hurried up the walk to Claire's door.
It was only after his arrival had been announced, and he was
following Jennings to the drawing room, that he remembered
his engagement to Claire was only a sham.

SIX

Claire smiled softly and shifted her position slightly so that she was able to gaze out the tall windows of the library at the darkened gardens. She had been closeted here for upwards of an hour and though her duties as Willow's mother were clear, she found that she could not seem to concentrate on the marriage agreements that Philip's solicitor was attempting so earnestly to explain. She was lost in contemplation of the exciting pleasures that she had enjoyed with John during the past fortnight and the details of Willow's marriage agreement seemed as dull as dust in comparison.

On the evening following their unexpected engagement, they had attended the opera, a superb production that should have delighted Claire's senses had her attentions not been thoroughly diverted by John's presence beside her in the box. Not even the play that followed, *The Farmer's Return,* with David Garrick, had served to claim her interest for more than a few brief moments. She had found herself instead observing John's strong profile and recalling the passion that they had shared in her small sitting room.

In the days that followed, John had arrived each day to introduce her to the varied delights of the city. They had spent an entire afternoon shopping, an activity that John, unlike most gentlemen of Claire's acquaintance, had appeared to enjoy. Claire had purchased a fine length of muslin and trimmings at Grafton's, a lovely china bowl from Wedge-

wood's shop, and tea from Twinings. In Gray's, the jewelers
on Sackville Street, Claire had admired an exquisite cameo
brooch. It had been far too dear and she had departed without
making the purchase, but John had arrived the very next day
to make her a present of it.

In the company of both Philip and Willow, they had enjoyed the horse-riding display at Astley's Royal Amphithea-
tre. They had also perused the exhibitions at the Liverpool
Museum and the British Gallery, where they had discovered
that their tastes in art were remarkably similar. There had
been several walks in Kensington Gardens and a marvelous
evening spent at Vauxhall pleasure gardens, where they had
rubbed shoulders with the general populace. They had
feasted on the thin slices of ham that had become so famous
and amused themselves by observing the varied groups of
revelers that had strolled by the open box that John had ac-
quired for them. Though the vocal concert had not been as
excellent as Claire had been led to believe, the tightrope artist
had been daring indeed, and both Willow and Claire had
been exceedingly delighted with the fireworks display.

Once John had found that both Claire and her daughter
enjoyed riding, he had provided superb mounts for them so
that they could explore Ladies' Mile in Hyde Park. They had
also taken part in the Promenade, Claire in John's curricle
and Willow in Philip's, and all four of them had spent one
entire day in John's well-appointed coach, traveling from one
point of interest to the next. But though Claire had found
these amusements most pleasurable, she had enjoyed even
more the time that she had spent conversing with John, learn-
ing of his interests and his preferences, and sharing similar
confidences of her own.

Most pleasurable of all had been the time that they had
spent in private; Claire was put to the blush as she remembered the sweet, stolen moments that they had shared. John's
lips had claimed hers more times than she could count and
they had achieved an intimacy that should have been most

improper had they not been engaged. It was while she was in the midst of one such recollection that Claire became aware of the lack of conversation around her. When she turned to glance at Philip and his solicitor, Mr. Watkins, she found them both regarding her with amusement.

"I see that you have returned to us, Lady Radcliffe." Mr. Watkins cleared his throat. "Is the settlement, thus far, to your satisfaction?"

Claire nodded quickly. "I am certain that it is. And I apologize to the both of you. I fear I have been wool-gathering and not giving this matter the attention it deserves."

"Your behavior is quite understandable, given the circumstances," Philip was quick to reassure her, and then turned to his solicitor with a smile. "Lady Radcliffe is also engaged to be married."

"My felicitations, madame." Mr. Watkins gave a slight nod. "When will this happy event occur?"

"We have not as yet set a date, Mr. Watkins." Claire repressed a sigh of longing. If only her engagement to John should truly end in marriage, she would be the happiest woman in all of England.

"Is there any of this agreement that you should like Mr. Watkins to further explain?" Philip looked a bit anxious and Claire knew he was eager to have the matter settled so he could spend the remainder of the evening with Willow.

"No, dear Philip." Claire smiled as she shook her head. "You have my full approval."

It did not take long to conclude their business and once Mr. Watkins had taken his leave, Claire rang for the tea tray. "I shall leave you now, Philip. I am certain that Willow is hovering anxiously in the hall and I shall send her to join you."

"Thank you." Philip nodded, a smile turning up the corners of his lips. "It is a fair agreement, you know, even if you did not hear the details."

Claire returned his smile. "I would expect no less, dear Philip, as you are Willow's perfect match."

"And she is mine." Philip responded quickly. "I am most eager to marry her and settle in at our estate. Perhaps you and Sommerset will agree to join us for a sojourn in the country when you return from your wedding journey?"

"Perhaps. I shall be sure to mention it to him. Your invitation is most kind."

Claire turned and hastened to the door so that Philip could not see the tears that sprang to her eyes. There would be no wedding journey with John. She had promised to cry off, once the gossip had diminished, and she could not break her vow.

Once Claire had sent Willow to join Philip in the library, she climbed the stairs to her bedchamber. An hour remained before she should see John again, and she was anticipating his arrival with pleasure. Only one thing was lacking in her engagement to John: Claire fervently wished that she could take back her promise and truly become his wife.

John sighed as he glanced at the clock that sat atop the mantel in Brooks's Circulation Room. It was eight in the evening and he could not join Claire until another hour had passed. No doubt she was still closeted with Ralston's solicitor in her library, mulling over the terms of Willow's marriage agreement. He had offered her the services of his own highly regarded solicitor, thinking to set the two lawyers together to accomplish the deed and spare Claire from the tedium. But though Claire had thanked him most sincerely for his offer, she had insisted that it was her duty to her daughter to accomplish the task herself.

He had arrived at Brooks's at four-thirty and had enjoyed a solitary dinner of marrowbones, accompanied by a fine glass of claret whose vintage had pre-dated his birth. At the conclusion of his dinner, John had adjourned to the Circulation Room, where he had requested a snifter of brandy and chosen an excellent cigar from the humidor. Ensconced in an armchair well away from any other members who might choose to intrude upon his privacy, he had perused the London papers until he had exhausted the club's ample supply. He had then spent the better part of an hour gazing alternately at the vaulted ceiling, the splendid chandelier, and the clock whose hands did not move rapidly enough to suit him.

John's father had joined the prestigious gentlemen's club when it had opened its doors in Pall Mall, in 1764. He had assisted Brooks in moving to the present site in 1778, and John had found a most interesting rhyme among his father's papers, concerning the founder's generosity to members in debt. It was a copy of a verse that had been sent to Brinsley Sheridan, himself the author of several witty comedies, *A School For Scandal* among them. John had found the verse so engaging, he had committed it to memory as it captured all that his father had told him of Brooks.

> Liberal Brooks, whose speculative skill
> Is hasty credit and a distant bill,
> Who, nursed in clubs, disdains a vulgar trade,
> Exults to trust and blushes to be paid.

Richard Brinsley Sheridan was also a member of Brooks's, though John's father had confessed that his election had been havey-cavey. A close friend of the Prince Regent, Sheridan had been put up for membership several times, only to be consistently blackballed by George Selwyn and the Earl of Bessborough. John's father had himself helped to hatch the stratagem that had gained Sheridan membership, and he had recounted the details to his son.

The plan had been set into motion on an evening when Sheridan's name should again be put forward. Shortly before the members were to vote on the candidates, a message had been delivered to Bessborough, stating that his house was on fire. After that gentleman had effected a hasty departure, Sheridan had arrived, arm in arm with the Regent. Sheridan had been shown into the waiting room for candidates and shortly thereafter, his arch enemy Selwyn had been told that the Regent desired a word with him. Once Selwyn had departed to answer the Regent's summons, the vote had been taken and Sheridan had been admitted quite handily.

Reviewing the history of his club did not hold John's interest for long. Thoughts of Claire took possession of his mind and he sighed deeply as he remembered the way that her generous lips had parted so eagerly when he had kissed her. She desired him completely, he was certain of that, and John had found it increasingly difficult to deny the passion that took hold of them both when they were together. Only a sennight remained until their engagement ball and John was on the verge of asking Claire to make their engagement real. They were perfectly suited and he truly desired to make her his countess.

She would agree, of that John was convinced. Claire was not the type to engage in feminine wiles and her response to his affections was honest and forthright. It was clear that she loved him, and he loved her in return. There was no reason why they could not marry and enjoy a lifetime of connubial bliss. He would declare himself tonight and propose that they plan a double wedding with Willow and Ralston. Though Claire's daughter and her fiancé had objected to his attentions at the onset, he had won their respect and it was readily apparent that they had come to regard him as a suitable match for Claire.

John's musings were interrupted by the sound of approaching footsteps in the hallway. He leaned slightly to the side and saw that two gentlemen had paused at the open doorway, their features hidden by the shadows. Thinking to discourage anything from intruding upon his privacy, John settled back into the cushions, well out of sight.

"You were right. There is no one here at this hour." The

first gentleman spoke so softly, John had to strain to hear him.

"Excellent!" the second gentleman, who sounded much younger, responded. "I should not like any to hear what I am about to divulge to you. I have agreed not to bandy it about, but it is such a good tale, I cannot keep it all to myself."

John frowned slightly. The voice of the older gentleman was unknown to him but the younger was vaguely familiar. He was about to stand up, to make his presence known, when the younger gentleman spoke again. "It concerns Lord Sommerset and I should not like to find myself on his dark side."

"Just so!" The older gentleman gave a wary chuckle. "I have heard that he is an excellent shot."

John grinned, settling deeply into his chair once more. There was much to be gained by keeping his presence unknown if these two gentlemen were about to discuss the latest *on dit* concerning him.

When the gentlemen had gained seats, the younger one spoke again. "You must promise never to divulge what I am about to tell you."

"Done." The older gentleman chuckled softly. "If this concerns Lord Sommerset, it is in my best interest to keep my tongue tightly reined. I should not care to serve as your second."

The younger gentleman laughed at this joke and then he cleared his throat. "I have told you of my secret engagement to Miss Fellows?"

John frowned at the mention of Miss Fellows's name. Had word somehow got out of her attempt to trap him into marriage in Aunt Marcella's gardens?

"You have told me and I approve. From what I have seen, Miss Fellows is a pleasing young miss and quite beautiful. Her family, however, is another matter. It is only a pity her father does not repair to his country estate and remain there."

"I could not agree with you more. It seems that Lord Fellows has spent the entire Season, thus far, at the gambling tables and his luck has been most unfortunate as he now finds himself facing utter ruin. Not even the moneylenders near Mecklenburgh Square will part with their coin in his behalf."

"I should hope not, for he would only gamble it away again." The older gentleman sighed deeply. "A sad case, Lord Fellows. I have observed him at Hazard and an unluckier fellow does not exist!"

"You have the right of it, uncle. Lord Fellows has only himself to blame for his troubles. But my dear Dorinda is the most generous of daughters, as well as the most loving. She came to me, some four weeks past, with the intention of crying off from our engagement. She was determined to set aside her own desires and marry a gentleman who possessed the means to save her father from bankruptcy."

"I see." The older gentleman sounded as if he did not see at all. "But your engagement to Miss Fellows still stands, does it not?"

"It does. I made it clear to her that I could not stand by idly while she sacrificed our future happiness."

The older gentleman gasped in alarm. "You did not go to the moneylenders yourself, Winslow!"

"No, uncle. Before I could even consider putting myself to those lengths, Miss Fellows's bosom bow, Miss Radcliffe, came up with a most unusual solution to our difficulty."

John raised his brows. It was no surprise that he had recognized the young man's voice. Willow had spoken to him at the opera and briefly introduced him to their group. He was Freddy Winslow, heir to his grandmother's fortune and a recently admitted member of Brooks's.

"Is this when Sommerset enters the picture?" The uncle was clearly intrigued.

"Yes, indeed. Miss Radcliffe was eager to arrange a marriage for her mother. Together with her fiancé, Lord Ralston, they settled on Sommerset as a likely match."

"Ah ha!" The uncle sounded most amused. "I should have known that Sommerset would not declare himself willingly. Did they set a trap for him, then?"

"A very clever trap. Miss Radcliffe and Ralston spread it about that my dear Dorinda was desperate to marry a wealthy gentleman to save her father from bankruptcy."

"Yes?" The uncle sounded puzzled. "But that was true, was it not?"

"It was. And that is one of the reasons why their plan was so clever. On the night of Lady Bollinger's ball, my dear Dorinda followed Lord Sommerset into the gardens and pretended to attempt to trap him into marriage."

"Pretended?" The uncle sounded even more confused.

"Yes. It was a sham, of course, all arranged by Miss Radcliffe and Ralston. They knew that Lord Sommerset would hear that Dorinda was desperately seeking a wealthy match, and thus he would not think to suspect Lady Radcliffe's motives when she arrived in time to save him."

"Save him? From your Miss Fellows?"

"Indeed." Winslow chuckled. "Lady Radcliffe arrived on the scene in the nick of time. She informed Dorinda that her hopes for a declaration from the earl were fruitless, as *she* was already engaged to him!"

"By *she* do you mean Lady Radcliffe?"

"Yes, indeed. Of course Lord Sommerset assumed that Lady Radcliffe's claim to be his fiancée was made solely to save him from Dorinda's clutches."

There was a long silence from the uncle and then he sighed. "It is quite complicated but I believe I have got the gist of it. But the earl and Lady Radcliffe are still engaged, are they not?"

"Most definitely. I am not privy to the full particulars, but I assume that Lady Radcliffe has promised to cry off once the Season is concluded. Of course she will not. And the earl will be forced to marry her to avoid further disgrace."

The uncle laughed long and hard. "It is simply masterful! Who is the author of this convoluted scheme?"

"Miss Radcliffe and Lord Ralston, with a good bit of help from my dear Miss Fellows. It could not have been accomplished without her aid. It is the reason that Miss Radcliffe has agreed to make dear Dorinda a loan of the funds that she will inherit on her wedding day."

"This sum will enable her to redeem her father's vowels?"

"Precisely." Winslow sounded most pleased. "And I shall repay dear Dorinda's debt when I claim my inheritance next year."

The uncle laughed and clapped his hands together. "This is a delightful tale, Winslow, but you must take caution not to divulge it to anyone else. It would go badly for your fiancée if her part in this scheme were made public."

"I shall be as silent as the grave." Winslow's voice was solemn. "I should not have told you, uncle, if I were not certain that you would also remain mum."

"That I will, boy. That I will. And now let us retire to White's, where I am to meet several friends whose acquaintance I should like you to make."

John remained in his chair until the sounds of their footsteps had receded, his mind spinning in shocked circles. Had he fallen into an elaborate trap set by Willow, Ralston, and Claire, herself?

Winslow's story had the undeniable ring of truth. All the facts that he had recounted to his curious uncle had been quite accurate. As Miss Fellows's secret fiancé, Winslow had been in a position to be privy to the scheme, and John found that he could not dismiss the charges that he had so gleefully uttered against the family he had come to think of as his own.

With great effort, John composed himself and gave a glance to the clock. Its hands had moved too far for his further contemplation. If he did not make haste, he should be late to meet Claire, and meet her he surely would. Lady

Claire Radcliffe, the scheming woman that he had come so dangerously close to making his wife, was about to receive the full measure of his legendary wrath!

SEVEN

Claire paced the floor in the drawing room, glancing at the clock every few moments. It was not like John to be late. On every other occasion, he had been a pattern card of promptness, arriving exactly when he had said he should. As the clock ticked on and the minutes passed in slow progression, Claire prayed that nothing dreadful had occurred to keep him from her side.

Willow and Philip had taken their leave a full hour ago, to attend a small gathering at the home of a friend. As there was no conversation to divert her, Claire found herself imagining the dire events that could account for John's unaccustomed delay. Foremost in her mind was the possibility of a carriage accident. Claire was well aware that this specter was due, in no small measure, to the disastrous event that had taken her parents' lives. She attempted to tell herself that such a disaster could not strike her a second time in one lifetime, but still she could not help but picture a broken carriage, smashed beyond all repair, and her beloved John lying motionless in the streets.

With great resolution, Claire banished these images and concentrated on some circumstance that might have caused John to linger at his club. Perhaps he had met an old friend and tarried with him, too engaged in their conversation to notice the lateness of the hour. There was also the possibility that he had stopped to assist an acquaintance, not realizing that the offer of his aid should cause him to be late. It was foolish of her to give way to her anxiety when there were so many small and insignificant events that could have caused his delay.

There was a knock on the open door and Claire turned eagerly, a welcoming smile on her face. Then her smile faded quickly as she saw that it was only Jennings with the tea tray.

"Your tea, madame." Jennings crossed the floor to place the tray on a table.

"Thank you, Jennings." Claire managed to hide her disappointment. In her concern over John's tardiness, she had completely forgotten that she had rung for the tea tray. "Has there been any word from Lord Sommerset?"

Jennings shook his head and Claire noticed that he also looked a bit anxious. "No, madame. If any such message is delivered, I shall make haste to carry it to you immediately."

Once Jennings had taken his leave, Claire poured her tea and sipped it anxiously, listening intently for the sounds of John's arrival. Several more minutes passed in agonizing silence and then she heard the rumble of carriage wheels rounding the corner. The carriage stopped outside her door and Claire gave a grateful sigh of relief. John had arrived, at last.

John frowned as he stepped down from his carriage and turned to his coachman. "There is no need to walk the horses. I shall not be long."

The coachman nodded and John strode up the walkway, the frown still present upon his face. During his short journey to Half Moon Street, he had considered the words that he should speak when he accused Claire of the double deception that she had perpetuated. It was only natural that she should attempt to explain, but he would remain deaf to her tearful apologies and brook no excuses from her lips.

As John stood at the door, waiting to be admitted, he vowed to remain calm, his demeanor as icy and forbidding as the peaks of the Pyrenees in his mother's homeland. He would not allow his emotions to become involved for he had no doubt that Claire should turn into a watering pot the instant that he accused her. She was not above using every means at her disposal to attempt to convince him that she was innocent of all wrongdoing.

When Jennings opened the door, he wore a welcoming smile, but John did not return it. Instead, he demanded an immediate audience with Claire and made haste to follow the butler down the hall.

As he walked through the familiar corridor, John reviewed the strategy that he had formulated. He would state quite clearly that he had tumbled to Claire's devious scheme and inform her that it could not succeed. Once she had digested that fact, he would demand that she continue the illusion of their engagement until the conclusion of the current Season. If she dared to object, he would threaten to expose the full particulars of her trickery, including her conspiracy with her daughter and Ralston.

Claire attempted to compose herself as she heard the sound of footsteps approaching in the hall. John was here and she had been as silly as a pea goose to worry about him. No doubt he had been detained through no fault of his own and should soon explain it to her. She rose from her chair, a welcoming smile on her face, as he strode through the doorway.

"John!" Claire's smile vanished as she noticed the cold expression in his eyes. Something was horribly wrong. "Whatever has happened?"

John waited until Jennings had left and then he faced her squarely. "Be seated, Lady Radcliffe. I must speak to you."

Claire stared at him in utter confusion. A stiff martinet had supplanted the friendly gentleman whom she loved so dearly. She opened her mouth, intending to ask for an explanation, but his scowling countenance caused her to sink back down in her chair, her query unuttered.

"You are clever, madame, and I find I must compliment you on the scheme that you hatched with your daughter and Ralston. It is far better than any that have been attempted in the past."

" But, John . . . I do not know what . . ."

"Enough, madame!" He flicked aside her words with a curt gesture and Claire fell silent in the wake of his wrath. His eyes glittered with contempt and she began to tremble violently. "I admit that you almost succeeded. Only tonight, I found myself contemplating the means to make our engagement real. I began to love you, madame. I freely confess it."

Claire felt her face drain of color. He had said that he loved her, but the contempt was still present in his eyes.

"Perhaps it was the eagerness with which you shared my kisses or the sweet, giving way that you came into my arms." His expression softened slightly, but then he seemed to shake off the memory for his angry expression took hold once again. "That was before I discovered the depths of your deception."

"Deception?" Claire could hear her voice trembling and tears began to gather in her eyes. "What deception? I have never deceived you, John!"

His voice was hard as he answered her. "I assumed that you would cry. It is a feminine trick that succeeds quite well with most gentlemen. But it will not succeed with me, madame, and it will be a waste of your time and energy to attempt it."

Claire sat mutely, blinking back the tears that threatened to flood down her cheeks. She did not understand in what way John believed that she had deceived him. Even worse, he seemed convinced that Willow and Philip were involved in some sort of conspiracy with her.

"You underestimate me, Lady Radcliffe." As Claire watched, the scowl on his face grew deeper. "Did you truly believe that I would agree to make you my countess without crying foul?"

Claire's eyes widened. He believed she was attempting to trap him into marriage! "I did not try to trap you into marriage, sir. You know full well that our engagement is a ruse. We both agreed that I should cry off at the conclusion of the current Season."

"But will you cry off? I think not!" He glared at her and then he smiled, a twisting of his lips a parody of that pleasant expression.

"But I shall cry off!" Claire's voice was shaking. "I shall cry off immediately if that is what you desire."

He laughed, a bitter sound that held no mirth. "You are most convincing, Lady Radcliffe, especially with that charming quaver in your voice. I have half a notion to put you to the test, but that will not serve my purposes. You will continue in our deception until I give my leave for you to do otherwise. If you fail to do precisely as I say, I shall expose all members of your conspiracy and hold them up to public ridicule."

"All members?" Claire repeated his words dumbly. Who did he believe was involved?

"Yes, indeed. I shall expose your daughter, Ralston, Miss Fellows, Winslow, and you, my dear. I shall take particular pleasure in exposing your trickery to the *ton*. And you needn't think that my part in the resulting scandal shall dissuade me. I find I am quite grown quite accustomed to the cuts of polite society."

"But . . . but surely you do not think that I . . . Why, my daughter would never . . . I assure you, sir, that . . ."

"Silence!"

Claire's mouth snapped shut as he glared at her. It did not matter what she said for he would not believe her. If she claimed that the sky was blue, he would proclaim that it was not.

"Do you agree to continue our ruse then, madame?"

Claire felt her anger begin to rise as he stood there glaring, his hands upon his hips. How dare he demand that she pretend to be his fiancée when he had accused her of something she had not done?

"Madame? I am waiting for your answer."

He tapped his foot impatiently against the floor, and Claire's anger reached an explosive peak. "I will *not* pretend to be your fiancée, sir! As of this moment, our ruse is concluded. Remove yourself from my presence and do not presume to return!"

"Ah, the lady has teeth." He gave a slight chuckle that set Claire's teeth on edge. "But before you bite, I would have you consider the effect my public accusation should have on your daughter and Ralston. Perhaps you do not care if you are shunned by polite society, but I daresay they do."

Claire gasped in shock and clasped her hands together to keep them from trembling. "You would ruin my daughter?"

"I should ruin any who dared to trifle with me, madame."

Claire felt the fear wash over her in escalating waves. Philip was obliged to remain in his father's good graces until the title passed to him. Lord Northrup would not allow his successor to be the subject of such scandal and Willow's fiancé should quickly be disinherited. Even if there were some way to prove that the gossip about them was not true, both Willow and Philip should suffer the slights of all who believed Lord Sommerset's accusations. They should have to retire to the country estate that Philip had inherited from his grandfather and live there in virtual isolation.

"Have you reconsidered your decision, madame?"

The amusement on his face caused Claire to clench her fists for fear she should pick up the jade elephant that sat on the table and hurl it at his head. She took a deep breath in an attempt to calm herself and nodded stiffly. "It shall be as you wish, Lord Sommerset."

"A wise decision." He dipped his head. "And I trust that you shall not tax my patience further by devising a new scheme to marry me?"

Claire stared at him in utter shock and she uttered the first words that entered her mind. "Marry you, sir? I shall marry you when pigs fly!"

"Well said, madame." He gave a stiff bow and marched to the door, pulling it open and turning to fire one final sally in her direction. "And I shall marry you when ladies wear breeches to a formal ball!"

EIGHT

"Please eat something, Mama." There was an anxious frown on Willow's brow and she regarded her mother with distress. "You did not take a single bite of Lady Yardley's supper last night. Both Philip and I observed you merely moving the morsels about your plate."

"I was not hungry, dear."

"But you must eat to keep up your strength." Willow's voice quavered slightly. "You will starve if you do not take sustenance and I could not bear that!"

Claire smiled ruefully. "One does not starve from a missed meal, my dear. It takes much longer than that."

"But you have lost flesh, Mama." Willow was insistent. "Madame Lanier told me that she was forced to take several inches from the waist of your costume for the ball."

"It is true that I am a bit thinner, Willow, but I am in no danger of becoming a wraith. And I am certain that my appetite shall return in full force once this dreadful engagement is past."

"Cook has made your favorite this morning." Willow gestured toward the plate of toast sprinkled with cinnamon and sugar that sat in the center of the table. "She will be most unhappy if you do not take a taste."

Claire sighed and removed a piece of toast from the plate. She stared at it for a long moment and then she obediently nibbled at a corner. Willow would plague her until she ate and she wished for a bit of peace. Both Philip and Willow had been insufferably solicitous during the past six days.

"Thank you, Mama." Willow smiled at her in a way that reminded Claire of the smile one gives a recalcitrant child when one's orders are at last obeyed. "Cook will be most relieved. I shall run to the kitchen and make certain that she is preparing your favorite dishes for supper."

Once Willow had left the breakfast room, Claire replaced the toast on her plate. The treat that she had enjoyed so thoroughly in the past now caused her stomach to churn alarmingly. It lay there untouched, silently accusing her with its very presence, and Claire picked it up again, carrying it to the French doors that led to the gardens and tossing it out among the bushes for the birds to enjoy.

When she resumed her seat, Claire sighed deeply and took a sip of the coffee that John had taught her to enjoy. She had dutifully accompanied him to several routs and balls, suffering his presence with a dignity that she had not known she possessed. She had been remarkably civil, smiling up at him whenever others were present, and dancing dutifully in his arms. Claire was certain that none had guessed the extent of her loathing for the man who had crushed her tender feelings so ruthlessly.

Claire frowned as she thought of the evening when John had accused her of duplicity. Once he had stomped from the drawing room, Claire had fled to her bedchamber to indulge in a bout of tears that left her pale and shaken. When she had managed at last to compose herself, she had vowed to get to the crux of his cruel accusations. John had believed that she had been deceitful and she should never forgive him for that. But someone had been guilty of fabricating the falsehood in the first place and that person was the true villain in the piece. Ringing for Jennings, Claire had instructed him to escort Willow and Philip to her sitting room the moment that they had returned.

Anticipating firm denials from both Willow and Philip,

Claire had been astounded when they had admitted their guilt. It seemed that they had indeed chosen John as a match for her, and had enlisted Miss Fellows to aid them in gaining their objective. The scene that Claire had witnessed in Lady Bollinger's gardens had been but a simulation performed solely for her benefit. Miss Fellows had harbored not the slightest intention of attempting to trap John into marriage.

"How could you, Willow?" Claire had stared at her daughter in utter shock.

"It was my doing, Lady Radcliffe." Philip had placed a comforting arm around Willow's shoulders. "I am solely to blame for choosing the earl."

"And I am solely to blame for wishing you married." Willow's voice had been thick with tears. "I am so sorry, Mama. I only wanted you to be happy!"

Claire had nodded, acknowledging the truth of her daughter's statement. "I know that, darling. But you should have told me. When John accused us of perpetuating this deception, I assumed that he was entirely mistaken."

"I will explain it to him, Lady Radcliffe." Philip had risen from his chair. "I shall call on him now and assure him that you were unaware of our scheme and would not have approved if you had known. We have been the cause of this dreadful misunderstanding and I am determined to set things aright."

Philip had left immediately and both Claire and Willow had waited anxiously as the minutes had ticked by. When Philip had returned, well over an hour later, he had worn a most dejected expression.

"He did not believe me." The anguish had been deep in Philip's eyes. "He assumed that my confession was but another trick that we had devised."

Claire had sighed, accepting the inevitable. The man she loved was lost to her and there was nothing she could do to reverse the damage that had been done. Drawing a deep breath, she had attempted to make the best of it, explaining

her necessity for continuing the appearances of her engagement and eliciting solemn promises from both Willow and
Philip that they should remain silent about the matter.

"Do you forgive us, Mama?" Willow's lip had trembled
and tears had run down her cheeks.

Claire had sighed, tears forming in her own eyes at the
sight of her daughter's distress. "Of course I forgive you,
my darlings. And it does not matter in the slightest, for I
should not have married the earl in any case. Our engagement
was merely a ruse."

"A ruse?" Philip had stared at her in shock.

"Yes, dear Philip. The earl and I entered into an agreement
to pretend to be engaged until this Season was over. It was
merely a device to save him from the unwanted attentions
of greedy mamas and their eager daughters."

"You truly intended to cry off at the end of the Season?"
Willow had dabbed at her eyes with the square of linen that
Philip had provided.

"Yes, dear." Claire had forced a smile on her lips. "So
you see that the earl's opinion of my character does enter
into the matter. I doubt that I shall ever have occasion to
meet him again, once the current Season is concluded."

Philip's eyes had narrowed and he had peered at her intently. "You do not love him then?"

"Love him?" Claire had struggled to assume a light tone.
"That is absurd, my dear Philip. I should never have entered
into my agreement with Lord Sommerset if he had engaged
my heart. It would have been far too painful to endure."

Claire sighed deeply as she recalled the words that she
had spoken. Meeting John each day and dancing with him
at parties and balls had indeed been far too painful for her
to endure. She had no doubt that it was the cause of her
sleepless nights and the reason why her appetite had vanished. She had survived in this manner for six long days,
striving to keep up the appearance of normalcy even as her

heart was breaking, but she did not know how much longer she could manage to hide her grief.

There was only one small circumstance that gave Claire comfort. Though she knew it was considered mean-spirited to take pleasure in the suffering of another, she could not help but feel her burden lift slightly when she observed how John had moved the food round his plate in a similar fashion, lifting not a morsel to his lips. His eyes had also borne black smudges beneath them, testifying to his lack of sleep, and the smile on his face had held no warmth as he had greeted his acquaintances. John was suffering, of that she was certain. He had said that he had loved her, and perhaps he loved her still. But even if he had come to believe her innocent of the accusations he had hurled at her, he would never confess that he loved her still, nor would he beg her apology for falsely accusing her. El Diablo was far too proud to admit that he was wrong. It was a classic scene from a tragedy, one worthy of Mr. Shakespeare. Oh, how ironic that two people could be so in love and neither of them admit it.

Claire considered the problem for a moment, but her privacy was rudely interrupted as Willow burst into the breakfast room, carrying a gown draped over her arm.

"Your costume for the ball has arrived, Mama." Willow held it up so that Claire could see. "I declare it is every bit as beautiful as any costume I have ever seen!"

Willow's smile was so eager that Claire forced herself to smile back. The costume was indeed lovely, a skilled rendition in golden silk of the gown that the Greek goddess Aphrodite would have worn.

"Every item is here, Mama." Willow pushed the remains of their breakfast aside and laid them out so her mother could see. "Here are golden sandals, a perfectly exquisite tiara, and the magical girdle that made her irresistible to Zeus. Madame Lanier has even seen fit to provide us with a packet of gold dust to sprinkle in your hair. It far outshines my shepherdess costume, Mama, though that is also quite lovely. You are pleased, are you not?"

"Yes, dear." Claire nodded quickly, but as she glanced at the lovely costume a daring concept popped into her mind. The very thought caused her eyes to sparkle and her smile to grow wide with pleasure. She had just found the perfect way to prove to John that she loved him every bit as much as he loved her. All she needed was the necessary courage to perform such a scandalous act.

"What is it, Mama?" The smile disappeared from Willow's lips and she stared at her mother in confusion. "You look so . . . so determined."

Claire laughed lightly and the anticipation of what she was about to do caused her cheeks to turn pink. "I *am* determined, dear. I have decided that I shall not dress as Aphrodite. The costume should look far lovelier on you."

"Oh, Mama! Could I wear it truly?" Willow's eyes began to sparkle with excitement. "We are almost precisely the same size and it should suit me perfectly. But are you certain you wish to appear at the ball dressed as a shepherdess?"

"No, dear. You may give the shepherdess costume to one of your friends. I shall dress in a costume that I shall fashion myself."

"But there is so little time, Mama." Willow began to frown. "The ball is this evening!"

Claire bit back the totally inappropriate giggle that threatened to erupt from her throat. "I am aware of that, dear, and it is the reason that we must make haste. Do you think that if we ask him nicely, Philip will part with a set of his formal clothing?"

"Of course, Mama. You know that Philip would do anything to make you happy. But why do you need . . ."

"I shall tell you when the time is right and not before." Claire interrupted what was bound to be a series of queries from her daughter. "Please send a message to Philip immediately, asking him to bring round a full set of his formal clothing."

Willow nodded. "Yes, Mama. But I still do not understand . . ."

"Do it immediately, Willow." Claire interrupted her once again and her tone brooked no nonsense. "If I am to be ready for the ball on time, there is not a moment to waste."

It was the day of his engagement ball and John frowned as he regarded his costume. When he had first commissioned it from his tailor, he had thought it fitting to attend in the garb of a pirate. Claire had confessed that when she had first caught sight of him, she had envisioned him as a pirate, engaged in daring adventures on the high seas. She had thought that her image was caused by the color of his skin, tanned darkly by the sun, and the thin, white scar that ran along his cheek. When he had explained the scar and the low branch that had cut him while on his first pony, she had begged him never to tell the tale. "Let all assume that the scar is from dueling," she had advised him with a smile, "and few shall possess the necessary sand to challenge you to a fight."

John scowled deeply as he thought of Claire and the cruel manner in which he had accused her. He had thought her like the other ladies of his acquaintance, grasping women whose sole aim was to ascend the social ladder, unscrupulous females who would use any means available to them to marry title and wealth. If he had only taken the trouble to consider it, he should have known that Claire was different.

He tossed the pirate costume on the bed and sighed deeply. He had stomped into Claire's Drawing Room with the intention of ringing a peal over her head. His stubborn pride had driven him to shout, and posture and intimidate her to the point where she had feared to speak. He had been an utter madman, already convicting her and deciding upon her punishment before he had even set foot in her home. Why had he treated her so high-handedly? John sighed again and dropped his head into his hands. He had done so because he loved her and he had not been able to bear the thought that she had deceived him.

She had loved him in return, John was certain. It would have been impossible for even the finest actress to simulate the sparkle that had appeared in her eyes each time that they had met. And it would have been even more inconceivable for her to feign her response to his embrace. Claire had loved him, and he had lost her love through his own failing. Rather than giving his temper full rein, he should have discussed the matter with her calmly and listened to her response with an open mind.

A fierce wave of guilt washed over John and he groaned deeply in his throat. His old nanny was used to say that his temper would someday cause his downfall, but he had not listened to her, either. And now it had happened. He had lost the only woman that he had ever loved.

There was a tentative tap upon the open door and Hartley's face peeped round the corner. "It is past eleven, my Lord. Should you care to break your fast?"

"Yes, Hartley. I shall dress now." John sighed as another wave of guilt assailed him. He had spent the past six days snapping at his staff for imagined transgressions and then apologizing profusely for his ill temper. His nerves were rubbed raw and tonight was to be the worst ordeal of all. Instead of the joyous occasion he had anticipated, he would once again be forced to face the pain in the depths of Claire's emerald eyes.

John watched impassively as Hartley chose his clothing. Once all was assembled, he stood as silent as a mute while his valet assisted him to dress. It was only when Hartley had brought his Hessians that John spoke. "If a man has lost the love of his lady, Hartley, what action should he take to regain it?"

"I . . . I do not know, sir." Hartley risked a glance at his master's face. What he saw must have reassured him, for he reached out to place a hand on John's shoulder. "He should admit that he was wrong, and beg her forgiveness."

"But what if she will not speak with him privately, Hartley?"

"That is indeed a problem, sir." Hartley thought about it for a moment. "If I were that gentleman, I should do something to make the lady laugh."

"Make her *laugh?*" John began to frown.

"Yes indeed, sir. A lady who laughs cannot be angry. The two emotions are quite the opposite, you see, and it is not possible for them to be present simultaneously. I presume we are speaking of Lady Radcliffe?"

John nodded. Hartley had been with him for too many years to be put off by his use of the hypothetical.

"Lady Radcliffe has a fine sense of humor, sir, and she has not laughed for a sennight. Mrs. York, her housekeeper, is quite anxious about her as she neither sleeps nor eats."

John did not bother to ask how Hartley had learned of this. He merely nodded and accepted it as fact. The servants in all the grand houses had their own lines of communication.

"If I were you, sir, I should attempt to make Lady Radcliffe laugh so uproariously that any remaining traces of her anger should disappear. If your joke is truly excellent, it should also serve as your apology."

John thought about it for a moment and then he began to smile. "Thank you, Hartley. You have just given me an excellent idea. Would you happen to know where I could procure a boar's head hat and a set of wings?"

Hartley's mouth dropped open and he stared at his master in utter disbelief. "A boar's head hat? And a set of wings, sir?"

"Precisely. I shall require them by this evening, Hartley. And I should like a pig's tail, too, for good measure. It must be one that I can pin to the back of my coat."

Hartley nodded. "It is to be a costume then, sir?"

"Yes, and I shall wear it to the ball. You must not fail me in this, Hartley. It may very well be my sole opportunity to make Lady Radcliffe my wife."

"Very good, sir."

John grinned as Hartley dropped the pirate costume and hurried from his chamber. His valet had worn a most determined expression and John was certain that he should spare no effort to secure the necessary items. The proof of Hartley's determination was in the pirate costume that lay in a crumpled heap upon John's floor. This was the first time in Hartley's long years of service that he had exhibited so little regard for an item of his master's clothing.

NINE

Claire gave a smile of satisfaction as she surveyed her image in the glass. She had closeted herself in her sitting room for hours, clipping and re-stitching the necessary seams to alter the items that Philip had brought to her. His formal set of clothing was now tailored to fit her slender form, but Claire found that she could scarcely face her reflection in the glass as she stepped back to assess the fit of the breeches.

A flush of heated color rose to cover Claire's cheeks and turn them bright pink with embarrassment. Most ladies of her acquaintance should be put to the blush if so much as an ankle were inadvertently exposed. Skirts swept down to the floor, thoroughly hiding the body beneath them. It was considered most improper to even refer to the mechanism that made it possible for a lady to walk.

Claire had laughed about this once with her husband, quipping that a proper gentleman must be quite shocked to discover that his bride possessed two legs of a design similar to his own. The shape of these limbs was never discussed and a gentleman had no certain way of knowing, until after he had spoken his vows, whether his wife's limbs should be fat and stubby, or long and graceful.

Hers were long and graceful, Claire decided, gazing at them critically in the glass. And her very appearance at the ball this evening should apprise every guest of that fact. It should be regarded as a scandal of the highest magnitude, but she could not dwell on that at this late date. All should be lost if her courage failed her now.

"Please, madame. You must reconsider!" Claire's dresser stood to the side, wringing her hands anxiously.

Claire glanced at her image once again, and then she shook her head firmly. "No. I am required to wear this. Nothing else shall do."

Her dresser's fingers trembled as she clasped the doubloon pendant around Claire's neck and made a final adjustment to her coiffeur. She looked ready to collapse in tears and Claire was reminded of another old saying that her late husband had been fond of repeating.

"It matters not whether I am hanged for a goat or for a lamb. The end result is the same." Claire reached out to pat her dresser's hand. "Fetch my silver cloak, Elise. It will conceal my costume until such time as I make my appearance. And tell Jennings to have the coach brought round."

"Yes, madame."

The dresser dipped her head and hurried to do Claire's bidding. Once the cloak was brought and fastened round her shoulders, Claire turned to face the glass again. Its voluminous folds covered her costume from head to toe, just as Claire had thought it would. None would know of her scandalous intentions until she removed it at the ball.

Claire swept down the stairs, her head held high and the color bright on her cheeks. She had sent Willow and Philip on without her, preferring to arrive unescorted. Willow had assumed that she desired only the material contained in Philip's set of formal clothing, and since neither of them had been permitted to glimpse Claire's finished costume, they had no suspicion that she should appear actually wearing Philip's breeches.

As Claire was handed into the coach, she took care that her cloak did not open. Once they were on their way, she leaned back against the squabs and drew a deep breath for courage. When she arrived, Willow and Philip should be every bit as scandalized as the other guests. It would be apparent to all that observed their shocked expressions that they had played no part in her disgrace.

It was only a short distance to Lady Bollinger's mansion and Claire forced a smile as she was granted admittance. She quickly sought out Marcella's dignified butler and handed him the urgent message that she had written earlier, requesting a private audience with her hostess.

"What is it, Claire?" Lady Bollinger rushed into the salon where the butler had secreted Claire. "You are dreadfully late, my dear, and the dancing has already commenced. You are well, are you not?"

Claire nodded quickly. "Yes, Marcella. But I thought it best that I show you my costume before I entered the ballroom. You must prepare yourself for a shock."

"Nothing could shock me more than my nephew's appearance here this evening." Lady Bollinger began to frown. "I have never seen him look so poorly. He smiles, but his smile does not reach his eyes. And when he dances, he merely goes through the motions of enjoying himself. You have quarreled, have you not?"

Claire nodded, beginning to unfasten her cloak. "Yes, and most dreadfully. He does not believe that I love him, Marcella, and I fear that I have lost his good opinion of my character. It is the very reason that I must wear this costume."

"Your costume cannot be any more ludicrous than his! My dear nephew is most dignified, you see, and for him to wear . . ."

Lady Bollinger stopped speaking abruptly and she gasped in shock as Claire drew off her cloak. Her mouth opened and closed several times in an attempt to speak, but all she could do was sputter helplessly. "Claire! But you cannot . . . Do you realize what . . . Oh, dear!"

"Please sit down, Marcella." Claire led the older lady to a chair. "I would spare you this outrage if it were possible, but I fear it is not. I will go to any lengths to regain John's regard for me. And wearing this costume is the only way I can prove that I love him above all else."

Lady Bollinger stared at Claire for a long moment and then she did something that caused Claire to fear for her sanity. Her lips quivered and a startled giggle emerged from her throat. Tears of mirth gathered in her eyes and then she threw back her head to laugh most uproariously.

"Marcella! Are you quite all right?" Claire rushed to the table to pour her hostess a glass of sherry. "I fear I have given you a nasty shock, and I apologize most sincerely."

Lady Bollinger waved the glass aside and struggled to regain control of her laughter. She succeeded, in part, though fits of giggles still caused her to sputter helplessly. "My dear, Claire! This is . . . Oh, my! It will be a . . . a scandal, of course. And your name shall be on . . . on everyone's lips."

"I know that, Marcella, and I think it best for you to claim that you had no prior knowledge of my intentions. I should not like your name to be linked with mine in this scandal."

"That is kind of you, Claire, and I suppose you are right." Lady Bollinger sobered quickly. "You say that you are obliged to appear in this *particular* costume?"

Claire nodded. "Yes, indeed. None other will suffice."

"Then you must do it, of course, and hang the consequences." Lady Bollinger rose to her feet and made her way to the door. She was about to open it when she turned back for one last word. "Your costume may be scandalous, dear Claire, but I must say that you do look undeniably ravishing in it."

John glanced around the ballroom once again, peering over the shoulders of several guests as he searched for Claire. He had danced with the two young ladies who had accused him last Season and thus silenced the tongues of the gossip-mongers, but Claire had not been present to see him perform this duty. And though the dancing had commenced nearly an hour ago, his presumed fiancée had not yet seen fit to put in her appearance.

He was about to avail himself of a glass of champagne from a passing footman when Aunt Marcella arrived at his side. John smiled politely, but his aunt merely nodded, an anxious frown upon her face.

"I must speak to you immediately, John."

John quickly led his aunt to a secluded spot behind a stand of potted palms and turned to her with some alarm. "What is it, Aunt Marcella? Do not tell me that Claire has sent her excuses!"

"No, indeed. Claire is here and she should be joining us very shortly. But it is most urgent that I speak with you before . . ." John frowned as his aunt stopped speaking abruptly. A dreadful hush had spread over the ballroom and he turned to his aunt in alarm.

"I am too late!" His aunt's voice was a mere whisper. "There is no doubt that Claire has arrived."

John rushed out from behind the green fronds and the sight that greeted him made his eyes widen in shock. Claire had indeed arrived and she was dressed in a set of gentleman's formal clothing!

As he watched, Claire entered the ballroom, moving quite regally onto the dance floor. The dancers scattered without a word, gentlemen pulling their partners back with great haste as if they were about to encounter one infected with the plague. The dance floor was deserted in a matter of seconds, leaving Claire as the sole occupant of the large space.

John's mind spun in shocked circles. Whatever had possessed Claire to dress in this scandalous manner? Though it was a costume ball and a certain laxity was enjoyed at affairs of this nature, she knew full well that ladies were not allowed to appear in breeches.

It was at this precise moment that John remembered the last angry words he had hurtled at Claire. *And I will marry you when ladies wear breeches to a formal ball!*

This was a formal ball. And Claire was wearing breeches. John stepped forward, into the wake of the dreadful silence that hung like a pall over the ballroom. He smiled at the woman who had risked certain censure to make clear her tender feelings for him, and bowed most genteelly to her.

Claire's eyes were fixed on the very top of the French doors that led to Lady Bollinger's formal gardens. She dared not look into any of the shocked faces for fear she would whirl on her heel and run from the ballroom to escape the scene of her disgrace. She had vowed to maintain her dignity at all costs, though it should be of no consequence to anyone but her. She should be shunned by polite society from this day forward.

The orchestra ceased playing abruptly, in mid-measure of a waltz. The utter stillness that enveloped her was dreadful, for none uttered a single word. As Claire moved through the crushing silence, she prayed that her knees would cease their trembling and the polite smile would remain in place upon her lips.

Small sounds became magnified in the absence of the usual noises. Claire heard the whisper of fans unfurling as proper ladies hid their eyes from the scandalous sight. There was the scrape of a chair, pulled out hastily for one who had grown faint, and more than a few startled gasps of outrage.

She had only to reach the French doors. Claire kept that encouraging thought foremost in her mind. Once she reached the sanctuary of Lady Bollinger's veranda, she could escape down the stone steps that led to the gardens and end this dreadful ordeal.

"My darling Claire. You have arrived at last."

A deep voice spoke, causing Claire to startle and drop her gaze. John was standing directly in her path, at the far end of the room, in the shadow of a stand of potted palms.

He was smiling, his knee bent in a bow, and Claire came

disastrously close to attempting a curtsy in return. At the very last moment, as she was about to reach for the edges of her skirt, she realized that this should be quite impossible. She settled for dipping her head in acknowledgment, and stood frozen to the spot, gazing at him uncertainly.

"How lovely you look this evening, my dearest fiancée. I am most proud to be your escort." His words were proper, just the thing a gentleman might say to his fiancée, but Claire heard the hint of laughter that lurked in his voice. And then, as he moved forward, out of the shadows, she caught her first glimpse of his costume.

He was wearing a boar's head as a hat, and a pair of wings stuck out from the sides from his coat. Marcella had been right. John's costume was most ludicrous. Such things as flying boars did not exist, even in myths and legends. It was at this moment, as she was pondering the question of why he had worn such a ridiculous costume, that Claire remembered the last angry words that she had spoken to him. She had said, *I shall marry you when pigs fly!* And John had dressed as a flying pig.

"No doubt you have surmised the reason for my costume." John smiled, and as he began to walk toward her, he turned to the side and flicked an appendage that was pinned to the back of his coat. "You see, my dearest, I have even gone so far as to wear the tail."

It was more than Claire could endure. Though she struggled vainly to maintain her composure, the sight of John's costume caused her to become quite undone. She gave a joyful whoop of most unladylike laughter and ran across the floor to his arms.

As they embraced, the silence in the ballroom was broken by a buzz of distraught comments. In a matter of moments, the noise grew to a roar, but Claire heard nothing but John's sigh of supreme contentment as he gathered her into his embrace.

"Does this mean that you will marry me?" His lips were warm against her ear.

"Oh, yes!" Claire's answer was a joyous exclamation. But then, as she realized the enormity of what she had done, she drew back with an anxious expression. "But I am ruined, John. The *ton* shall never forgive me for the scandal that I have caused here tonight. Are you certain that you wish to marry a social pariah?"

"Yes, my darling Claire. I should never allow such a small thing as a scandal to keep us apart. But you will not be ruined, my dearest. Before the conclusion of this ball, all shall come to regard you as a lady of great courage and supreme loyalty. I have a plan, you see, to turn our mutual disgrace into a great entertainment, one that shall be the talk of the *ton* for years to come."

"You do?" Claire's spirits began to rise as she looked up into his smiling countenance. "How will you accomplish that?"

"I shall confess to our guests that we had quarreled and broken off our engagement by mutual consent and you shall tell them exactly what you said to me."

"I shall marry you when pigs fly?" Claire's eyes widened and an impish smile crossed her lips.

"Precisely. And I shall repeat my answer to you, that I would marry you when ladies wore breeches to a formal ball."

Claire nodded quickly. "That will explain our costumes, but will they forgive me the scandal?"

"Yes, indeed. Most members of the *ton* have grown jaded and they continually seek new amusements. Our unusual reconciliation shall amuse them greatly and they will be even more delighted when I invite them all to be guests at our wedding tonight."

"Tonight?" Claire gasped.

John gazed down at her fondly, a smile on his lips. "Now

that I have you in my arms once more, I intend to keep you there. Will you marry me tonight?"

Claire felt a smile of pure joy flood across her face. "Yes, John. Are we all to travel to Gretna Green?"

"There is no need. I procured a special license and if you agree, we shall exchange our vows at the conclusion of the ball."

"In our costumes?" Claire began to giggle. "You do look quite ridiculous, you know."

"And you look quite fetching. But there will be ample time for us to dress for the occasion. Willow has offered to fetch any gown of your choosing and Philip will accomplish the task of obtaining suitable clothing for me."

Claire's eyes widened in surprise. "Philip and Willow knew that you planned to marry me tonight?"

"Yes." John smiled down at her. "I asked for their assistance this very afternoon and they were most happy to oblige me. The only question was whether you would agree to become my countess, and that was answered most convincingly when you appeared at the ball wearing breeches."

Claire laughed and then she reached up to hug him, nearly dislodging his boar's head hat. "I love you, John."

"And I love you, Claire. I shall prove it to you every day of our life together. And now, before we redeem ourselves in the eyes of our wedding guests, shall we afford them the sight of a flying pig waltzing with a lady in breeches?"

"Yes, indeed."

Claire felt her smile take on epic proportions as John signaled to the orchestra and they struck up a waltz. John held out his arms, Claire stepped into them, and they began to dance their very last waltz together before they became husband and wife.

SWEETER THAN CANDY

by

Regina Scott

To my mother, Rosann Brown—
her story on her day with all my love.

ONE

Panting, Daniel Lewiston heaved himself up the last two steps to the Kinsle terrace and collapsed onto the stone bench in delighted exhaustion. Voices, young and strident, echoed his name across the emerald lawn and set the swans to fluttering in the placid lake below. His best friend Jonathan Kinsle glanced up from his week-old copy of the *London Times*. "I trust you're enjoying this debacle?"

Despite the fact that he could barely catch a breath, Daniel grinned. "Immensely," he managed. He grabbed the crystal glass of lemonade Jonathan's manservant had poured for him earlier and gulped the tart liquid down. That seemed to help the spasms in his chest. He really ought to see about getting more exercise if a brisk game of ball could so wind him. Refusing to allow his state to ruin a perfect summer's day, he leaned back against the terrace balustrade and tried to pretend he didn't notice the two small figures stealthily approaching the steps. "You should join us."

Jonathan reached out a languid hand to pick up his own china teacup and quirked a blond brow. "Heaven forbid. I wouldn't dream of spoiling your fun, old man. Duck."

Daniel bent over as a blue cloth ball sailed past the spot where his head had been moments before. Someone cried out in vexation below, only to be quickly shushed. Daniel bent lower to retrieve the ball, wincing as his stomach protested the compression. *Exercise more often and eat less,* he amended.

"You might find you enjoy it," he chided his friend as he straightened. "These nephews of yours are simply ingenious." He lobbed the ball over the top of the bushes and heard a quite satisfactory yelp of dismay.

"Entirely too ingenious," Jonathan muttered as the bushes shook with obvious plans for revenge. He flicked a displaced leaf from the otherwise immaculate sleeve of his navy coat. "Seriously, Danny boy, if you hadn't taken such a shine to them, I don't know how we would have managed these last three weeks with Cynthia in London."

Daniel ran a hand back through his already tousled brown hair and shifted his weight along the bench to the right. He heard the protest from the seat of his dun-colored trousers and felt the back of the bush snag on his own navy coat, which was far from immaculate. *More exercise, less food, and a new tailor.* "It was no great burden, I assure you. I haven't had this much fun in years. In fact, I can't remember when I ever had this much fun." He shot to the left, and the ball neatly missed him again. Feeling a bit more satisfied with his performance, he bent to retrieve it.

Jonathan chuckled. "Yes, you were the most pitied boy in the neighborhood, growing up with all those sisters and a mother who was determined to protect you against any calamity, especially any that were any fun."

Daniel smiled as he rolled the soft cloth back and forth in his large hands. "She *was* rather over-protective, God rest her soul."

"Thank God Cynthia has more sense," Jonathan sighed. "Although there are times I see the similarities between your mother and my sister. She seems to have kept the boys close, but I suppose that's natural in a big city like Bristol and so near the docks. Can't have been a very savory environment, if you take my meaning. It's a shame our parents weren't more willing to forgive Cynthia for her elopement. We might have been able to teach them some manners."

Daniel shook his head at the reproof. "They're no worse than you were at that age, Jonny."

Jonathan raised an eyebrow. "I beg your pardon? I may have been an active child, but I don't recall chasing our neighbor about the back lawn."

"That's because your neighbors consisted of four fatherless girls and a boy who wasn't even allowed to leave home for school." Keeping an eye out for his would-be attackers, he leaned closer to his friend. "Although I understand from young John that Cynthia may be marrying again. I realize she most likely wants a father for them, but isn't that a little soon? Their father has been dead less than six months."

Jonathan shrugged, crossing long legs without so much as creasing his fawn-colored trousers. "What would you have her do? He left them next to nothing, and she knows I'll be hard pressed to keep them. If this business with the Admiralty comes to naught I'm not sure how we'll get along unless she remarries. Mind you, I hadn't heard her mention any gentleman in particular, but it wouldn't surprise me. Cynthia may be past her prime, but she's not bad looking."

"Spoken like a true brother," Daniel teased. "Your sister was always a diamond of the first water, and I can't imagine a few years has changed that."

"A few hard years, old man," Jonathan sighed. "Nathan Jacobs may have been a devoted husband and father whenever he happened to return from the sea, but he wasn't a very good provider if I'm any judge of things. You might want to aim for that mulberry."

Daniel rose casually, then twisted to hurl the ball into the bushes at the bottom of the terrace. A chorus of complaints rose in its wake. He gazed thoughtfully down at the quaking vegetation. "Let's talk no more about this with present company, eh, Jonny? He was their father, after all."

Jonathan shook his head and reached once again for his

tea. "Never could stand to hear an unkind word said about anyone, could you, Danny boy? You even speak highly of Enoch McCreedy and everyone knows what a tartar he is. This tendency will come back to bite you one day, you see if it doesn't. There are scoundrels in this world that deserve to be recognized."

"And there are three little boys who deserve to have a bit of fun," Daniel countered, a frown creasing his brow. "Although, at the moment, I only seem to be able to locate two of them."

Inside the manor, the third boy crept stealthily up to the terrace doors. He was so intent on secrecy that he didn't hear the front door open or the manservant murmur a welcome. He plucked the dusty gauze curtains aside and reached for the tarnished gilt handle.

Cynthia Kinsle Jacobs was shrugging out of her pelisse in the entry hall, bone weary of traveling and dejected by her failure. She caught a movement in the pier glass above the nearby hall table. She blinked, and the picture came into focus. "John Wesley Jacobs," she barked from long practice, "what are you doing?"

The ball was instantly out of sight around his back as he turned to smile at her, his slender face as pale as the worn curtains behind him. Cynthia knew she ought to be cross with him for making mischief in Jonathan's house, but it was difficult when she'd missed him and his brothers so much the last three weeks. She had kept envisioning them as they had been since moving from Bristol: pale, quiet, listless, more like three little statues than the active boys she had raised. She supposed that rather than being cross she ought to be thankful that he was playing again. But instead she found herself looking over her shoulder for Jonathan.

Jonathan was the least indulgent of uncles. She supposed it was her fault for not trying to reconcile with her family sooner. He had been no more ready to be an uncle when she had shown up on his doorstep a month ago than she had been to become a mother at seventeen. She had had nearly nine years to get used to the idea; Jonathan had had less than six weeks. He was obviously trying to do his duty and just as obviously finding that duty entirely too trying. He had grown used to the quiet solitude of the house since their parents had passed on, and three little boys were three children too many.

If only the Admiralty had been able to tell her what had happened to Nathan's effects! She had been counting on some money coming to light so that she might be able to continue to live with her sons alone. Now that was impossible. They had no choice but to remain here, and any misbehavior by her sons would only make that situation more difficult.

And John was clearly up to something. Even if she hadn't just caught him in the act of some mischief, he looked entirely too much like his father had, after breaking his promise and shipping out for the fifth time, to be even remotely innocent. She'd often thought the only thing missing from her husband's wide-blue-eyed look of innocence was a halo over his curly, blond hair. At least he had that now. That and three sons who looked just like him. She forced the thought to the back of her mind and focused on John.

"Oh, hello, Mother," he nodded politely, edging away from the terrace door. "You're back a bit early."

"Too early for you, I'm sure," Cynthia replied, schooling her face to firmness. "Shouldn't I have to go upstairs to find you at this time of day, sir? What have you done with your Uncle Jonathan?"

John's blue eyes opened even wider, but he didn't stop moving away from the terrace door, threading his way around the three dark chairs and settee. "Why, nothing. He's about somewhere."

With a swirl of her black widow's gown, Cynthia stepped

to cut off his escape through the open door of the sitting room. "And will I find James and Adam in that same somewhere?"

"I believe they're out on the terrace," John pointed with his free hand, his shoulder shaking only a trifle as he balanced the ball with the other hand. "Perhaps you should go check on them."

And he was as creative as his father about getting out of scrapes as well, she thought, laying a hand on his shoulder and propelling him back across the matted carpet toward the terrace door. "Let's go see them together, shall we? Unless, of course, you'd like to explain what you're doing in the sitting room with a ball in your hand?"

Her son sighed, deflating in defeat. "Oh, very well. If you must know, we were having a game with Mr. Daniel."

"Mr. Daniel?" Cynthia frowned, absently smoothing her dark blond hair back into the coil at the nape of her neck.

"You must have met him, Mother," John insisted. "Uncle Jonathan said he's known you since you were born."

Cynthia blinked, her thoughts momentarily arrested as time seemed to slip backward. She sank onto the settee. "Not Daniel Lewiston?"

John nodded. "Yes, that's him. I knew you knew him. Uncle Jonathan said you were going to marry him before you met Father."

Cynthia shook her head with a twinge of melancholy. That was one subject she had thought long settled and one person she had thought never to meet again. But she should have realized she'd meet him if they continued living here. "Your uncle says entirely too much," she managed. At her son's frown, she felt compelled to explain. "Your grandmother and grandfather wanted me to marry him, John, but please believe me when I say that Daniel Lewiston and I would never have suited."

To her dismay, she saw her son regarding her with narrowed eyes as if he very much doubted the truth of her last statement.

She couldn't imagine why, but she felt a blush heating her cheek. "Now, John, this is none of your affair. All you need know is that the only man I've ever loved was your father."

"Of course," John nodded complacently. "But now that Father's dead, you have to marry again. Uncle Jonathan . . ."

"Said so," Cynthia finished for him, deciding to say a few things herself when next she saw her dear, devoted brother. "I've heard entirely too much on that score from your uncle, the vicar, and every matron in London, so don't you start on me, too."

He crossed his arms over a narrow chest and affixed her with a stern gaze. "Surely you must see reason, Mother. Uncle Jonathan has no use for us. And he says we do not have enough money to live on our own."

She met the forthright gaze with difficulty. How dare Jonathan tell her son such things! For all that they were true, it was too heavy a burden for an eight-year-old boy. From an early age, John had been a help to her when Nathan was gone, going with her to the nicer parts of town to carry the socks and clothing she mended to augment Nathan's pay and later caring for his younger brothers while she made the rounds herself. Lately, however, she had noticed that he seemed intent on taking control of more and more situations, bossing his brothers incessantly and trying to do the same for her. It was as if he no longer trusted the adults around him.

"We'll do all right, John," she told him, praying God would understand the need for her lie. "I don't want you to worry about such things. Haven't I always taken care of you?"

"You are an admirable mother," he replied, small chin so high she didn't know whether to laugh or cry at the mature words. "But I'm the man of the family now that Father's gone. And it is my duty to take care of you."

Pride swelled along with a lurking desperation. "That is very brave of you, John," she murmured.

He bowed his head in noble acknowledgment and strolled

toward the door. Just as he reached it she remembered he still held the ball. "John," she began, rising.

The terrace doors burst open, flooding the room with light. Cynthia jumped in surprise. Then, heart pounding in her throat, she fell back from the huge, dark shape that stumbled toward her. One of the chairs toppled over with a crash, and she reached out instinctively to protect John. Surely some sort of a madman had blundered into the house! She could hear Adam and James shouting and peered closer but all she could make out in the bright sunlight was a misshapen form that seemed to have three heads.

"Ah ha!" the largest of the heads yelled at her oldest son. "Now I have you!"

"No, you don't!" John contradicted, pulling away from her to dash into the entry hall and clatter up the stairs. The creature made to follow him and as it ambled past her, she finally brought it into focus. A tall man, heavy, disheveled, and thoroughly out of breath, with Adam riding one shoulder and James the other. She was so surprised that they were past her before she could stop them.

"James, Adam!" she commanded, gathering her wits. The behemoth slid to a stop at the foot of the stairs, one hand clutching the carved newel post. His massive shoulders straightened as if he knew he was in trouble as well. Not a madman, then. She couldn't imagine who would be so bold as to dash about with her sons on his shoulders, but the game clearly had to stop before Jonathan caught them. Two heads swung back with wide blue eyes in an uncanny mimic of her late husband. She offered them her sternest gaze, ready to scold both her sons and the man who carried them. "Is this how you behave in your uncle's house?" she demanded.

Seven-year-old James looked thoughtful, reminding her more of Jonathan than her Nathan. Four-year-old Adam wiggled on his perch, further wrinkling his black short pants.

"I'm afraid it's my fault," rumbled the gentleman in a voice that was familiar, although deeper than she seemed to remember it. He turned carefully so as not to upset the boys, and Cynthia realized it was Daniel Lewiston.

He was much changed since the last time she had seen him, then a young man of eighteen whom she had found impossible to understand. His mahogany brown hair was shorter, although that only made the waves more noticeable. His eyes seemed darker, but then the gray had always reflected his emotions. She wondered what he was feeling now—embarrassment, if the crooked smile on his large, full-lipped mouth was any indication. However, probably the biggest change was the state of his usually tidy clothing. Now there wasn't a patch that wasn't snagged, smeared, or rumpled. But then, her sons in the best days seemed to have that effect on people.

"Good afternoon, Mr. Lewiston," she smiled, finding her concerns fading. Surely Jonathan would know he was playing with the boys. Daniel had obviously had a hand in helping her children recover their usual high spirits, although whether that was a blessing or a curse just now she wasn't sure. "It's good of you to take the blame for these antics, but I very much doubt you had to hold my sons' feet to the fire to get them to agree to this game."

Daniel found it harder to smile back. Cynthia Kinsle had always been able to send a shiver up his spine. It wasn't so much that she was beautiful, although that might have intimidated others. Her hair, soft and rich as the honey of its color, those thick-lashed eyes as dark as violets, and her slender figure would have made her the toast of the *ton,* if she had ever come out as expected. She'd certainly broken every heart in the neighborhood before eloping with a handsome naval officer of dubious family. His mother and hers had mourned, so sure were they that she and Daniel would make a match. He had never had such delusions. Cynthia was clever and spirited, and she delighted in making fun of a certain gangly youth. Just standing near her made him feel maladroit. They would never have suited.

But there was something different about her now, standing

there with the sunlight making her widow's weeds look nearly purple. Perhaps it was the dark circles under her eyes or the way her long fingers plucked at the dress, a dress that reminded him of why he was playing with the boys in the first place. "You'd be surprised how much coaxing it took to get them to have a little fun," he replied. Adam wiggled again, and he reached up and set the little fellow on his feet, with James beside him.

"No," she said quietly, "I would not be surprised in the slightest. Unfortunately, Mr. Lewiston, my sons do not have the luxury of having fun whenever it so pleases them. James, Adam, go find John and take yourselves upstairs to your room. I'll join you shortly."

Daniel offered them a smile, but they hung their heads and shuffled upstairs. He supposed they were in for a scold, and he turned to Cynthia to explain again that any misconduct was entirely his own fault. The unshed tears in her violet eyes stopped him.

"Are you all right?" he felt compelled to ask.

Cynthia refused to let him see her cry. She was tired from the journey and suddenly sick of being the one to stop the games and never the one to play them. Most likely he hadn't meant to criticize how she was raising her sons, but the words stung just the same. Like it or not, they were no longer on their own. They would have to live according to Jonathan's rules. "I assure you, Mr. Lewiston," she managed, "I'm quite all right. Thank you for taking time to play with the boys. Now if you'll excuse me."

"Of course," he bowed her out, telling himself he ought to be relieved. But if anything, he was more troubled than he had been in days and he wasn't surprised to find, as he turned to the terrace, that clouds had moved in to spoil his perfect summer day.

TWO

In the library doorway, Daniel's butler cleared his throat with a phlegmy rattle. "They're here again, sir."

Daniel glanced up from his perusal of the plans for the new school he was building for the village. " ' They,' Evenson?"

"The young Masters Jacobs, sir." Daniel could see that his man was trying to keep the impassive demeanor his position required, but his graying hair looked wilder than usual and there seemed to be a tic working on his firm jaw. Nevertheless, the library seemed suddenly brighter. Daniel arose eagerly, shrugging into his old tweed coat. "Splendid. Where have you put them?"

"I hesitated to put them in the withdrawing room without anyone there to watch them," Evenson replied. "Especially after the incident with your great-aunt's vase."

Daniel made a face, remembering their game the day before. While it was easier for him to have them visit here where he had no fear of disrupting Jonathan, the house was definitely taking a beating. "Were you able to find enough of the pieces to get it back together? The Countess dotes on it so . . ."

"Your great-aunt will never know the difference," Evenson assured him, "so long as she doesn't pick it up."

"Very good, Evenson." He paused in the doorway to listen, glancing up and down the darkly paneled hall, but his fortress of a mansion was as quiet and still as usual. He glanced back at his man with a frown. "So, where did you put them?"

From down the corridor came a deafening crash of metal on hard wood. Daniel was dashing toward the sound with Evenson at his heels before the first echoes started reverberating to the arched ceiling.

Three pairs of wide blue eyes met his in front of the door at the end of the hall. Daniel rolled his own eyes before turning to Evenson. "The Armory?"

Evenson cleared his throat again. "Yes, well, I thought it would keep their interest, and it was my understanding that everything was nailed down."

"And so it was," James said calmly, looking slightly less pale than the other two. "All except him."

Daniel looked to where he pointed. What had been an ornamental suit of armor just inside the doorway was now a haphazard jumble of dented metal. "Ho, what happened to Sir Cedric?"

"Adam did it," John declared.

Adam gasped and immediately burst into tears. "I . . . did . . . not!" he wailed, setting the echoes jarring through the house once again.

"Easy now," Daniel said as calmly as he could, his glance taking in all three of them. James was biting his lower lip in exactly the same way Jonathan had used to do when he was about to get caught for some misdeed. Adam was sniffling pathetically, his baby face awash in self-pity. John was studying the wall of swords on his right with remarkable intensity. It was impossible to tell who had caused the disturbance, but then, Daniel reflected, it probably didn't matter.

"No harm done," he assured them. "I'm sure we can put Sir Cedric back together again. In fact, wasn't there some rhyme to that effect?"

" 'All the King's horses and all the King's men couldn't put Humpty Dumpty together again,' " James quoted helpfully.

"Nonsense," Daniel declared in their skeptical faces. "Who needs a lot of soldiers anyway? What say we have a go at it, just the four of us?"

Adam nodded, brightening over hiccuped sobs. James looked pleased at the idea. John narrowed his eyes. "Can't we just leave it for the servants?"

Daniel put an arm around his shoulder and guided him farther into the room. "Never leave your mistakes for another man to fix, John. Besides, I'd wager the three of you know far better what a proper knight should look like than our friend Mr. Evenson here."

"Assuredly, sir," Evenson obligingly agreed.

"There, you see? We'll work here for a bit and when we're done, Mr. Evenson will have tea and cakes awaiting in the withdrawing room."

Luckily, Sir Cedric was far easier than the infamous Humpty Dumpty to put back together again. The wooden frame on which the various pieces of armor had been hung had merely been tipped over. Once righted, the boys were able to identify the pieces and hang them back into place, with much merriment as gauntlets were mixed with stockings and the breastplate with the helmet. By the time they retired to the withdrawing room, they were in a much happier mood.

"This surely is a fine, big house," John commented as they sat munching on the cakes Evenson had brought them, their voices echoing in the large, drafty room. "Of course, it isn't quite as fine as Colonel Hathaway's, is it, James?"

James frowned. "Colonel Hathaway?" He jumped suddenly, and Daniel had the distinct impression that John had pinched him under cover of the tea tray. "I . . . I'm not sure who you mean, John."

Daniel smiled at the boy's attempt to tell the truth and still support his brother.

"You remember Colonel Hathaway," John insisted. "Mother's beau?"

Daniel found he had little interest in hearing about Cynthia's latest conquest, and he cleared his throat in a warning to change the subject.

"Mother has a bunch of bows," Adam piped up.

"That's right, Adam," John encouraged, casting a sidelong look at Daniel but ignoring the obvious hint. "And her favorite is the Colonel."

Adam frowned, but John pushed another cake onto his plate, and he turned his attention to attacking it eagerly.

Probably another charming military man, Daniel thought, but the bitterness of the thought surprised him.

"In fact," John declared boldly, "Colonel Hathaway is probably going to be our new father."

The last bite of cake was suddenly hard for Daniel to chew. James choked on his own piece. Adam's blue eyes widened.

"He is," John insisted, somewhat belligerently, Daniel thought. "I heard Uncle Jonathan say Mother had to marry. He doesn't have the blunt to keep us all, isn't that so, Mr. Daniel?"

"I'm sure your uncle can care for you as long as needed," Daniel assured him, although he knew how strapped Jonathan must be with four extra mouths to feed. The smaller Kinsle estate had never been prosperous, and what little had been left, Jonathan had poured into his library on inheriting. He had hardly expected his sister, who hadn't been home in nearly ten years, to suddenly appear with three nephews he hadn't known he possessed.

"I don't recall whether I like Colonel Hathaway," James remarked thoughtfully.

"Oh, he's all right," John shrugged. "I daresay he'll be gone as much as Father was. And even when he is in the country, he'll be out at his club. We won't see him much."

"Mother won't like that," Adam pouted.

"Mother doesn't have a choice," John informed him. "She has to marry whoever asks her. Uncle Jonathan said so."

The conversation was definitely unsuitable for young gentleman, and he wasn't entirely sure it was suitable for his own hearing. But he wasn't their father, and the best he could do was rattle the dishes on the tea tray to focus their attentions elsewhere.

"Poor Mother," James sighed, ignoring him.

"Poor us," John amended. "Father may not have been home much, but at least he loved us. We won't be so lucky this time."

Adam's bottom lip trembled, but he sucked it in manfully as he slid down from the leather chair to the Aubusson carpet. "Colonel Hathaway might love us." When John scowled at him, he stuck out his chin. "He might! We're lovable, aren't we, Mr. Daniel?"

Something constricted in the vicinity of Daniel's heart. "You are indeed, my lad, all three of you."

"If you were our father I daresay you wouldn't leave us for some silly club," James asserted with a sniff.

"All fathers need time to themselves," Daniel tried to explain to them. "But I'm sure whoever is lucky enough to be your new father will want to spend time with you."

Adam had wandered closer to him and now climbed happily into his lap. "Why can't you be our father, Mr. Daniel?"

He should have seen it coming. The spark in John's eyes told him the conversation had been manipulated in just this direction. James and Adam were waiting eagerly for his answer. He'd have to pick his words carefully if he were to keep from depressing them further.

"Any man would be proud to be the father of three such fine, smart boys," he assured them.

It was obviously not enough. Adam frowned. "Then why don't you ask Mother?"

Daniel kept a determined smile on his face. "Well, your mother and I have known each other since we were children, Adam, but we've never been particularly attached to each other."

"But she's awfully pretty," Adam argued.

"And she has a pleasant disposition," James asserted.

"And she can bake better cakes than this," John muttered, setting the confection firmly on his china plate.

Daniel glanced around at their earnest faces. The idea was too farfetched to go any farther. "Well, gentlemen, I'm quite flattered by this regard, but I assure you your mother wouldn't have me."

"Don't see why not," James replied. "You're a much better choice than this Colonel Hathaway fellow. And you like us."

Daniel ran his hand back through his hair. Why couldn't he seem to get them off this subject? Was some part of him actually entertaining the notion that he could court and win a beauty like Cynthia Kinsle? She'd laugh him out of the house. "Truly, my lads," he insisted. "Your mother and I would never suit."

John's frown was more of a pout. "Why do you both keep saying that? Mother's the mother and you'd be the father. You just need to explain that to her."

"It's hardly that simple, John. Surely your mother would expect a gentleman to court her properly." He realized he wasn't convincing anyone in the room, including himself, and hurriedly added, "I wouldn't even know what to say to her."

John was quick to reply, reinforcing Daniel's opinion that the boy was masterminding this affair. "You need to visit her at Uncle Jonathan's. Talk about things ladies find interesting, like clothes."

Daniel kept a straight face although the thought of discussing the merits of silk over kerseymere with Cynthia was laughable in the extreme. "Clothes, eh? Somehow I don't think . . ."

"Or gardening," John insisted as if sensing reluctance. "You can talk about your gardens." He nudged his brother. "Couldn't he, James?"

James, always solemn, nodded. "Yes, that should suffice."

The grin broke free as he tried to imagine Cynthia rhapsodizing over rosebuds. "Your mother likes gardens, does she?"

"And you should bring her presents," John encouraged him. "Everyone likes presents. A package of pins, perhaps, or a tea strainer."

"Really?" He tried to look appreciative of the well-meant advice, but his mouth hurt from holding back the laughter.

"And candy," chimed in Adam. "There's nothing sweeter than candy." He sighed longingly, and Daniel, seeing the obvious hint, reached obligingly for the nearby crystal candy dish, allowing a chuckle to escape. As they helped themselves all around, he was relieved to hear them return to their usual conversation about whose turn it was to pick the game and how they might elude their uncle the next day. As he listened to them, a part of him kept toying with the idea of courting Cynthia, but he shook his head. He had courted a number of young ladies over the years but none had stirred his heart enough to offer. He had decided the love spoken of by the poets was obviously beyond him. Yet, a companion would be pleasant and certainly he was beginning to realize what a hole would be left in his life when Cynthia eventually remarried and the boys moved away. But did he care for them enough to risk a life with the redoubtable Cynthia as his wife?

He kept the boys busy the rest of the afternoon with a "tiger" hunt through the grounds. It wasn't until he had called for his carriage to take them home that John broached the subject again.

"So, Mr. Daniel, when shall we tell Mother that you're going to call?"

There they were again, three faces raised entreatingly to his. He wondered how any parent ever found the strength to say no. But say no he must before this madness went any farther. He was about to do so, with as much force as necessary, when he noticed the tension in John's face. His blue eyes were over-bright, and there was a decided tremor in his lower lip, not unlike the way Adam looked before he cried. He'd never seen the boy want anything so much, and he found he couldn't be the one to deny him.

"Perhaps I can find time in the next few days," he heard himself say. "I suppose it wouldn't hurt for your mother and me to get reacquainted."

THREE

Cynthia watched her sons working at their copy books, the sunlight from the high windows in the schoolroom making halos on their golden heads. The creak of her rocker kept up a steady rhythm. She blinked to keep herself from falling asleep.

"Done," her middle son declared, and she rose, putting aside the sock she had been mending to look over his work. The neat letters marched across the page in orderly rows.

"Very nice work, James," she smiled, giving his narrow shoulder a gentle squeeze. Of all her sons, he least reminded her of Nathan. James's temperament more closely resembled her brother's—meticulous, thoughtful, and self-contained. She did not have to worry that when she set James a task it would not be completed to her own and his satisfaction.

Next to him, John hunched over his own work and quickened his pace, but not before she caught sight of the ungainly scrawl. She shook her head. If James was the cautious one, John was more likely to throw caution to the wind. He was entirely too much like his father, a fact that endeared him to her as well as worried her.

"This isn't a race, John," she cautioned. "Take your time and do it properly. James, you may read while we wait for John and Adam to finish."

Adam sighed gustily and bent back over the copy book, pudgy fingers straining on the pencil. He was still young for this work, she felt, but if there was anything Adam hated, it was being treated like a baby. He wanted to study everything his brothers studied, do everything his brothers did, be everywhere his brothers were. The current bane of his existence was that he still wore short pants. She had been saving for material to make him long pants, but so far it had been much easier to cut off the tattered legs of pants his brothers had outgrown and refit them to his chubby body.

Someone coughed politely in the schoolroom door. Turning, she saw her brother standing there, his narrow face closed as usual. "Good afternoon, Jonathan. What brings you up to see us?"

"You have a gentleman caller," he replied, moving into the room with his manservant behind him. "If you would be so good as to come with me? Tims can watch the boys."

Surprised, she nodded and smiled encouragement to the boys. As she followed him back into the corridor, she wondered who could possibly be calling on her. It couldn't be news about Nathan. How many times had she tensed to a sudden knock at the door, thinking this was the day they would tell her he had been killed? When it had finally happened it had almost been a relief. But surely the only other reason a man would call on her would be regarding Nathan's effects. Had the Admiralty learned something new?

She hastened her steps to catch up with Jonathan but she hadn't made it to the stairs when a hiss pulled her up short. Jonathan didn't seem to notice, continuing on. Looking back, Cynthia saw John hurrying after them, her hairbrush in one hand.

"Here." He shoved it at her. "You'll want to look your best."

Frowning, she accepted the implement. "Thank you, John. You followed me just to give me this?"

He looked away, shuffling his feet. "Well, I thought you needed it."

Cynthia had a sudden vision of him putting some creature

in her bun as she was bent over James's work. She reached up to touch her hair. Nothing seemed to be moving. "John," she said slowly, eyes narrowing, "is there something I should know?"

He backed out of reach. "No, why do you ask?"

"No reason, I suppose," she replied, attempting to hand him the brush. "But if I am hideously embarrassed at this meeting, young man, you will answer for it this evening."

He swallowed. "Just be nice, Mother. Please?"

She frowned again, but he was already turning to hurry back toward the schoolroom. She slipped the brush into the pocket of her gown for retrieval later—and use on the seat of a certain young man's britches if her suspicions proved true—and continued downstairs.

She wasn't sure what she had been expecting, but it certainly wasn't the sight that met her eyes. Daniel Lewiston was pacing her brother's austere sitting room. For once his clothes, a dark blue superfine coat and matching trousers with a lighter blue waistcoat, were immaculate. What was more out of character, however, was that his meaty hands clutched an obscenely large box with lettering identifying it as coming from a famous Wells confectioner. It was obviously chocolates and could only be a present for the boys, one he wasn't sure she'd let them accept. She decided to put him at his ease.

"Mr. Lewiston, how nice of you to call," she smiled.

He started, then managed a smile. "Mrs. Jacobs. Very good of you to receive me."

"Yes, it was, wasn't it," Jonathan quipped, seating himself in one of the Hepplewhite chairs near the windows overlooking the terrace.

Cynthia quelled his amusement with a frown and took a seat on one of the closer chairs to give Daniel the excuse to sit as well. He glanced at the chair across the room near Jonathan, then sighed and chose the one closest to her instead. Offering her a weak smile, he pushed the candy box toward her in much the same way John had just pushed the brush.

"I . . . I thought you might like these."

"Me?" She stared at the box in surprise. "I thought they were for the boys."

Next to her, Daniel felt himself blushing. Blushing, of all things! By God, was he such a coward? He straightened himself and set the box into her lap. "No, Mrs. Jacobs," he replied firmly, "I assure you they are for you." When she continued to stare at the box, he couldn't help adding, "Of course, you may share them with the boys if you desire."

Cynthia glanced up at him in confusion. The intent look he gave her back offered no clues. "Thank you," she replied for lack of anything better to say.

Satisfied, Daniel sat back in the chair. She continued to divide her attention between the box of candy and his face, and he realized the silence was stretching. He wracked his brain for something to say.

"They're very good chocolates," he tried. *Look at me, I'm reduced to prattling!* "If you like chocolates, of course."

"Actually, I prefer stick candy," Cynthia replied. "I've always had a sweet tooth for rock." *What an inane conversation! Whatever is his purpose?*

Daniel nodded. "A wise choice. Doesn't get your fingers nearly as dirty. Not that you'd ever dirty your fingers, of course."

Cynthia felt a laugh bubbling up. Luckily, Jonathan responded for her.

"You'd be surprised how dirty her fingers get taking care of those boys, Daniel."

He managed another weak smile at the sally. Cynthia frowned her brother back into silence. The quiet stretched once more. She was obviously waiting for him to say something. Daniel squared his shoulders.

"The boys tell me you like to garden."

Cynthia blinked. "Garden? Mr. Lewiston, I haven't been

near anything resembling a garden in ten years. Certainly nothing like the rose gardens your mother used to tend. Do you still have them?"

There was something decidedly wistful about her tone of voice. He supposed she couldn't have seen many gardens at that, not if she'd been living near the Bristol docks as Jonathan had intimated. "Yes, the gardens are still there, although I admit I don't spend much time in them. I'm not all that keen on roses."

She smiled. "Oh, but who couldn't like roses? I always thought your mother was so fortunate: all those bushes, all those colors and shades. There must have been enough blooms to brighten every room in the house."

So, she did like gardens. It was a pleasant surprise. No one had been able to do justice to the roses since his mother had passed on. His sister Clementine had scolded him about their sad state on her last visit. Perhaps if he married Cynthia . . . He cleared his throat and attempted to change the subject. "Actually, I far prefer the maze."

She hadn't thought of the Lewiston maze in years. She could feel herself brightening just remembering the fun they had had there. "Oh, I'm so glad to hear you kept that as well! After all the times we lost you in there, I'd have thought you'd want to tear the thing to the ground!"

He smiled, sharing the memory. "You five were scamps, no doubt about it. But for all Jonathan and I shouted and chased you about, it was a great deal of fun. To tell you the truth, I miss it."

Cynthia frowned, but he seemed sincere. "You cannot mean it. Your sisters and I were awful to you, Daniel. I don't know how you put up with us."

He looked away. "I suppose one is willing to put up with a great deal when one is lonely."

She started, and although he still refused to meet her eye she found she had to believe him this time as well.

"Well," Jonathan put in, "I'm sure our Cynthia has out-grown all that."

Looking at her in the black widow's weeds, Daniel could almost believe him. "Then that's a pity."

She felt herself blushing under his steady regard and lowered her eyes. He seemed to understand how she had been feeling lately, that there seemed so little to enjoy in her life outside the boys. A rose garden to tend or a maze to wander through would have been most welcome.

"But surely you came here to discuss something more than gardens, old fellow," Jonathan prompted.

Daniel frowned at him. He knew he wasn't making tremendous headway, but Jonathan's prodding would not help. Perhaps he'd said enough for one day. He rose. "No. I just wanted to bring your sister the chocolates."

"I don't understand," Cynthia replied, returning his frown.

He smiled at her. "No, I didn't think you would. Good day, Mrs. Jacobs, Jonathan."

She rose and Jonathan rose with her. Together they saw him to the door. "Yes, well, thank you for the candy, Mr. Lewiston," Cynthia told him, relieved that the confusing visit was at an end. "I will be sure to share it with the boys."

"Yes, you do that," he nodded as Jonathan opened the door. "Tell the boys I look forward to their next visit."

Her brow cleared. That was it. The candy was a bribe to keep the boys coming to visit. She supposed she had been a bit forceful the first time she had seen him again. "I'll let them know. Good day."

As soon as the door closed behind him, he sighed in relief. He really should have known better; he shook his head as he climbed into his waiting carriage. Cynthia no more saw a suitor in him now than she had when they were both teenagers. He was a fool to let three little boys convince him he could succeed in winning her. Even desperate as she was, she could do far better.

And she was desperate, he could see that clearly. He didn't

usually notice clothing, but it was hard to miss the fact that the boys were quickly either outgrowing or wearing out every stitch of the black mourning clothes, which he was beginning to believe was all they had. And Cynthia's mourning dress, for all its careful hemming, had obviously been made for someone larger and taller than she was. He could remember a day when she would not have allowed herself to wear the same frock twice in a month. Yet he had seen the same dress both times he had visited.

But that doesn't mean she's willing to take you, my boy, he chided himself. Our Cynthia can whistle up a prince. Small chance she'll settle for a frog.

FOUR

The boys were good as gold for the rest of the afternoon, and, as if that wasn't enough to make Cynthia suspicious of their motives, they asked to go to bed early that night. She was not completely surprised then to find that when she retired some time later, there were three rather large lumps under the quilt on her bed.

The temptation to tease them was strong, but she forced herself to stride to the bed and thump on the largest of the three shapes. "John, James, Adam, come out of there at once."

The lumps wiggled, and John's head appeared from under the quilt, James and Adam shortly behind him. Cynthia put her hands on her hips.

"What am I to do with you? Why aren't you in bed?"

John straightened and affixed her with a stern eye. "We had important matters to discuss with you."

James nodded seriously. Adam hiccuped.

Cynthia sank onto the bed beside them. They seldom felt the need to confront her like this, so it must be important. "I see. Is something wrong?"

"Not wrong," James started.

"Yes, wrong," John interrupted insistently. "Mother, we have decided that we need a father."

Cynthia glanced around at the serious faces. "You had a father. He died." The words came out colder than she had intended and to cover it up she reached for Adam and pulled him into her lap. "Why do you want another one so soon?"

"Has it been so soon?" James asked thoughtfully. "I remember Father, but it seems as if he's been gone a very long time."

Cynthia gathered him closer, too. "I know, James. He was out at sea so often, I'm sure it seems as if he's been gone much longer. But it has been barely six months. I'm still wearing mourning." She plucked at the hideous black dress.

"It does not signify," John insisted. "We would like a new father. You have to marry him."

"I see," she nodded, trying not to bristle at his authoritative tone. However, she couldn't help adding, "And have you picked out the gentleman and chapel as well?"

It was the wrong choice. "Yes, we have," John replied. "You will marry Mr. Daniel in the Wenwood Church." He quailed before her frown. "Please?"

"Yes, Mother, please?" Adam chimed in, baby face turned entreatingly to hers and making it impossible to scold John. She took a deep breath and smiled at the three of them.

"I'm very glad you like Mr. Lewiston so much, my sweets, but I assure you, we would not suit."

"Why not?" John demanded, crossing arms over a puffed-out chest. "He's very good to us."

"He gives us cakes," Adam piped up, "and candy." He sighed gustily. "There's nothing sweeter than candy."

"He has the most wonderful house," James put in. "With a very large library full of books, almost as many as Uncle Jonathan."

"He has a large estate, a French chef, and thirty thousand pounds per annum," John summarized. "And I heard he thinks you're a diamond of the first water."

Cynthia suddenly had the image of Daniel's visit that morning. Good heavens, had he been attempting to court her? She blushed at the thought that she hadn't even realized it until now. She was so agitated that she set Adam off her lap and got up to pace the room.

"You must be mistaken, John," she tried to explain. "Daniel Lewiston may be pleasant to you, and he certainly has been pleasant to me, but he cannot be interested in making me his wife. The last he knew of me, I was a rather giddy young girl. In fact, I hate to tell you this, but his younger sisters and I tormented him to no end. We used to play the most shameful tricks on him."

John bounced to the foot of the bed and watched her with wide eyes. "Like what?"

Cynthia was almost afraid to confess how shallow she had been, but if it would convince them that she and Daniel could not make a match of it, then it was worth a try. "Well, we used to tell him tea was later than it was so that when he arrived his mother would scold him for being late. We must have played that trick on him at least a dozen times, and he never seemed to catch on. And once Daphnia, his closest sister, actually bribed the footman to put a snake in his bed." She shuddered even now at the thought of waking to find oneself beside a slithering serpent. "But I think the worst thing we ever did was sneak into his room while he was sleeping, steal all his clothes, and hide them in the maze. He was the most pitiful sight, bumbling through the branches in his nightshirt."

"Why didn't he have the servants go fetch them?" John frowned.

Cynthia cocked her head in wonder. "You know, I never considered that. We never had all that many servants here, but the Lewistons seemed to have dozens. He could have called upon any number of footmen or gardeners or stable hands. Odd that he chose to do it himself." She remembered his comment that morning about doing anything to keep loneliness at bay and suddenly realized why he had never told his mother of their pranks. She didn't have time to consider it further for John had obviously decided he had had enough of reminiscences.

"I still don't see," he pouted, "why you cannot marry."

She was tired, but she had to try not to let him exasperate her. "John, this truly is none of your affair. *If* I remarry, I would like to decide on the husband, thank you very much."

"And how exactly do you plan to do that?" Jonathan asked from the doorway. Cynthia frowned at him, but if he noticed, he didn't let it deter him.

"This isn't a proper conversation for children," she sniffed.

He leaned against the doorjamb and crossed one slippered foot over the other. "I quite agree. If the infantry will please decamp?"

Adam started to protest but John hushed him, herding his brothers before him to the door. She would have sworn he winked at Jonathan in passing.

"You don't honestly think they'll return to bed without help, do you?" she asked.

"Most likely not, but you can check on them after you answer my question. I just caught the end of that conversation but I take it you still have the same objections to Daniel Lewiston as a suitor as you had when you were a girl."

Remembering a similar conversation with her parents ten years ago, she blushed. "I was afraid Mother and Father would force me to marry him. I said awful things, as I recall."

"You said he was fat and stupid and nothing would induce you to so much as dance with him, let alone marry him."

She thought of the kind man who had rekindled her sons' joy in life and cringed. "That was badly done. He was patient when we were children, and he seems even kinder now. In truth, Jonathan, I think I've always admired him for that. But if I remarry I want more than kindness. I would want a good provider, someone who would take care of all of us." She forced herself to put Nathan's handsome face from her mind. "Someone who would stay around this time, who wouldn't leave for adventure or fame. Someone who'd love us and want to be with us more than anything else. Someone who'd bring little presents . . ."

"Like candy," Jonathan put in.

She had a sudden vision of an impossibly large box of chocolates and felt herself blushing. "I warn you, Jonathan," she told him sternly, "do not throw him at me again. I'm quite capable of choosing a second husband, *if* I decide to remarry."

Jonathan straightened to go. "Of course you are, my dear. But you'll forgive me for believing that you couldn't do better than Daniel Lewiston for a husband. I hope you'll give it some thought."

Whether it was Jonathan's suggestion or otherwise, she found herself thinking about the issue a great deal over the next couple of days. She saw Daniel Lewiston at church services in Wenwood, but he didn't seem to pay her any particular notice. She decided that Jonathan's assumption about Daniel's visit had been wrong. Daniel obviously just enjoyed watching her sons play, and he wanted to keep himself in her good graces—no more than that. She supposed it was logical. After his father had died, his mother had been so fearful of losing him, she had almost locked him in the house. Besides occasional visits by Jonathan and the tormenting by her and his sisters, he had had no interactions with other children. His mother had even had tutors at the house rather than send him away to school as was usual with other sons. Small wonder he was enjoying her sons' childhood when he had had none of his own. Still, it was a little disappointing to think that she had so effectively depressed any feelings he might have had for her all those years ago that he had no interest in courting her now.

She was pleased, however, to see that her sons seemed to be settling in at her old home. They smiled and nodded to the other families at services as if they had lived there all their lives, and John went so far as to spend some time visiting with several of the elderly widows of the village as the congregation was filing out. Like his father, he got along well with everyone, and she was glad to see he was putting his gift to good use.

She was forced to reconsider her luck at settling in when that very afternoon saw the beginning of a string of rather interesting callers. First it was the Widower Trent, a large, red-faced man who she remembered owned a considerable farm on the other side of Wenwood. His intentions were obvious from his leering grins, but it was his suggestion that the boys would be best put to work on his farm, saving him a great deal in laborer's wages, that prompted her to have Jonathan show him out.

The second caller arrived Monday afternoon, his footman helping him across the threshold and assisting him to perch on one of the chairs in the sitting room. Mr. Lassiter, it seemed, had not been able to find a girl to suit him in all his 75 years, but rumor that her husband had left her wealthy had encouraged him to call. She saw him to the door herself.

The third caller arrived Wednesday morning, straightening his cravat and trying to hide a cut on his chin where someone, presumably himself, had been attempting to shave the beard he had yet to grow. Young Mr. Pittley stammeringly explained that young women made him nervous; therefore, he wanted an older woman to wed because she would be able to teach him the finer points of life and would not mind when he then took younger mistresses. He left of his own accord when she began laughing hysterically.

"I never knew Wenwood boasted such a crop of idiots," she confessed to Jonathan that evening. "One would almost think there were no decent marriageable men for miles."

Jonathan shrugged, putting his feet up before the fire. "I don't suppose there are. With Squire Pentercast and his brother married, that only leaves Tom Harvey, but he seems to have his eye on Mary Delacourt, lucky dog. I thought she'd prefer Daniel to him, but Daniel seems to have abandoned the field. It simply points out that your choices are limited, my dear. If you decide to remarry, you can't afford to be choosy."

The idea had no appeal, but she decided not to think about it. Word had obviously gotten out that she was too top-lofty, for her sudden popularity disappeared almost overnight. She tried to focus her energies on her sons, overseeing their schooling, looking through trunks in the attic for older clothes or material that might be made into clothing for them, and making sure Jonathan's cook prepared dishes the way they liked. From time to time, she allowed them to go over to the Lewiston estate to visit, but as they almost always came back ready to take up the fight for Daniel to be their father, she was loath to let them go very often. She was therefore surprised to find them missing entirely when she returned one afternoon from an outing to Wenwood in search of buttons for a new coat for John.

She found Tims dozing in the rocker, the schoolroom otherwise deserted. The two of them had searched the house and then the grounds with mounting concern. Jonathan was unable to shed any light on the matter. He insisted that they must have gone to visit Daniel, but she kept visualizing the nearby River Went with three bodies washed up on the bank. Determined to set her mind at ease, she demanded the carriage brought around and set off for the Lewiston estate.

FIVE

Gravel biting through the knees of his trousers and the palms of his gloves, Daniel peered around the corner of the maze. He wiped the sweat from his brow as he hurriedly checked behind him and before him once more, his breath coming in deep rasps. The path before him stretched empty to the exit. He listened, but heard only the faint summer breeze rustling through the close-cropped laurel. Heart pounding, he scrambled to his feet and raced toward freedom. Behind him, he heard shouts of pursuit and doubled his speed.

"Halt, or I'll shoot!" John yelled, leaping into his path. Daniel skidded to a stop. James and Adam leaped onto his back, and he went down laughing under the weight. As soon as all three of them were on top of him, he wrestled James and John to his chest and tickled them unmercifully while Adam whooped in delight.

"Mercy, mercy!" James giggled.

"I give up!" John shouted, squirming.

Daniel released them and they crawled off him, collapsing on the path, laughing. As their merriment faded, he heard the sound of hooves on gravel and knew they were in for it.

John sat up, eyes wide. "Mother!"

Adam sobered immediately, and James rolled to his feet. "Are you sure? How did she know where to find us?"

They all looked so worried that he rose and wrapped his

arms about the three of them. He was surprised that he seemed to feel as guilty as they looked, though he wasn't sure what any of them had to feel guilty about. He supposed his own feelings came from remembering how his own mother had reacted when he came in with dirty or torn clothes. But was having a little fun really such a heinous crime?

Knowing they couldn't very well avoid their own mother, he shepherded the boys toward the exit and across the small stretch of lawn to the edge of the drive. The Kinsle carriage did indeed stand within the arch by the front entryway, with Evenson and one of the footmen hurrying out to greet the arrival.

Cynthia was just alighting on the footman's arm as Daniel led the boys forward. Her slender body in the black dress was tensed, and as they drew near he could see that her lovely lips were set in a tight line, her finely etched brows drawn together in a frown. The stern look did not ease as she caught sight of the boys; Daniel felt John hesitate beside him.

"Mrs. Jacobs," he managed with a bow over the boys' heads, "a pleasure."

"That I do not believe," Cynthia told him, her voice as stern as her face. It was obvious the boys were safe and well, although she couldn't remember when she'd seen so much dust on their clothes. Even Daniel's tweed jacket and dark trousers were caked with the stuff, and he seemed to have a twig of laurel sticking out from behind one ear. Still, it was hard to forgive them for scaring her half out of her wits. And it was even more difficult to forgive Daniel for continuing to encourage them in these escapades. She had to make them understand. "Boys," she stated firmly, "you cannot run away like this. Anything could have happened to you and no one would have been any wiser. I realize you enjoy coming to visit Mr. Lewiston, but I can assure you this incident will not repeat itself. Say your farewells and get in the coach at once."

Adam's lower lip was trembling again, James was biting his, and John was pale and still. "Goodbye, Mr. Daniel," he muttered for them all.

Daniel very much wanted to tell her that they were no trouble, that surely they were allowed to have some fun, but somehow he sensed she would not thank him for interfering. Perhaps if he could speak with her without the children present his comments would be seen as less of an intrusion.

"That was well done, John," he nodded, looking up to meet Cynthia's frown. "But I think we would be very rag-mannered to have your mother come all this way without offering her some refreshment."

"I don't need anything . . ." Cynthia started, wanting only to get the boys home, but he purposely turned to the hovering Evenson to forestall her.

"Evenson, do we have any more of those delightful cakes we had the other day?"

Evenson opened his mouth but John was shaking his head violently no. "I . . . I believe they are all gone, sir, but I'm sure Monsieur Henri can find something else suitable for the lady."

"Excellent." Daniel offered Cynthia his arm. "Shall we?"

She bit her lip—did all the Kinsles have that habit, he wondered?—and glanced around at the three upturned faces. He added his pleading look to theirs. *I suppose there's no harm in it,* Cynthia thought with a sigh. "That would be very nice, Mr. Lewiston. Please lead the way."

Daniel tried to ignore John's look of triumph as he walked them into the house. He escorted them all down the long, twisting hall to the withdrawing room and murmured pleas-antries while Evenson arranged for tea. It arrived a short while later along with a game of nine pins, which Evenson erected in the corner, nodding to Daniel to entertain the lady. It was nicely done, but somehow Daniel felt Evenson had gotten the easier end of the deal.

Cynthia sipped her tea slowly, glancing about the room.

It did not seem to have changed much from what she remembered. In fact, it was almost as if the room had been abandoned on the day she had eloped, so thick was the dust on nearly every surface, from the walnut credenzas on either side of the marble fireplace to the grouping of sofa and chairs in the center of the room to the farther corners of the polished wood floor. The corner the boys were playing in at least seemed to have been dusted, but she wondered if perhaps it had been by the seats of their pants. She took another sip of her tea, listening to the polished oak pins clatter to the base amidst the rise and fall of children's voices. Across from her, Daniel offered her the kind of smile he used to use when she and his sisters had pulled a prank on him. She felt instantly contrite, lowering her cup to the silver tea tray.

"I'm so sorry the boys keep intruding on you, Daniel," she told him. "It's just that there's so little to do at Kinsle House right now and . . ."

He held up a hand. "Please, Mrs. Jacobs, you mustn't apologize. I asked you in to explain that I enjoy being with the boys. Please don't ask them to stay away on my account."

Cynthia stared at him, but his round face was earnest, his gray eyes sparkling, and his smile rather endearing. "You, you actually like them?"

His smile deepened. "Of course I like them. They're intelligent, fun-loving, adventurous little jackanapes. I've always wanted brothers. I guess I'll have to settle for nephews, and surrogate ones at that."

Cynthia felt something thaw inside her. "You don't know how good it makes me feel to hear someone praise them. They really are darling boys. If only Jonathan realized that."

"Jonathan and Colonel Hathaway," Daniel muttered, although he reached for his tea so quickly she wasn't sure she'd heard him correctly.

Daniel took a sip of the tea to steady himself. He had been calling himself a coward for several days since his half-hearted attempt at courting her. Evenson reported that several of the eligible Wenwood bachelors had already been calling, making his chances even smaller. But each time he sent the boys home, he wondered if it would be the last time. Each time they left, the house seemed larger and more empty. And he was beginning to realize that the boys needed him as much as he needed them. There weren't many men who would understand how it felt to be raised only by a mother. For all their sakes, he had to try again to get Cynthia to see him as a suitor.

A cheer went up from the bowlers, and Cynthia smiled at their enthusiasm. It took her only a second to realize that Daniel was sharing her smile. *He really does like them,* she thought, warmed more by his caring than by anything that had happened since Nathan's death. Daniel seemed to have noticed her regard, for he paled and cleared his throat.

"Mrs. Jacobs," he began.

Cynthia couldn't stand his nerves. She had obviously been overly stern in her dealings with him, and guilt smote her anew. "Daniel, please, you've known me since I was born. We grew up together. I know I was a dreadful child, always helping your sisters tease you, but I hope you can see I've grown beyond all that. You can call me by my first name. In fact, I wish someone would. It would be nice to remember I have a name other than 'Mother.' "

Her speech only served to make him more nervous. She was being far too kind when he had expected resistance. It somehow made things more difficult. He adjusted his cravat self-consciously and swallowed again. Perhaps it was best to just get it out in the open. "Very well, Cynthia. I understand that you may be thinking of remarrying?"

Cynthia took a deep breath to keep from screaming in vexation. Not him, too! All her good intentions disappeared. "That, Daniel, is hardly your concern."

Now, that was the Cynthia he expected. And she was entirely right. "Not normally, no," he agreed with her. She looked so fierce that he was forced to take another fortifying sip of tea. Even she had to notice that his hand shook as he set down the cup. How could he be so craven? "Dash it all," he exclaimed and was rewarded by a look of surprise. "I never could do anything right around you. Cynthia, if you must remarry, would it pain you too terribly to consider me as a candidate?"

She stared at him. This could not be happening. Daniel Lewiston, courting her? He could not be in love with her, not after having known her as the giddiest girl in the neighborhood. And it had been a very long time since she had thought of seriously considering anyone as a husband but Nathan. She shook her head and looked at him more closely. For the first time she didn't see an overgrown version of the boy she had known, she saw a man. She could feel her own teacup start to tremble and set it hastily down. Then she noticed that he looked no more delighted with the matter. Sweat was beading on his upper brow, causing his dark hair to curl on his forehead. His gray eyes were stormy with emotion, but she'd have termed it fear rather than love. "You don't really want to marry me, do you, Daniel?" she asked softly.

He inhaled slowly, focusing on her face. There had been a moment when a light seemed to shine in her eyes and at that moment he had been surprised to find that he very much wanted to marry her. But the moment had passed and he reminded himself that he was doing this for the boys. "I didn't think I particularly wanted to marry anyone, at least not right now," he replied truthfully. "But I've never been happier than the last two months since your boys arrived. I'd hate to lose them to someone who didn't even care about them. Not that you'd marry that sort, but sometimes widows don't have the luxury of choosing. I just wanted you to know that if you must marry, I'd be proud to be the boys' father."

Tears welled behind Cynthia's eyes, and she looked hastily away from his kind face. "Thank you, Daniel. I don't think you can know what that means to me. It's very kind of you."

"Kind, but not wanted," he murmured. She couldn't meet his gaze. "Cynthia, are you already in love with someone?"

She shook her head, blinking the tears away. "No, no, of course not. I don't want to get married any more than you do." She glanced up in time to see him start.

"Then why . . ." he began, but his brow cleared suddenly. "John was right. Jonathan can't keep you."

Embarrassed, Cynthia held out her hand in entreaty. "Please don't let anyone know. Nathan tried to take care of us. He always brought enough money home from his trips to see us through a year or two. He was hoping this last trip would put him in a position to share in prize money. It also put him in more danger. When he was killed in battle, I was sure there would be something put aside for us in his belongings, but the Admiralty swears there was nothing. Jonathan will do what he can for us, I'm sure. It's just that three growing boys . . ."

Daniel nodded in understanding. "Then we should marry."

"Well, I like that," Cynthia exclaimed, drawing back in surprise. "Don't I have something to say in this matter?"

He had the good sense to look abashed. "I'm sorry if I seem to be making decisions for you, but can't you see our marriage would be for the best? This place is huge, I've got plenty of blunt with nothing useful to spend it on, and truth be told I think I've always been lonely. Don't you see—we both get what we need."

It was quite logical. She could see that. Jonathan and his sisters would be delighted with the match—in fact, one of the reasons she had teased him so unmercifully when they were younger was that their parents kept insisting he would one day offer for her. Sometimes she thought she had just been building up an excuse as to why he wouldn't offer. But now he had offered, and if she accepted him, the boys would have a father, one who would dote on their every act, and a steady, reliable source of income. It was perfect for the boys and for Daniel. But would it be perfect for her?

She smiled politely at him. "You've given me a great deal to think about, Mr. Lewiston."

He raised an eyebrow. *"Mr.* Lewiston? I was just plain Daniel at the start of this conversation. Have I been demoted for my audacity?"

"No," she laughed. "I'm sorry, Daniel. It's just that this is a very serious decision. I need time to think."

"Take all the time you like," he replied, returning her smile. Another cheer went up from the bowlers. "Just so long as you allow them to keep coming by while you do it."

SIX

For the next week, she thought. She thought on long walks through the Kinsle/Lewiston fields while the boys were studying with Tims. She thought while she sat up rocking Adam to sleep. She especially thought every time the boys disappeared to Daniel's house. The logic of his proposal seemed flawless. The benefits to him and the boys were numerous. The benefits to her were not inconsiderable.

Daniel had made it plain that he would take an active part in raising the boys. While she could not gainsay Nathan's love for his sons, his voyages, which usually kept him away from them for eighteen months or longer, made it impossible for him to help raise them. A part of her couldn't wait to share the burden. And a very selfish part of her couldn't wait to live in a house with servants at her beck and call. She could not say she was sorry about never having to darn another sock, never having to plead with the authorities for money, never having to cook her own dinner from food that was barely fit to eat in any circumstance. She could have fine clothes again, someone to fix her hair, a rose garden! And the boys would have the schooling that befitted gentlemen.

And what would she have to give up to provide this life of luxury for herself and her sons? Every time she reached that point in the argument she found herself shivering. Nathan may not have been home much, but the eleven months in total they had spent together had given her a pretty good idea of what daily life was supposed to be like between husband and wife. She had run away with Nathan because she was madly in love. She could not make the same claim about Daniel, for all that she admired his character. Could she be intimate with a man for whom she held no romantic feelings? And if she found that prospect daunting, did that give her the right to deprive her children of such an opportunity?

As far as she could see, the only way to settle the matter was to explain her concerns to Daniel. Her courage failed her twice before she forced herself to accompany the boys on one of their visits to the Lewiston estate. Evenson answered the boys' knock and escorted them with proper solemnity through the house to the back garden, where, he explained, Daniel was overseeing the replanting of a hedge that had been damaged in a spring storm. She tried not to let the deference shown her and the boys influence her determination to get answers to her questions, but when Daniel was so obviously glad to see them and quite willing to listen to her, she found it even more difficult to begin.

"Now then," he smiled when he had led her to a secluded stone bench away from the gardeners but within earshot of the scampering boys, "what can I do for you?"

She could smell the nearby rose gardens. It ought to have been a good omen, but she felt as nervous as he had looked the day he had proposed. "I've given a great deal of consideration to your proposal," she told him. "And there are several issues we must discuss before I can give you my answer."

Daniel wasn't sure whether to be alarmed or pleased that she was taking him seriously at last. He changed his smile to a solemn look. "Of course. Please continue."

She took a deep breath and plunged in. "First, I realize that you are proposing this marriage for my sons' welfare. I think you should understand that this is a long-term proposition. They will need to be sent to school, to be assured a place in the world. They would be assured a much greater place if you were to adopt them. I do not think their father would have objected." It was a great deal to ask, and she knew it. But it would show her whether his intentions toward her sons were sincere.

"I would be honored to have them become Lewistons," Daniel replied warmly, relieved that the issue had been so easily resolved. "With your permission, I'll have the papers drawn up before we are married, and we can sign them on our wedding day. I will also have my will changed for your review, leaving everything to them."

"Oh, my," she gasped at the enormity of his gesture. "Daniel, I wouldn't dream . . ."

"I would," he smiled. "They'll be my sons, after all."

"Yes, I suppose they would." She sat for a moment, stunned.

Somehow, he didn't think that was all there was to it. "Was there anything else?" he prompted.

Cynthia blinked. "Yes, but it is much more difficult to discuss."

He leaned back on the bench. The day was warm and sunny, he could hear birds singing in the trees of the garden, and he was moments away from becoming a father. "I am at your disposal."

She rose and paced, making him feel a little less sanguine about his chances. She seemed to realize how nervous she looked, for she forced herself to be seated beside him on the bench. "I think you know that I ran away with Nathan Jacobs because I adored him. You and I have a different relationship. I like to think we are . . . friends?"

He nodded. "Certainly. And partners for the boys' well-being."

"Yes." She tried to take strength from his calm demeanor, but her palms were sweating within her gloves. "I hope you will understand, then, that I am somewhat reluctant to resume a wifely role?" She looked at him pleadingly.

So, he'd make an excellent father even though she couldn't bear the thought of him as a husband. That was really the heart of the matter. He couldn't compete with the dashing Nathan Jacobs when the man was alive, and he didn't seem to be able to compete with him now that he was dead. Yet, if she could be so forthright about her feelings, so could he.

"You've had more experience being a wife than I have being a husband," he replied. "But isn't marriage supposed to be about more than simply caring for children?"

He hadn't meant it as a criticism of her first marriage, but she obviously took it so. "Nathan and I shared a bond that went far beyond our children," she told him haughtily. "Did you expect me to immediately form such a bond with the first eligible bachelor who proposed?"

He refrained from pointing out how quickly she seemed to have formed the bond with Nathan, leaving family and friends behind for nearly ten years. "Of course not. But if you put constraints on our marriage, will you keep that bond from ever forming?"

She got up and walked to the edge of the hedge. This was not how she wanted this conversation to go. She had loved Nathan, would always love Nathan. For all that Daniel was gentler, more forthright, and much more dependable, he had not captured her heart. "I'm sorry, Daniel," she murmured. "But I'm simply not ready to be so intimate."

She had not said it, but he seemed to hear the word "yet" echoing after her declaration. He could also hear the boys calling in the greenery and tried to remind himself again that he was doing this for their sakes, after all. He had no right to assume that Cynthia would be his reward. But if she were here, with him, would he have a chance at winning her heart? The desire to do so was suddenly overwhelming.

"I understand completely," he lied, doing his best to keep his usual smile in place. "Please, Cynthia, let me assure you that I did not make that proposal to put you into any kind of compromising situation. If you wish our marriage to be platonic, I will honor your request. But you must not ask me to give up hope that one day you will change your mind."

She wasn't sure why that frightened her, but it did. She glanced back at him. He was smiling warmly and the sunlight glinted off the rich mahogany of his hair. He looked even more innocent than her sons. But if he was plotting mischief, it would be more dangerous to her than anything her sons tried. If Daniel succeeded, she would lose her heart again. She wasn't sure she'd ever be ready.

She heard John call to James and Adam and forced her fears aside. The man was being more than generous in agreeing to all her terms. What did she have to complain about?

"Very well, then, Daniel," she replied with a bright smile. "I accept your proposal. I will marry you."

They were married two weeks later in the church in Wenwood, Daniel having procured a license from the local bishop. A pleased Jonathan hosted a wedding breakfast at Kinsle House, then Cynthia, the boys, and their assorted belongings were packed into the carriage and trundled down the drive, around the bend, and up the road to the Lewiston estate.

The boys ran laughing into the hall when they arrived, their voices echoing to the hammered beams a full story above their heads. Daniel knew they had already begun to see the house as their home, but he still detected a change in their attitudes, as if they had suddenly been set free in a new world. They wanted to explore and touch and demand an explanation for everything from the Tompion marquetry clock in the library to the gilt-framed Lawrence painting of his Great-aunt Chloe upstairs in the portrait gallery. In following them from room to room, he had to admit he had never realized what a fascinating house he had.

Cynthia found it difficult to share her sons' joy in their new home. The lofty Gothic ceilings with their open carved beams, the dark wood that seemed to panel each room, and the thick-limbed, many-knobbed furniture with the scarlet upholstery seemed broodily depressing to her. Odd that she had never noticed it as a child, but then most of her memories of being in the house with Daniel's sisters were pleasant. Now the dust she had first noticed in the withdrawing room was everywhere, and the thought of cleaning it from so many rooms depressed her further, until the footmen began marching past with her belongings and she remembered she would not have to lift a finger if she didn't want to. She trailed behind the procession up the massive central stairway, gazing at the rich-hued tapestries, oriental vases, and Greek statues that lined the long halls, until Evenson stopped her at the doorway to a large bedchamber.

"Your room, Mrs. Lewiston," he intoned.

The name sounded surprisingly lovely on his lips, and she smiled as she stepped past him. Then her smile froze on her face. Staring at her in the center of the chamber was a huge box bed whose burgundy and gold hangings reached to brush the high ceiling. There were twin dressing tables on either side of it, the elaborate carvings of twisting dragons on their fronts matching the headboard of the giant bed. The size and complexity of each piece of furniture was overwhelming enough, but what upset her far more was the tortoiseshell comb and brush set on one of the dressers, with all the accouterments a gentleman might need to shave and dress in the morning. A young woman in a black dress and white apron was setting Cynthia's brushes and belongings on the other table.

"This," Cynthia said in icy tones, "is not my bedchamber."

Daniel was chasing Adam down the corridor that held the family bedchambers when he was pulled up short by Cynthia's voice. It wasn't so much that it was any louder than usual; if anything, it sounded oddly stilled.

"I assure you that there has been a mistake," she was telling Evenson, who stood erect and proper just inside the door to the master bedchamber. "This cannot possibly be my room."

"Hey, ho," he called, moving to his butler's side. "Is something amiss?"

One look at her confirmed his suspicions. Under the pale pink rosebuds on the rim of the fetching straw bonnet she had worn to their wedding, her chin was as firm as Adam's when he was determined to have his way. Even the ladylike flounce of her pink silk wedding gown failed to hide the fact that her dainty foot was tapping in agitation.

Evenson cleared his throat. "Madame does not find the bedchamber to her liking."

"Oh?" Daniel glanced around the large chamber. He didn't immediately see anything that might trouble her in the heavy polished walnut furniture or burgundy bed linens; but then he'd seen it every day since he had been eight. "If it's the decor that bothers you, Cynthia, we can easily have it redone. I suppose it is a bit on the manly side."

She was alternating between blushing and paling, and he knew something must be seriously wrong.

"Evenson," he remarked casually, "go see what the boys have found to amuse themselves with so quietly, would you?"

Evenson bowed with obvious relief. "With pleasure, sir."

As his man hurried off down the hall, Daniel stepped to Cynthia's side. "Now then, suppose you tell me what's troubling you."

She glared up at him, anger rising as she felt a tear trickle down one cheek. How could he stand there and pretend the only thing troubling her was the color of the bed linens? She had once thought him lack-witted, but now she wondered whether he was a lecher as well. "You promised!" she hissed.

Daniel blinked. "Promised?"

She stepped back from him, livid. "Don't pretend you

don't remember. To think I trusted you. Call the carriage at once. The boys and I are leaving."

"Cynthia!" He caught her hands in his, and she pulled them quickly out. "I don't understand. If you don't like this chamber, you have only to pick another. Gads, there must be at least twenty in this monstrosity."

Arrested, she stared at him. "Choose another?"

"Yes, please, if that's what's troubling you."

She stepped a little closer, peering up into his face but saw only earnest concern. He stood as still as possible, wondering what on earth had happened to make her so skittish.

"Where are you sleeping?" she asked, eyes narrowed.

"I asked Evenson to move my things down the corridor closer to the nursery stairs," he told her honestly. "I thought you'd need the bigger room. But if you don't like it . . ."

She expelled her breath slowly and forced her fists, which were balled at her sides, to open. "No, no, this chamber is fine. I'm sorry I made a fuss. You see, this is obviously the master's bedchamber, and I noticed your things on the dresser and that made me think . . ."

"That I was installing you in my bedchamber," Daniel finished, understanding at last. "I'm sorry I'm such a slow-top. I should have explained it to you. In fact, I probably should have let you make the arrangements. It strikes me now that perhaps you'd rather the boys slept on this floor, near us."

She picked at the lace on the sleeve of her gown, afraid to ask him for even such a small favor after making such a silly mistake. "Would you mind?"

"Not in the slightest. As I said, we've plenty of space. I daresay John at least is of an age at which he'd like his own."

"My own room!" John gasped in the doorway.

Daniel smiled at his face. Despite the look of astonishment, it was cheerier now than any time he could remember. It pleased him to think he might have had some hand in that. "Your very own, if you'd like it."

"I'll say!" John declared. "Hear that, you two?" he called to his brothers, who were hurrying up the corridor with Evenson puffing at their heels. "I'm to have my own room!"

"I want my own room, too!" Adam demanded.

James looked thoughtful. "I don't think I should like to sleep alone just yet. Especially in a strange house."

"It's not a strange house," Adam pouted. "It's our home, isn't it, Mr. Daniel?"

"It certainly is, my good man," Daniel told him, scooping him up and depositing him on his shoulders. He caught Evenson grimacing at the gesture and grinned. "There are at least eight bedchambers along this corridor. You may have your pick of the lot—with your mother's approval, of course."

Cynthia nodded, and John and James dashed off in opposite directions, whooping in delight. Daniel felt Adam wiggling.

"Hurry up, Mr. Daniel. We don't want them getting the best rooms!"

Evenson cleared his throat. "Might I be excused, sir? If you're going to be making alternative living arrangements, I really should be letting the staff know."

Daniel shooed him out of the way, heading out into the corridor while Adam cried out impossible directions. It felt a little odd being pointed by a child hanging onto his ears, but Adam wasn't a heavy burden and they were quickly in the midst of the search.

It took over an hour for them to inspect each of the chambers in the family wing and decide on a likely grouping. John picked a corner chamber with a turret window overlooking the west fields. After some consideration, James and Adam decided they would share the larger chamber next door for the time being, as it had a connecting door to a chamber that could be used as a playroom. With some relief, Cynthia settled on the chamber opposite theirs and next to John's. The single large, south-facing window let in plenty of light and when she looked out, she could see the rose gardens below. The yellow and green bed hangings and upholstery on the chairs and stool near the white stone fireplace made the room seem much cheerier than the master bedchamber. The only problem was that Daniel chose the chamber next door. He caught her eyeing the connecting door with obvious misgivings. As the boys discussed where they would put their few belongings, he drew her aside, hoping to calm her fears once and for all.

"Interesting architecture, don't you think?" He nodded toward the offending door.

She managed a polite smile. "I suppose it was to allow visiting couples to reach each other more easily."

"Undoubtedly. But the Lewistons of the past were a practical lot. Just in case the couples weren't all that interested, the door can be locked from either side." He reached up over the doorjamb and took down the brass key that was kept there. "Here. You keep the key. If you ever need me, just use it."

She paled again, and for a moment he thought he had gone too far.

"You are too good to us, Daniel," she breathed, eyes bright with unshed tears. "I promise you, I'll repay you somehow."

Adam dashed up suddenly, hugging Daniel around the legs. "This is the best day yet, Mr. Daniel. We have our own rooms and we get to be with you always."

Daniel felt the now familiar constriction near his heart. He glanced from Adam's beaming face to Cynthia's watery smile. "Believe me, my dear, you already have."

SEVEN

Cynthia's watery mood barely lasted through the first course of lunch. It seemed impossible to believe that after nearly ten years of exile, she was finally to have the pampered, comfortable life for which she had been raised. The very thought made her feel a bit like a traitor to Nathan's memory, but the sight of veal on her plate for lunch somehow pushed the guilt away with the memory. If she had to trade love for a mess of porridge, at least it was to be very good porridge.

Of course, that's what she had assumed. It was well known that the Lewiston estate boasted a real French chef, and she had naturally supposed that the food would be beyond anything she had ever tasted. One mouthful made her reach for the damask napkin in dismay. Farther up the long table, which could easily have seated thirty, she saw that Adam was attempting to push the overcooked peas around his plate with his utensils and only succeeding in mashing them further. Across from him, James was chewing the cheddared potatoes, although with difficulty, and near Daniel, John had pushed the Yorkshire pudding away in disgust. Only Daniel at the head of the table was calmly eating as if nothing untoward was happening.

"Is this normal fare?" she called up from the foot of the long table, where her place had been set.

Daniel swallowed and nodded. "Seems to be Henri's favorite lunch. I believe we have it on a regular basis."

"Every Wednesday, sir," Evenson supplied from his station at the side table, although Cynthia thought even he looked disgusted by the fact.

"Every Wednesday?" John gasped. James swallowed, then reached quickly for water to drown the lump. Adam smashed the last pea triumphantly.

Daniel glanced around at the obviously displeased faces around him. "Don't you care for it?"

Cynthia's frown turned the boys' eyes back to their plates. "I'm sure it's quite adequate, Daniel. The boys and I have learned to make do with far less. However, I admit I'm curious. Do *you* like it?"

Daniel glanced down at the gray lump that was the veal. "To tell you the truth, I've never actually thought about it. Luncheon and any other meal was just something to get through."

Cynthia felt a sudden stab of pity. She could picture him rattling about this great house, conducting his estate duties alone, eating alone, reading himself to sleep alone, and waking up alone to do it all over again. She might not be able to keep him company at night, but she could certainly make sure that his home was clean and his food edible.

"I think it's safe to say we can do something about this," she smiled to everyone at the table. "Evenson, I shall want a word with Mr. Henri this afternoon."

Evenson cringed. "Of course, madame. However, I think you should know that Monsieur Henri takes a nap every day from noon to three, and then of course he's busy with the dinner preparations, so perhaps I might suggest . . ."

"One o'clock," Cynthia smiled, but the boys had the good sense to lower their eyes once again. "In the library."

Evenson swallowed, and bowed himself out.

* * *

She didn't wait until one. Once she saw that the boys were safely engaged in a protracted tour of the picture gallery with Daniel and one of the more trustworthy-looking footmen, she changed from the soft pink wedding gown Jonathan had magnanimously purchased for her into her mourning gown. She had hoped never to don the thing again, but it was guaranteed to look far more serious than the pink gown and she needed to look as serious as possible for this interview. She supposed she ought to meet all the servants at some point or at least discuss arrangements with Evenson. For now, she would have to settle for handling "Monsieur Henri."

She hadn't reached the ground-floor landing before she heard the shouting. The fact that it was in French and filled with a considerable number of words her mother had never taught her only caused her chin to rise a few more inches. She followed the noise down the back stairs and swept into the kitchen. The scullery maids huddled by the door scattered. Evenson withdrew to a discreet distance, and the two footmen who had been attempting to restrain the portly chef dropped their arms and bowed to her. She smiled sweetly, then stepped forward, holding out her hand.

"Monsieur Henri, I came as soon as I could."

She knew the other servants were exchanging glances of puzzlement. Her appeasing attitude stopped the Frenchman in mid-tirade. She continued before he could recover. "My dear sir, you cannot know how delighted I am to be so fortunate to have an artiste of your caliber on my staff. *Je suis enchanté!*"

She knew her French, though rusty, was near perfect. The little man's head came up, and a look of delight spread across his pasty face. "I assure you, madame, the honor is all mine."

"Oh, but you are too kind. A man of your skill, here, is nothing short of miraculous." With the other servants wide-eyed about her, she stepped closer and lowered her voice, continuing in French. "I realize, of course, that my husband must have been a sad trial to you. His palate, alas, is not very refined, *non?* But I assure you, I will be a much more discerning judge."

The Frenchman swallowed, catching the steel behind her velvet words as she had hoped he would. "I will attempt to please, madame, of course."

"I know you will. I will expect recommendations from you each Monday morning for every meal in the week to follow. We will meet in the library at precisely eight. I ask that you consider we are feeding three young boys with un-schooled palates as well as two adults. Given that this is Wednesday, I will waive the recommendations for this week. I hope you will use this time to show me exactly how skilled you are."

"Oui, madame," Henri muttered, breaking into a sweat.

"Excellent. And Henri, if you ever serve my husband the slop you provided for lunch today, it will be the last day you serve my husband. Do I make myself clear?"

"Oui, madame," he managed in a choked whisper.

Cynthia beamed at everyone around her, switching back to English. "It was delightful to meet you, monsieur. I know our home will be better for having you here." She nodded to the others and swept out of the room.

Once back in her new bedroom, she sank down on the embroidered stool near the empty fireplace and broke into delighted laughter. The look on Monsieur Henri's face had been priceless, but the shocked look on Evenson's usually impassive face had been even better. That should teach the man to treat her Daniel with anything less than respect!

She choked on her laughter. *Her* Daniel? What was she thinking? For that matter, what was she doing meddling in his affairs? She was acting as giddy as the child she had once been. Daniel Lewiston had been master of this house for years. What right had she to walk in her first day and order his staff around? True, the cook had been shirking his duties, but was it her place to correct him? She was mistress of this house under the flimsiest of pretenses. By this evening, she had no doubt every servant as well as most of her neighbors would know that the Master and Mistress of Lewiston House kept separate rooms. While this wasn't unheard of among the gentry, it still made her feel guilty that she somehow wasn't repaying his kindness. She supposed she would simply have to get used to the idea that the best thing she could do for Daniel Lewiston was to ensure that he had a well-run household.

With this thought in mind, she approached Daniel in the withdrawing room that evening after a much improved dinner. James was reading aloud a book he had found in Daniel's "excellent" library to a rapt Adam, and John was sitting on the hardwood floor with knees to chest, staring dreamily into the fire. She sat down next to Daniel on the nearby sofa and lowered her voice so as not to disturb her sons.

"Thank you for being so good to us," she murmured, gathering courage from the smile he gave her back. "I have been thinking about our lives here, and I wondered if you'd mind if I made a few changes?"

His smile deepened. "If they're anything like the change you made in Monsieur Henri, I'd be delighted. That was the best dinner I think I've ever had."

She blushed. "Your chef and I simply reached an understanding. I don't know if I'll have such luck elsewhere."

"Oh, I don't know," Daniel encouraged her. "What else do you wish to change?"

"Well, for one thing, would you mind if we sat a little closer at the dining table?"

He chuckled. "It *is* a bit of a shout when we try to converse. I'll tell Evenson to set all five places near the head. What else?"

"Do you think the boys might have a tutor?" she ventured.

Daniel nodded. "Certainly. Although I wondered about Mr. Wellfordhouse's classes at the vicarage. They'd have a chance to meet other children that way. The class is small now, but it will grow once we have the school built."

Cynthia was surprised to find how easy it was to talk to him about matters. Whenever she'd raised such issues to Nathan, he had laughingly scolded her for worrying too much. "I think the vicarage school would be wonderful," she agreed. "There are some things, however, the good reverend won't be able to teach them, such as horsemanship."

"We used to have an excellent stable," Daniel replied thoughtfully. "I rode every morning for years, but I somehow lost interest after my sister Cerise married. I suppose it was just one more thing to do alone. I'd be delighted to take the boys riding whenever you'd like. And you, too, of course."

"You'll have to get us riding outfits, then," Cynthia laughed. "There isn't much call for horsemanship on the Bristol docks."

"Done," he grinned. "We'll have a tailor and seamstress in from Wells tomorrow."

But even when the tailor and seamstress had measured them and scurried off to make riding outfits and several other items Daniel commissioned, riding proved to be difficult. Daniel took the boys and Cynthia down to the stables to inspect the horses; however, Cynthia was disappointed to find the animals old and entirely too docile for all but Adam. Seeing her disapproval, Daniel suggested they purchase suitable mounts. Cynthia brightened, until he called for the carriage to take them to visit Enoch McCreedy.

Mr. McCreedy was well known about Wenwood for two things: fine horses and a foul temper. Even when he was a young man of twenty her father had refused to deal with him, and she could only assume that Jonathan had followed suit. She remembered her mother sweeping her skirts aside to keep from touching him as they passed in the village. He had leered at her and spat on her shoes. It took a strong person to deal with Enoch McCreedy and come out the better for it. She wasn't sure Daniel had that strength.

She managed to convince him to leave the boys at home with Evenson and the footman to watch them, soothing the boys with the idea that the exact color of their horses would then be a surprise. She kept him busy during the ride across the village by asking him questions about his sisters—when they had married, how they were getting on, how many children they had by now. She nodded and chatted, but all the while her mind was elsewhere. She kept trying to think what skill she possessed that might allow her to help Daniel. She had learned to bow and scrape to the servants of the merchants in Bristol so that she might earn a living darning socks and mending clothes. She seemed to remember how to behave with arrogance befitting gentry if her handling of Monsieur Henri was any indication. But would either approach allow her to help a kind man like Daniel purchase horses from a tyrant like Enoch McCreedy?

Daniel was more than happy to recount tales of his many nieces, all his sisters having had daughters so far, but he knew by the way Cynthia's eyes kept darting to the window that her thoughts weren't entirely on what he was saying. He supposed she'd heard stories about Enoch. The man certainly had figured largely in local lore. Daniel had met him a few years ago at a horse auction and struck up a conversation. He had been the only one to stay when the man began cussing and spouting bile, amazed by how easily Enoch vilified anyone who crossed his path. It was obvious to him that the man was as alone as he was, and once he had shown Enoch he wasn't to be turned aside so easily, they had struck up an odd friendship. He had little doubt the man could sell him some prime blood, but he wasn't sure how Cynthia would react to the man's personality.

"Perhaps you should wait in the carriage," Daniel tried when they arrived at the farmstead. "It's a bit dusty, and I wouldn't want you to ruin your gown."

As she had chosen to wear the black dress again, she could hardly agree with him. "I'm not afraid of a bit of dust. I would like to help you select the horses for the boys, if you don't mind."

He could hardly gainsay her. Glancing out the carriage window, he saw that several horses were already out in a paddock some distance away from the main stable. "All right, then. Suppose you go with Jeffers to have a look at the mounts and I'll see if I can't scare up Enoch."

It wasn't exactly what she had had in mind, but she couldn't find a reason to argue. With great misgivings, she allowed the footman to lead her over to the fenced area where she could survey the horses.

Daniel let her go with equal misgivings, then hurried into the dark stable to find his friend. Enoch was exactly where he'd thought he'd find him, back in one of the stalls, checking on one of the stallions he used for stud service. The tall, thin, craggy man glanced up as Daniel neared, running a hand back through black hair that was graying at the temples and narrowing his sharp blue eyes.

"Didn't think to see you so soon," he muttered, setting down the stallion's hoof and patting the brute as he exited the stall. "Married folks usually have better things to do."

"Nice to see you again, too, Enoch," Daniel grinned at him.

He stumped along the aisle, and Daniel fell in beside him. "I suppose she made you come."

"We need horses. Where else would we go?"

He spat into the straw at his feet. "I heard she was a tartar. You were lucky when you were a lad—she ran away on you before you had to offer. Should have learned your lesson then."

Daniel couldn't imagine why, but for once Enoch's words stung. He tried to ignore it and focus on what he had come for. "So, what would you recommend for three boys and a lady?"

They were out in the sun now and Enoch waved toward the paddock. "Looks like she already made the decision."

Cynthia saw them coming. The man beside Daniel was taut as a halyard and as hard as a whetstone. She'd dealt with his kind many times in the Admiralty. Arrogance was the only approach they understood. She drew herself up to her full height for the oncoming battle. Unfortunately, that only put her eyes on a level with Enoch's collarbone. She craned her neck to meet his gaze as Daniel introduced them.

Enoch spit at the ground only inches from her feet. She refused to move. "Well, which horses do you want?"

Even though she had been expecting it, his insolence annoyed her. "I'm sure my husband knows what we need for our stables."

"Your stables, eh?" He quirked a bushy eyebrow. "Last time I checked, they were Mr. Lewiston's stables."

She started to bristle, but Daniel slipped an arm about her waist and she froze in surprise. "Now, Enoch, you know how things are with newlyweds. We do everything together. And right now we'd both very much like your advice on horses."

Cynthia sucked in her breath, but whether it was a result of Daniel actually treating this creature politely or how warm his arm felt all the way through her black gown, she wasn't certain. "I'm sure you're quite capable of determining which horses we should purchase, Daniel," she murmured as firmly as she could.

"He wouldn't know good horseflesh if it sat on him," Enoch grumbled. "Any more than he knows a good woman when he sees one."

Daniel shook his head. It was obviously not one of Enoch's better days. The only thing he could do was take Cynthia home before matters worsened. "Never mind, Enoch. I think we've seen enough for one day. Cynthia, let's go home."

Cynthia trembled in suppressed rage. How dare the man speak that way about Daniel? How dare he imply that she was less than a good wife to him? "You're quite right, dear," she sniffed, head high as she turned away from the paddock.

Enoch chortled. "Give it up, missy. You just like to let him think he's running things. Everyone knows who wears the pants in your house. The only shame is, Daniel doesn't get to see what goes into them."

Cynthia turned bright red. There was nothing for it. Daniel turned and slugged him right in the jaw.

Pain shot through his hand and he hopped back out of reach before Enoch could return the swing. The older man's head had rocked back with the blow, but he didn't stumble. He rubbed his jaw and winced. "Well then, I guess we all know how things stand. The three ponies, I think, for the younger ones, and the bay mare for the lady. No charge. They're my wedding present to you. I'll have one of the boys bring them round tomorrow morning. Good day to you both." He knuckled his forelock in Cynthia's direction and turned back to the stables.

Daniel stared after at him, hand smarting and thoroughly confused. He realized Cynthia was staring at him, eyes wide, all color fled, and he could only hope she didn't think him as great a beast as Enoch.

"Oh, Daniel," she cried, throwing herself into his arms. "That was magnificent!"

She was so close he could smell the scent of roses in her hair. Her body next to his was soft and curvy and seemed to fit against him in all the right places. It took every ounce of strength he possessed to force himself to push her gently away before she could see how she was affecting him. "Thank you, my dear," he managed, wincing at the pain in his right hand. "But would you mind returning with me to the carriage? I'm not feeling particularly well."

Cynthia found she wasn't feeling particularly well, either. The feel of Daniel's arms about her had been surprisingly good and the summer day had suddenly felt much cooler when he had set her back from him. She tried to reach out to him but he turned quickly before she could touch him. Self-conscious, she let her hand fall to her side and followed him back to the waiting carriage. Yet, she could not help marveling again at what she had seen. Daniel Lewiston, knight errant. It was a side of him she had never suspected existed. Could she have misjudged her husband after all?

EIGHT

Daniel's defense of Cynthia's good name was not the last of the surprises in store for her. She soon found that she didn't really know her new husband well, if she had ever known him at all. Growing up, she had assumed his timidity and awkwardness around her was part of his personality, that he approached everyone that way. Certainly nothing that had occurred until his gallantry at the stables had led her to believe otherwise. But a number of events over the next few weeks made her realize that there was a great deal more to Daniel than she had ever thought possible.

The first event was the arrival of the horses from Enoch McCreedy. True to his word, he had sent sturdy ponies for Adam, James, and John, and a darling spirited mare for her. In earlier days she would have thought the idea of Daniel riding the brute of a stallion Enoch sent as a surprise for him preposterous, but Daniel had no trouble mounting and galloping about the estate with evident glee. Soon she and the boys were cantering alongside him on a daily basis, the boys proud in their matching black trousers and jackets, and Adam proudest of all in his long pants. And she had to admit, as she admired the way the sky blue wool riding jacket and skirt flattered her figure and coloring, that Daniel's taste in clothing was bang up to the mark as well.

The second event was a visit by several of the village matrons, including Squire Pentercast's wife Genevieve and her

sister Allison, to congratulate her on her marriage and welcome her formally to Wenwood. Since she had run away to
be married to Nathan and neither his family nor her own had
ever approved of the match, she had never had such a visit
in her life. She wasn't at all sure what to say or do, but
Daniel welcomed the women to their house. He chatted with
them about their own families as if he'd known them for
years, which of course he probably had, and in general let it
be known that he was utterly enchanted with his new bride
so that the ladies left singing her praises without her having
so much as to remember to pour the tea.

If she had thought Daniel was impressive at home, she
was equally surprised to find him adept at social gatherings
as well. Allison had ordered Daniel to bring Cynthia to the
next assembly at Barnsley Grange, but Cynthia had hardly
taken that seriously. She hadn't danced in years, and she
certainly didn't want to subject Daniel to something he might
find uncomfortable. Besides, except for her pink wedding
dress, all her dresses were much too dark and of poor material to make a good showing even at a country dance.

She was therefore surprised to return from a ride with
Daniel and the boys to find a rather large box sitting on her
bed.

"Oh, a present!" Adam squealed, having followed her into
the room before continuing to his own to change. He clam-
bered up onto the bed and bounced on his knees, setting the
box to rocking. "Open it, open it!"

James and John crowded in the doorway. John frowned.
"A present for Mother?"

Daniel put his arms across their shoulders and bent to
speak in their ears. "Certainly. After all the toys we've
bought, not to mention the new horses, don't you think she
deserved something all for herself?"

Cynthia frowned at him, then at the box. "Well, I don't
think I deserve it. What have you done, Daniel?"

His gray eyes twinkled with blue. "Open it."

Grimacing, she reached down and shook off the lid. Whatever was inside was wrapped in yards of white tissue. She glanced back up at him. He grinned at her.

"Open it, Mother!" Adam urged, bouncing again in his excitement.

She shook her head in exasperation and began unpeeling the wrapping. As the tissue began to open, she caught sight of rose satin, as soft as the petals of a flower. Eagerness seized her, and she practically tore the last of the paper off. In her hands lay the most beautiful dress she had ever seen.

All of it was made of the delicate rose satin, with darker rose ribbon in triple rows around the high waist and full skirt. The rounded neck and small puffed sleeves were edged with intricate embroidery of white roses on emerald leaves. In the center of each rose was a small pearl. Similar roses seemed to climb from the ribbon at the hem to blossom under the gathered bosom.

"Oh," John grunted dismissively, "it's just a dumb dress."

"Very nice, Mother," James nodded dutifully before John pulled him across the corridor toward the well-furnished playroom. Adam reached out and patted the soft material.

"It's very pretty, Mother. You'll look just like the roses in Mr. Daniel's garden."

Cynthia smiled at him, feeling her eyes moisten. "That's right, Adam."

He crawled down from the bed and skipped off across the corridor. Watching him, Cynthia glanced up to find Daniel watching her.

"I don't know what to say," she murmured, oddly embarrassed. "It's absolutely beautiful."

"Good," Daniel nodded. "Then you'll have no trouble accompanying me to the assembly this Wednesday."

"No, I suppose I won't," she couldn't help laughing.

And she had worn it to the assembly, with a nosegay of rosebuds at her wrist and roses entwined in the braid in her hair. And Daniel had danced every dance with her, and she had felt more beautiful than she had ever felt—even the night she had met Nathan. In fact, Nathan had never seemed farther away and for once the thought didn't terrify her.

Daniel couldn't help noticing the change in her. All his efforts to bring them closer were beginning to work. She was laughing again, not the teasing laughter he remembered as a young man but a joyful sound that did something to his heart to hear it. He ordered a dozen more dresses, each in a different style and all in shades of violet and blue and pink that complimented her fair coloring. Whether it was the dresses or laughter he didn't know, but he was pleased to see that the dark circles disappeared from around her eyes.

He was also pleased and a little surprised to find that virtually none of his own clothes were fitting. Between the improvement in Monsieur Henri's cooking and the exercise he was getting with the boys, he had lost a good fifty pounds. When he put on the new clothes he ordered for himself, he had to admit that he cut a rather dashing figure. Perhaps Cynthia hadn't married herself such a frog after all.

There was one thing more he felt he must try to change, however, and that was Cynthia's inability to play with the boys. While he would cheerfully wrestle and dash about the house with them, Cynthia always watched from a distance. She watched with an indulgent smile on her face, that was true, but she refused to join them. At first he wondered whether she was hampered by her new gowns, but she didn't seem more likely to enter their games when she wore the hideous black dress, which was rarely now. More likely, he decided, she had had to be both mother and father for so long that she was unable to unbend to be herself even long enough to play a game of hide-and-seek. It seemed to him a symbol of their relationship—while it was pleasant, the joy was missing. If he could get her to unbend in one area, perhaps the other would follow.

His opportunity came one afternoon when he had been playing a boisterous game of touch and run with the boys through the hedges of the maze. He had stopped to catch his breath near one of the entrances when he heard Cynthia calling to the boys to come in for tea. James and Adam dutifully appeared from behind various shrubs. A half-hearted scuffle behind him could only be John. He held out one arm to stop them and put a finger to his lips.

"Let's see if we can't get your mother to play for a bit," he whispered. All three of them brightened and they scampered off into hiding. Daniel sauntered out of the maze right into Cynthia's path.

"Hello, my dear. Did I hear you calling?"

Cynthia smiled at him over the basket of roses in her arms. She had to admit that even with his new clothes powdered with dust and thoroughly rumpled, he was looking rather handsome. She'd never realized in fact how handsome he really was. His jaw was firm, his profile strong, his shoulders were impressive, and his legs long and powerful. The strength of her possessive feelings surprised her and she had to look away with a blush that rivaled the blooms in her arms. "Yes, well, I've finished with the roses for the day and I thought it must be time for tea."

"Well," Daniel grinned at her. "If you really want tea, you'll have to come fetch us." He tapped her gently on the arm. "You've been touched."

She blinked, and Daniel pelted off into the maze, his husky laughter floating behind him.

"Daniel, this is ridiculous," she sniffed, peering into the bushes in first one direction and then the other. Really, couldn't the man be serious? The path stretched empty in all directions. "Boys, come out immediately."

"Boys," Daniel's voice countered from somewhere on her right. "You will do nothing of the kind until your mother touches one of us."

Somewhere to her left someone giggled. Adam, she thought, eyes narrowing. "Very well, then, have it your way." She set the basket on one of the stone benches that dotted the maze and tiptoed toward the sound. Carefully she peered over the top of the bushes. There was no one there. Frustrated, she sank back onto her feet.

"Nah nah nah," John teased from her right. She whipped about in time to see him disappearing around a turn in the maze. She lifted her skirts and dashed after him.

For the next few minutes it was pure anarchy in the maze. Children raced around corners and dove into bushes. Daniel actually leapt over one of the lower hedges to avoid her touch. Determined, she pursued him deeper into the maze, his laughter always just ahead of her. Adam escaped by crawling under a stone bench. James ran away so quickly he lost a shoe, and she only paused long enough to scoop it up and slip it in the pocket of her gown. John had the uncanny knack of letting her get within a finger's breadth before sprinting past her and disappearing again. Her hair came undone from its pins, she trod on the flounce of her gown, and she had never had such a wonderful time in all her life.

She was about to get the jump on John at last when she caught sight of Daniel heading for the center of the maze. Letting her son escape, she edged along the hedge and peered around the corner. Facing away from her, Daniel was bent over the stone bench at the center of the maze to catch his breath, one foot up on the bench. She tiptoed up behind him and placed both hands on his broad back. "I have you!" she shrieked triumphantly.

Daniel grabbed her around the waist and pulled her into his embrace. She was so surprised that she could only gasp out an "oh" and with her mouth in such a perfect position, he kissed her.

It was a quick peck, nothing more. But it caused the strangest sensations in her stomach and all she could do was stare at him. He had the oddest expression on his own face, his gray eyes suddenly dark, and she had the distinct impression that his breathlessness had nothing to do with the game.

"Cynthia," he managed. "Say something, please."

She blinked. "Thank you?"

He laughed shakily. "Thank you? Is that for the game or the kiss?"

"Both?" She felt shy suddenly and dropped her gaze. The feel of his arms around her was wonderfully comforting, and she found she had no desire to move. What she did have a desire for, however, was another kiss, and the thought was enough to shock her into silence.

Daniel had no idea how things had gotten to this pass. Here he stood with Cynthia in his arms in the middle of the garden, of all places, the feel of her mouth under his still fresh in his mind. *Fresh* . . . it was overpowering. He found himself staring at those lips, warm, dusted with moisture like dew on the petals of a rose. All he'd have to do was lower his head once again and . . .

"Awww, she caught him!" Adam cried from the hedge. "Do we *have* to go to tea now?"

Daniel forced himself to let go of her. Cynthia smoothed down her skirts and stood a little straighter. He had to bite his lip to keep from laughing. Her effort was completely in vain with her hair wild about her shoulders and dust caking the hem of her skirt.

"That's only fair, Adam," she told her son with a smile. "I did catch Daniel, and he promised we'd go in when I caught one of you."

"All right," Adam sighed. Within minutes, they had rounded up James and John and were headed back to the house with Daniel in the lead. Cynthia picked up her basket and trailed behind. She told herself she was quite glad she had managed to get them to return to the house, but suddenly she had lost all interest in tea, and she couldn't wait to get some time to herself to think.

NINE

She didn't get time to herself until after the boys had retired. Daniel seemed disappointed that she didn't choose to
stay up and play chess or billiards with him as had been their
wont of late, but today's kiss in the maze had thoroughly
unnerved her and she found it impossible to be alone with
him until she knew why.

After she had departed, Daniel sat staring into the fire,
thoughts unfocused, or rather refusing to focus on a particular incident. He nodded at Evenson, who came in to check
the windows and doors before going to bed. "Is there anything more I can do for you, sir?"

"Can you explain women to me, Evenson?" Daniel asked.

Evenson sighed. "If I could do that, sir, I would no longer
be your butler. I'd be the richest man in England."

"In the world," Daniel amended.

"Just so, sir. Good night."

Daniel nodded again as he left. He continued to sit in front
of the fire, watching the red coals dimming one by one to
black. Around him the room grew still and cool. He had
spent many such nights before Cynthia and the boys had
come into his life, but the memories were far from pleasant.
His life was richer and better with them in it. He had thought
he was content with his lot. But after the kiss this afternoon,
he knew he could never be.

He had fallen in love with Cynthia.

He shook his head. How could he have been such a fool? He had wanted to win her heart, but somehow he had never considered that he might lose his own. He'd thought the poets mad, but now he knew they were no madder than he. The frog was hopelessly in love with the beautiful, clever, wonderful mother of his sons. If she had felt for Nathan half of what he was feeling for her, he suddenly understood how she could run away and leave everything behind.

Most likely it had been creeping up on him all summer long, only he had just noticed it this afternoon when she had run up behind him. He really hadn't been intending to kiss her, but with her mouth so delectably close he hadn't had much choice. And the taste of her and the feel of her had been so sweet. He closed his eyes just thinking about it. God, how could he ever be in the same room with her again without wanting to hold her that way once more?

He leaned back on his elbows. He couldn't face her without saying something, that much was clear. But what was he to say? "My dear Cynthia, I know I made a bargain when I married you, but I've changed my mind. I want ours to be a true marriage. You will report to my bed this evening." He shook his head. That would hardly do. Yet he balked at the idea of simply telling her he loved her. Surely she would just smile politely and tell him to go to blazes.

"They're all right about you, my lad," he sighed. "How much of a man can you be if you can't even tell the woman you love that you love her?"

Upstairs the woman he loved was having a similar conversation with herself. It was equally plain to her that she had fallen in love with Daniel, although she couldn't remember when it had happened. She looked at herself in the mirror of the dressing table and a slow smile spread across her face. In love! She had never thought to feel this way again. A blush was spreading with the smile. She was in love with her darling, gentle, sweet-natured husband. But was he in love with her?

The smile and blush faded as quickly as they had come. True, he had kissed her, and he seemed to have been as affected by it as she had. And she had realized some time since that his awkwardness around her was a sign that her presence meant more to him than he wanted it to. But did that truly mean that his heart was engaged? Men did not necessarily love where they lusted, she had heard. Should she trust him with her heart when she did not know his?

But how could she face him without blurting out her feelings? And what was she to say? "Daniel, I know I asked you for a marriage of convenience but would you mind if I shared your bed?" The blush returned in full force. She would sound like a veritable wanton!

And yet she had to do something. They had been rather cozy together this summer, but everything was changed with the kiss. She could try to ignore it, but she feared it would only fester. The best thing for all would be to tell him the truth, that she was hopelessly in love with him and wanted to make theirs a true marriage. Knowing her Daniel, if he felt otherwise, he would be very gentle about telling her so.

She resolved to speak to him as soon as the boys were off to the vicarage school that next morning, then spent so sleepless a night worrying about his answer that she arrived at the breakfast table late and feeling haggard. She took some comfort in the fact that Daniel did not look as if he had slept well, either. There were bags under his stormy gray eyes and his hand stirring the honey into his tea shook on the spoon. The boys did not seem to have noticed the difference; they sat eating and laughing as they usually did.

"We are going to the pond to fish this morning," John announced, cramming a piece of toast in his mouth and speaking around the wad. "Wanna come, Mr. Daniel?"

Daniel managed a smile. "I'd love to, but isn't Mr. Wellfordhouse expecting you at the vicarage?"

John avoided his eyes. "I'm sure he'd understand if we took a day off."

"Fishing!" Adam exclaimed, waving the spoon from his porridge in the air. "I'm gonna catch a whale!"

Cynthia smiled at him and motioned him to put the spoon down, which he did with a contrite look.

"I do not believe Mr. Daniel's pond carries whales," James interjected. "Sturgeon would be the best one could hope for, I would imagine."

"Minnows, more likely," Cynthia told him. "But I quite agree with Daniel. Fishing will have to wait. You need to go to school."

John set down his spoon and frowned at her. "Mother, there is more to life than school. Isn't that so, Mr. Daniel?"

"A great deal more, John," Daniel nodded. "However, you won't be in much of a position to enjoy it if you don't have a decent education. I know the pond is calling, but it will be here tomorrow and the day after that. Today you need to go to school."

John glanced between the two of them. "Is something wrong?"

Cynthia could feel a blush heating her cheek and hastily looked away from the knowing blue eyes. "No, John."

"Everything is fine, John," Daniel agreed, although his voice sounded a little shaky to Cynthia. "And I'd be delighted to take you to the pond this afternoon when you return from the vicarage."

John slumped in his chair and poked at his porridge. "Oh, very well."

Daniel nodded. "I'll look forward to it, then. I hope you understand about the vicarage school, John. You more than any of the others need to be attending, because it will prepare you to go to Eton."

"Eton!" Cynthia gasped. "Oh, Daniel, how wonderful!" He beamed at her. "It's the least I could do."

"What's eatin'?" Adam demanded. "I want to go, too."

"And so you shall, my lad," Daniel nodded. "First John,

then James, then you. And after that, Oxford or Cambridge if you like."

John was frowning again. "I don't know those places. Are they near Barnsley?"

"No, they're much farther than that," Daniel explained. "They're fine schools, John, where you'll meet lots of fellows just like you. Your Uncle Jonathan attended Eton. So did the Duke of Wellington. I always wished I could. These are places you'll be proud to say you were graduated from."

John paled and rose from his chair. "You're sending me away?"

"Daniel is sending you to school, love," Cynthia said soothingly, reaching out a hand. John shrugged it away. "John, it's more than I'd ever hoped for you."

"*You* want me gone, too?" John cried. James stared at them all, and Adam trembled in his chair.

"John," Daniel said firmly, hoping to make the boy see reason before the whole lot of them started crying, "no one wants you gone."

"Perhaps this isn't the time to talk about this," Cynthia put in, seeing her oldest son shake with suppressed emotion.

"Why, because you don't want me to talk?" John demanded.

The boy was obviously beyond logic. "John," Daniel said quietly. "I think that's enough."

John turned on him, eyes wild, and Daniel had to fight not to flinch away from the betrayal staring back at him. "I know why you're doing this!" the boy shouted at him, blinking away hot tears. "You want to spend more time with her! You like her better than you like us! Well, she wouldn't even be here if I hadn't told her to. I did everything! I told the ladies in the village she wanted a husband so those awful men would call. I got you to go over there when you didn't even want to. I got her to marry you. She doesn't even like you. She thinks you're fat and stupid!"

"John!" Cynthia gasped, hands flying to her mouth.

The constriction by his heart that the boys' concerns usually caused was gone and Daniel felt only pain inside him. He had been right all along. It didn't matter how princely he behaved or how lordly he looked. To Cynthia, he would always be a frog. It would have been easy to give up and go back to his quiet life before they had arrived, a life with small chance of hurt and even smaller chance of love. He straightened under John's glare. He refused to give up on them.

He rose and went to kneel beside the boy to put himself at John's eye level. John's small chin stuck out and his fists were balled at his sides. His thin chest heaved as he gulped back sobs. "John," Daniel said carefully, "this isn't about how I feel about your mother. My idea of you going away to school is entirely about my love for you. When I married your mother, I gladly took on the responsibility of raising you and your brothers. I take that responsibility very seriously. It is my duty to help you grow up to be a gentleman you'll be proud of. A good education is a requirement for such a gentleman."

"But why must I go away?" John sniffed, dashing the tears away with the back of his hand. "Why can't I stay here and get an education?"

Daniel could feel all three boys waiting for his answer. He tried not to look at Cynthia. "You can get a good start at an education with Reverend Wellfordhouse," he explained. "Perhaps that will be all you want or need. But very likely you'll want to go on to learn more, whether at Eton or Harrow or some other good school. We have over a year before we have to make that decision. And rest assured, we will consult you on the matter. Now, do you think you can apologize to your mother for your behavior and get yourselves off to school?"

The boy nodded, sniffing away the last of his tears. He threw himself into Cynthia's arms for a hug. Adam and James scooted out of their seats, eyes wide, and followed John from the room. Like it or not, Daniel knew that left him to face Cynthia.

"I think perhaps I'd better see that they make it to school," he murmured, hurrying after them and hating himself for being so craven. He promised himself he would come back that afternoon, as soon as he could figure out a way to start rebuilding their relationship.

Cynthia watched him slink from the room and sank back against her chair in defeat.

TEN

Sometime later, Cynthia stopped her pacing about the library and peered out the window hoping to catch a glimpse of the returning Daniel. After her sleepless night and John's outburst that morning, her nerves were on edge and she wanted only to get her declaration over and done with. Especially after John's damning statement, she couldn't let Daniel think she so despised him.

But Daniel didn't come home that morning. Nor did he arrive in time for luncheon, although she had a distraught Monsieur Henri delay the meal twice. In fact, she did not see him again until she had descended for dinner and found him and the three boys boasting about their fishing of that afternoon. By then she was ready to scream.

For once, Daniel was content to avoid Cynthia. While the boys were at school, he had found a way to tell Cynthia he loved her. He waited anxiously through dinner, but she made no mention of the package he had left on her mantel, and he realized with a sinking heart that she hadn't found it yet. He let the boys stay up later than usual, hoping that she would retire to her room, but she seemed intent on confronting him. At last he took the boys up to bed and slipped into his own chamber. He managed to change into nightclothes, but he found it impossible to sleep and perched on his bed, listening for her footfall in the corridor.

Cynthia couldn't understand Daniel's attitude. He had to

know she wanted to talk to him, yet he let the boys stay up later than usual and insisted on taking them up to bed himself. She paced the withdrawing room, waiting for his return, and was just about to go up after him when Evenson came through on his rounds to close up the house. He was plainly surprised to see her, but made to bow himself out.

"Evenson," she demanded, "where is my husband?"

"I believe Mr. Lewiston retired for bed some time ago, madame," Evenson replied. "Shall I wake him for you?"

"No," Cynthia sighed, feeling every bit as dejected as John had that morning. "I might as well retire, too, then. Good night, Evenson."

She didn't wait to hear him respond.

Upstairs, she dismissed the young lady Daniel had hired to serve as her lady's maid, and began taking down her hair herself. She had combed out her tresses and put on her white cambric nightgown before she saw the box on the fireplace mantel.

"And don't think a present will get you out of discussing this, my man," she muttered to herself as she took down the box and carried it to the bed. Still, Daniel's presents had always been wonderful, and she hurriedly pulled the lid off the oblong box. Inside lay a half dozen white sticks of candy, each thicker than her thumb.

She shook her head. "Where on earth did he find rock here in Wenwood?" she wondered aloud. That had been one of her few joys in living in Bristol, the rock candy made by the town's leading confectionery. She vaguely remembered telling Daniel something about it when he had first called. Grabbing one of the sticks, she took a long lick and let the sweet taste roll down her throat. Hope filled her with each swallow. Perhaps there was a chance for them if he was still willing to buy her such a present. She had taken perhaps three such licks when she noticed that the end of the stick had red marks on it. Looking closer, she saw that the marks formed letters, letters that read, "I love you."

She stared at the stick for another second before climbing to her feet. The candy trembled in her grip. She started for the door to her chamber, then stopped, turning toward the door that connected her chamber with Daniel's. Heart pounding, she moved toward the door and reached up over the jamb for the brass key. She transferred the candy to her left hand and, sticky fingered, unlocked the door with her right. The lock protested with a loud screech. He would know she was coming.

The rest of her was shaking with her hand as she pushed the door open. Daniel was standing at the side of his bed, his green satin dressing gown obviously thrown on in haste, hair tousled. "Cynthia, is anything wrong?"

Wordlessly, she held out the candy to him, lettering first.

"Oh," he smiled sheepishly. "You found it. You had said you liked it better than chocolate. I hope you don't mind."

Cynthia swallowed, feeling the lingering taste of the sweet on the back of her tongue. "Do you know what it says?"

He nodded, standing a little taller. "Yes. I asked the candy maker to put in the words. The candy is special, you know. No matter how long you lick it, the words will still show. And it will say 'I love you' until the very end, just as I will."

The stick fell to the ground as Cynthia cast herself into his arms. Daniel hugged her close, finding her mouth once again so near to his. She tasted of the candy, and more.

And that night they both learned that Adam was wrong. There was indeed something in life far sweeter than candy.

LOOK FOR THESE REGENCY ROMANCES